London, 1814

A season of secrets, scandal and seduction!

A darkly dangerous stranger is out for revenge, delivering a silken rope as his calling card. Through him, a long-forgotten scandal is reawakened. The notorious events of 1794, which saw one man murdered and another hanged for the crime, are ripe gossip in the ton. Was the right culprit brought to justice or is there a treacherous murderer still at large?

As the murky waters of the past are disturbed, so servants find love with roguish lords, and proper ladies fall for rebellious outcasts until, finally, the true murderer and spy is revealed.

Regency Silk & Scandal

From glittering ballrooms to a Cornish smuggler's cove; from the wilds of Scotland to a Romany camp—join the highest and lowest in society as they find love in this thrilling new eight-book miniseries!

Dear Reader,

If you met Hal Carlow in the first of this Silk & Scandal miniseries, *The Lord and the Wayward Lady,* you will remember him as an incorrigible flirt and a shocking rake.

As the younger son, Hal feels under no pressure to settle down—and besides, he is having far too much fun as it is. I realized that he is so used to fast young ladies, dashing matrons and wicked widows that none of them was ever likely to fix his wandering attention long enough for him to fall in love.

It would take a Good Girl to bring Hal to his knees, and in Julia Tresilian I found one. A wicked blue-eyed devil of a rake is the last thing Julia is looking for—she and her mama are on the hunt for a respectable gentleman of moderate fortune. And when a young lady has attracted a trio of rather stuffy suitors, the last thing she needs is the man with the worst reputation in Brussels scaring them off.

The Battle of Waterloo is going to turn their lives upside down and have them both breaking the resolutions they have made so painfully. I loved discovering the honorable and heroic officer inside the rakehell and the courageous and determined woman inside the very proper young lady, and I hope you enjoy following them from the balls and picnics of Brussels society through the mud and carnage of the battlefield and back to fashionable London.

With best wishes

Louise

Louise Allen

THE
OFFICER
AND THE
PROPER
LADY

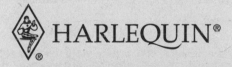

HARLEQUIN®

TORONTO • NEW YORK • LONDON
AMSTERDAM • PARIS • SYDNEY • HAMBURG
STOCKHOLM • ATHENS • TOKYO • MILAN • MADRID
PRAGUE • WARSAW • BUDAPEST • AUCKLAND

Recycling programs
for this product may
not exist in your area.

ISBN-13: 978-0-373-29620-0

THE OFFICER AND THE PROPER LADY

Copyright © 2010 by Melanie Hilton

This edition published by arrangement with Harlequin Books S.A.

For questions and comments about the quality of this book please contact us at Customer_eCare@Harlequin.ca.

® and TM are trademarks of the publisher. Trademarks indicated with ® are registered in the United States Patent and Trademark Office, the Canadian Trade Marks Office and in other countries.

www.eHarlequin.com

Printed in U.S.A.

Look for these novels in the Regency miniseries

SILK & SCANDAL

And coming January 2011

Chapter One

May 20th 1815. Brussels

His eyes were an unsettling blue-grey, like a sky threatening storms. How Julia Tresilian knew that, when the possessor of those eyes was quite twenty yards away, lounging with a group of fellow officers around a park bench, she was not precisely certain.

Nor had she any idea why she was staring in such a brazen manner at a strange man. Miss Tresilian was, above all else, a perfectly proper young lady. Every day, weather permitting, she would walk in the Parc de Bruxelles with her young brother. And every day, she would exchange polite greetings with her acquaintances, play with Phillip, do the marketing and return to Mama in their apartment on the Place de Leuvan. She did not speak to unknown gentlemen. She most certainly did not stare at them.

And most of the gentlemen she saw on the streets of Brussels were unknown to Julia, she acknowledged with an inward sigh. The arrival of the British refugees fleeing Paris ahead of Napoleon's return in March had certainly enlivened the scene. It made the Tresilians thankful that they had already obtained genteel lodgings, but the newcomers did not much improve the social life of a widow of modest means and her daughter without connections or introductions. The new residents crowding into every house for rent in the desirable Upper Town were from quite another strata of Society to their own.

Then the military had arrived in ever-increasing numbers, both in the city and in the surrounding countryside, culminating only three days before in the Duke of Wellington establishing himself in a house on the corner of Rue Royale overlooking the Parc.

The sight of the commander in chief of the Allied forces sent the civilian population into what Mrs Tresilian described acidly as a tizzy. Such a celebrity in their midst could only be exciting, and the knowledge that they were under the protection of a great general filled everyone with confidence. But it also reminded them that this corner of Europe was where the inevitable confrontation with the French Tyrant would take place.

And to a large extent, the outcome of that confrontation would depend on men like the young officers relaxing so lightheartedly in front of her. Julia realized that she was still staring at the one man—and that he had become aware of her regard. His gaze sharpened and focused as he lifted his head to look at her. She felt the colour flood her cheeks and discovered that she could not look away.

He did not smile, yet his direct stare held no insolence. He looked as she felt, that he had seen someone he recognized at a level far deeper than simple acquaintance. He seemed faintly puzzled, or perhaps intrigued, but not disconcerted by their silent exchange. But then, he did not look like a man who was disconcerted by much. Julia, on the other hand, could not recall feeling more flustered in her life. Her breath was short, her heart was pounding and she felt absurdly shy. She should look away. Unfortunately, it seemed that she could not.

'Julia?' *Phillip, thank goodness.* With the sense of being pulled out of a trance, Julia bent down to hear what her four-year-old brother wanted.

'Yes, my love?'

'Throw my ball, please?'

She took the dusty yellow and blue ball and tossed it for him towards the largest empty expanse of grass. With a whoop, he gave chase, tumbled over, picked himself up and ran on. Julia brushed off her gloves, turned her back on the disconcerting officer in his blue uniform and pretended to admire the formal bedding lining the gravel walk.

'Miss Tresilian. What a happy chance.'

'Major Fellowes.' She shifted her gaze from the marigolds with reluctance. 'Hardly chance. I walk here every morning, after all.' *And will change to the afternoon if that is what it takes to avoid you.* His manner over the past weeks had grown uncomfortably familiar for someone met by chance at a mutual acquaintance's house. She wished she had brought their maid to accompany her, but she had never felt the need before.

'Frederick, please. You know I wish you would use my given name.'

'We are not on such terms that it would be seemly, Major.' Julia opened her parasol with a snap and deployed it as a barrier between them. She had been naive to think him merely a nuisance. Even to someone with her sheltered background, this had reached the point where his intentions were blatantly obvious. His very dishonourable intentions.

The major countered by moving to her other side. 'But you know I wish we were, Julia.' He ignored her tightened lips and lack of response. 'A young lady, alone in a foreign city, needs a man to protect her.'

'I am not alone, sir.' Julia tried to look bored and sophisticated. She suspected she merely looked embarrassed and alarmed. Vulnerable. She had no experience to help her deal with this.

'A widowed mother, a baby brother? What protection are they?'

'Sufficient. Or they should be, if a lady were surrounded by *gentlemen*.'

'My dear Julia, you will find that gentlemen do not flock to the side of young ladies who are living on the continent for reasons of economy and who cannot offer a dowry to accompany their undoubted charms. In those circumstances, a more businesslike relationship is appropriate.'

'And what, exactly, would it take to send you about *your* business, Major? How much clearer do I have to be that I do not wish for your company?' Julia demanded. There was at a tug on her skirts and she looked down, forcing a smile for her brother.

'Throw the ball, Julia.'

'Of course, Phillip.' She tossed the ball a good distance, and watched him scamper off, before she turned on the man at her side. 'You should be ashamed, not only to proposition me but to do it with a child present!'

'My dear Julia, consider.' Major Fellowes laid a hand on her arm, and she stiffened. 'Just what is your future without me?'

'Respectable.' She glared at his gloved hand protruding from the gold-braided cuff. 'Will you kindly unhand me? Nothing, believe me, will make me agree to be your mistress.'

'You will not be so very respectable if word gets around that you are open to negotiation,' he suggested. 'I would only have to drop a word in a few ears that we have had this conversation and the damage would be done.'

Julia tried to shake off his hand, but he closed his fingers, drawing her towards himself. 'Let me go, people will realize something is amiss,' she hissed.

'No doubt, any onlooker will merely deduce we are discussing the price.' His face bore an expression of such self-satisfaction that she was tempted to strike it. But that could only make matters worse. She had to get rid of him before Phillip came back. But how, without creating an even worse scene?

'Bet against Thomas's mare over that distance? You must be all about in your head,' Major Hal Carlow said to the man at his side who was earnestly explaining the merits of a chestnut gelding belonging to a certain Lieutenant Strong.

Captain Gregory launched into details lost on Hal as he watched the young woman on the upper walk—the apparently respectable young woman who had been staring at him as though she knew him. He had never seen her before, so far as he knew, although, as she could hardly be described as a Diamond of the first water, it was possible she had escaped his attention. In which case, what was so attracting him now?

'Carlow?' He ignored his companions, still watching the young woman. She had been joined by an officer in a scarlet coat. Foot Guards. He narrowed his eyes: 92nd Foot and not someone he recognized. And not someone *she* wished to recognize either, judging by her averted head and her stiff body. The man put a hand on her arm.

'I'll see you back at the Hôtel de Flandres,' Hal said abruptly, abandoning his plans to go and catch up on his sleep. He took the steps up to the wide lawn at a stride and strode off to intercept the small boy with the ball. 'Good morning.' He hunkered down to eye level, managing the unwieldy length of his sabre without conscious thought. 'Is that your governess in the green pelisse?'

'My sister Julia.' Big brown eyes stared back solemnly, grubby hands clasped his toy. 'Are you in the cavalry, sir?'

'Yes, 11th Light Dragoons. My name is Hal Carlow.' Hal scooped the child up in his arms and began to walk towards the path. 'And what is your name?' He liked children—well enough to ensure his frequent adventures left no by-blows to haunt his somewhat selective conscience.

'Phillip Tresilian and I'm four.'

'A big boy like you? I thought you must be six at least.' Hal stepped over the strip of marigolds and walked up to the couple on the path. Close-to he could see the flush on her— Julia's—cheeks and the distress in her eyes, large and brown like her brother's. The other officer still had his hand on her arm.

'Miss Tresilian! You must have quite given me up, I do apologise,' Hal said cheerfully as he came up to them. Her eyes widened but she did not disown him. 'Shall we go on to the pavilion for tea? I expect Phillip would like an ice as usual.'

'Not in the morning, sir! You know he is not allowed ices before luncheon,' Miss Tresilian said in a rallying tone.

Good girl, he thought, as he extended his free arm for her to rest her hand on, then feigned surprise at seeing the other man was holding her. He let the good humour ebb from his face and raised one eyebrow. 'Major? I believe I have the prior claim.' Now what had he said to make her blush like that?

'Miss Tresilian was walking with me, sir.' The infantry officer bristled. He outweighed Hal by about a stone and had a good three inches of height on Hal's six foot.

Hal met his eyes and allowed the faintest sneer to cross his features. 'And now, by appointment, she is walking with me.' The small boy curled an arm around his neck in well-timed confirmation of his friendship with the Tresilians. 'I believe I do not have the pleasure of your acquaintance, Major? Nor, I suspect, have my friends.' Hal let the slightest emphasis rest on the last word and saw his meaning go home.

The other man released Miss Tresilian's arm. 'Frederick Fellowes, 92nd Foot.'

'Hal Carlow, 11th Light Dragoons.' That went home too. Something of his reputation must have reached the infantry. 'Good day to you.'

Miss Tresilian rested her hand on his sleeve. 'Good day, Major Fellowes,' she said with chilly formality. She waited until they were out of earshot before she said, 'Please, sir, do put Phillip down, he is covered in dirt.'

Hal set the boy on his feet and threw the ball to the far end of the lawn for him to run after. 'Are you all right, Miss Tresilian?'

She looked up at him, her face still flushed beneath the brim of her plain straw bonnet. He studied big brown eyes and a nose that had just the suggestion of a tilt to the tip, a firm chin and a neat figure. No great beauty, but Hal had the sense of a vivid personality, of intelligence and humour. He felt a desire to make her blush again, she did it so deliciously.

'I am now, thanks to you, Major. I do not know what I would have done if you had not rescued me—hit him over the head with my parasol, I expect—and then what a figure I would have made of myself.' Her eyes crinkled with rueful amusement as he smiled. 'And how clever of you to get our names from Phillip. Did you really mean by that reference to your friends that you might call Major Fellowes out?'

She was quick on the uptake, this young lady. And lady she was, for all her lack of maid or footman and her simple gown and spencer.

'Of course. Fellowes lacks address: it really is not done to persist where one is unwanted, even when a lady is so temptingly pretty.'

She ignored the automatic compliment. 'Not with discreditable offers it is not,' she said with feeling, then blushed again. 'Oh dear, I should not have mentioned that, should I? But I feel I know you, Major Carlow.'

'Is that why you were looking at me just now?' he asked. 'I hoped you wanted to make my acquaintance.'

She bit her lip in charming confusion. 'I really do not know. It was very brassy of me, but there was something about you I thought I recognized.' She recovered her composure a little and her chin lifted. 'And you stared right back at me.'

'True.' Hal stooped to pick up the ball and sent Phillip chasing towards the fountain in its octagonal basin. 'But then, I am a rake and we are *supposed* to stare at ladies and put them to the blush.'

'You are? A rake I mean?'

'Indeed. I am precisely the kind of man your mama would warn you about and, now I think on it, you may have leapt from frying pan to fire. I am absolutely the last man you should be seen walking with in the Parc.'

'No, Major Fellowes is that,' she retorted. 'You rescued me.'

Hal was not given to flirting with young unmarried ladies. For a start, whenever he hove into sight, their mothers herded them together like hens with chicks on seeing a fox. And he had absolutely no intention of finding himself confronting a furious father demanding that he did the decent thing by his compromised daughter.

Society was full enough of carefree widows and dashing matrons—and the *demi-monde* of skilled lightskirts—to keep a gentleman of an amorous disposition amused without him needing to venture amongst the ingénues adorning the Marriage Mart.

But Miss Tresilian was not one of those young ladies either. She was, to his experienced eye, a good three and twenty, her manner was open and her wits sharp. She was not one of the fashionable set either: he did not recognize her name and her bonnet was a Season out of style. There was something about her that argued both virtue and a lack of sophisticated boredom.

'My reputation is worse,' he observed, reverting to Major Fellowes. 'I have not heard of him—but he had heard of me.'

'And he was very wary of you.' Miss Tresilian nodded. 'So you are a notorious duellist as well as a rake?'

'I confess I fight, gamble, drink and amuse myself with some dedication,' Hal told her with a shrug, feeling he might as well be hanged for a sheep as a lamb so far as his reputation with Miss Tresilian was concerned. He did not have to mention loose women in his list of sins: the slight lift of one eyebrow showed that she could add those herself.

A shadow passed over her face. 'Gamble? What on, Major?'

'Anything, everything. Cards, dice, horses, what colour gown Miss Tresilian will wear for her next appearance in the Parc.'

'Do you often win, Major?'

'Almost inevitably.' She raised the brow again. 'I play cards well, but I have the knack of calculating odds even better. I enjoy gambling, not throwing money away. You disapprove of gambling, Miss Tresilian?'

'My mother and I are in Brussels on what is called the *economical plan*,' she said, wrinkling her nose in distaste for the term. 'In other words, we are compelled to live abroad where it is cheap in order to husband our resources. Many of the British community are here for the same reason, and for most of them, it is because the head of the household has gambled away a fortune.'

'Your father is not with you?'

'Papa died just before Phillip was born.' Miss Tresilian looked round, sighting her brother standing hopefully in front of the refreshment stand. His nankeens, Hal saw with amusement, were now an absolute disgrace. 'Thank you, Major Carlow, for rescuing me and for your escort. I am sure you must be wanting to rejoin your friends now.' Whatever her reasons for staring at him so fixedly before, they were evidently nothing to do with flirtation. She was now intent on politely disengaging herself.

'Not at all. At least, not until I have put a stop to any tittle-tattle that you being seen walking with me might arouse.' Hal scanned the array of elegant ladies gathered in little parties around the pavilion. 'What we need is a matron of influence and reputation. Ah yes, just the person.' He tucked Julia's hand under his arm and led her across the gravel to a lady sitting alone, delicately spooning vanilla ice from a glass. Behind her, in the shadows of one of the trees, stood her maid.

'Lady Geraldine. How very lovely you look today.'

'Major Carlow, a delightful surprise to see you doing something as tame as walking in the Parc, and at such an early hour! Perhaps you never got to sleep last night.' Her ladyship smiled wickedly from under the brim of her hat as Hal bowed, returning a smile every bit as wicked.

'May I introduce Miss Tresilian, ma'am? Miss Tresilian, Lady Geraldine Masters. I have just rescued Miss Tresilian from a rather slimy dragon. I have done my utmost not to flirt with her, but she will now have been observed by the censorious walking with me for quite ten minutes.'

'And requires some respectable chaperonage? Indeed. Do sit by me, Miss Tresilian. My first duty is to warn you against associating with bloods of Major Carlow's ilk. However, I must congratulate you upon escaping from a dragon's clutches. Major, take yourself off so I may restore Miss Tresilian's reputation as required.'

'Ma'am.' Hal bowed, repressing a smile at the expression of barely concealed alarm on Miss Tresilian's face. Lady Geraldine, daughter of the Duke of Wilmington and wife of the indecently wealthy Mr John Masters, was one of the leading Ladies of the Park, as the reigning English set in Brussels Society were known. She was a handsome woman in her late thirties, kind, outspoken and apt to be amused by handsome young men of address of whom she had a number in her train. Her devotion to her husband was, however, in no doubt. He should know, he had tested it personally. 'I leave her in safe hands. Good day, Miss Tresilian.'

'Good day, Major. And thank you.' She smiled, an expression of genuine sweetness, and her face, that he had thought merely pleasant, was transformed.

Hal swallowed, bowed and took himself off, pausing to direct a waiter to send ices and tea across to Lady Geraldine's table. He handed the coins to pay for it to Phillip. 'Settle the account, there's a good chap,' he said, amused by the delighted expression on the small boy's face as he followed the waiter, the coins clasped tight in his grubby fist.

A charming pair, the Tresilians, he thought as he strode towards the Place Royale exit, heading for his hotel and a couple of hours' sleep. One grubby urchin and one respectable young lady. One *virtuous* young lady, he thought and told himself to forget about her.

'Tell me about your slimy dragon, Miss Tresilian.' Lady Geraldine fixed her eyes on Julia's face and smiled. Her regard wavered as someone approached their table.

'My brother, ma'am,' Julia apologised as Phillip marched

up, waiter in tow, a huge grin on his grubby face. 'He is not usually such a ragamuffin.'

'Boys will be boys,' her ladyship remarked, with a glance at Major Carlow's disappearing figure. Julia dragged her own eyes away from broad shoulders in dark blue cloth. Did every officer have his uniform tailored to such a pitch of perfection? If they did, she had never noticed before.

'However,' Lady Geraldine continued, 'I am sure he does not need to hear the tale of the dragon. Monique!' Her maid came forward. 'Please take Master Tresilian to a table in the shade to eat his ice. There, no-one can overhear us. Now tell me, what necessitated your rescue by Major Carlow?'

Julia could see no way out of telling her everything. 'I presume Fellowes thinks that because we are not well off and I have no male relatives in Brussels, I am open to such offers,' she concluded. 'It is very lowering to think such a man assumes something like that about one.'

'It is nothing to do with your appearance or manner,' Lady Geraldine said soothingly. 'After all, Major Carlow obviously recognized you as a respectable young lady, or he would not have brought you to me. And if the worst rake in Brussels sees that, then you have no need to fear.'

'He warned me he was,' Julia said with a frown. 'Not that I have any experience of rakes, but he did not seem so very shocking.'

Although she had been very aware of a faint, and very feminine perfume when she had taken his arm and there had been a smudge of what might have been face powder on his shoulder. And perhaps the tiny red mark on his cheek was rouge and not a shaving nick. There had been dark shadows under those beautiful blue eyes: it was beginning to dawn on her that the gallant major had probably come straight from a woman's bed to join his friends in the Parc.

'Charm is a rake's stock in trade. He did not flirt with you?' Lady Geraldine appeared surprised.

'I don't think so, ma'am.'

'Extraordinary.'

Julia told herself that her good opinion of Major Carlow would have suffered if he *had* flirted, but she had the uncomfortable suspicion that she might have enjoyed it. No-one had ever flirted with her, and the fact that such a notorious rake had not attempted it was disappointing. Unflattering, even. From a purely academic point of view, it would have been interesting to see what all the fuss was about.

'May I have your direction, my dear?'

Julia jerked her wandering attention back from Major Carlow and opened her reticule. 'Mama's card, ma'am.' Lady Geraldine was hardly likely to call on the Tresilians, although Mama would want to write and thank her for her help.

'A good address,' Lady Geraldine observed.

'I know. We were lucky to arrive before the rush.'

'Indeed you were. After all, the Richmonds have had to settle for that barn of a place on Rue de la Blanchisserie in the Lower Town.' Something in her ladyship's smile hinted that she was not over-fond of the Duchess of Richmond. 'When does Mrs Tresilian receive?'

Goodness, she *did* intend to call! 'Between two and four on Mondays, Tuesdays and Thursdays, ma'am.' But their usual callers were modestly circumstanced people such as themselves, not Society ladies. 'Thank you for the tea, and for lending me countenance, Lady Geraldine. I must take Philip home.' Julia gathered up her reticule and her scattered wits and shook the proffered hand in its tight kid glove.

'Will we meet the major again?' Phillip demanded, as they left the Parc and negotiated the crowd outside the Duke of Wellington's house. 'I liked him.'

So did I...'I shouldn't think so,' Julia said. 'But he had a lovely uniform: you must tell Mama all about it.'

'And a great big sword for killing Boney with,' Phillip said with a bloodthirsty chuckle, dancing off down the pavement swinging an imaginary weapon. Julia followed, suddenly sombre.

Chapter Two

Two days later, Lady Geraldine duly called and was received by Mrs Tresilian and Julia, Phillip having been deposited with the landlady and a litter of kittens in the kitchen.

'My niece has just gone back to England to be married,' Lady Geraldine observed once tea had been poured. 'I find I miss having a young lady to go about with quite dreadfully—I have no daughter of my own, you see, and I do so enjoy the company of young people.' Mrs Tresilian made sympathetic noises. 'So, if you would lend Julia to me, I would be delighted to chaperone her to parties and so forth.'

'Lend?' Mrs Tresilian said faintly. 'Parties?'

'And balls: we seem to have them every night, after all. Routs, receptions, picnics. You know the sort of thing.'

'Me?' Julia felt she had to add something, however inane.

'You do enjoy parties, Miss Tresilian?'

'Yes, ma'am. But I know no-one in Society…'

'But I do. Mrs Tresilian? I would not be depriving you?'

'Not at all,' Mrs Tresilian said with emphasis. 'I live very quietly, which is so dull for Julia.'

We cannot afford to live any other way! Julia thought in alarm. *Parties? Balls? Picnics? That means gowns and silk stocking and gloves and...money. What is Mama thinking of? I cannot spend like that just to enjoy myself!*

Lady Geraldine stayed the regulation half hour then departed in a froth of green muslin leaving promises of invitations, a wave of chypre perfume and two astonished Tresilians behind her.

'Mama! I have not got a thing to wear.'

'Well, that would present an original appearance!' her mother observed with a smile. 'Let us make a list of what you will need. We can trim up some things with fresh ribbons, and we can look at my lace, see what can be done with that. But a ball gown is essential. A new afternoon dress, a walking dress. And something for half-dress occasions. We will make a list.'

'But how can we afford it?'

'It will be an investment. This is a miraculous chance, to be here just now when Brussels Society must be full of men who do not need to hang out for a rich wife. It will not be as it has been up to now, with so many people like us, here to save money. Diplomats, confidential secretaries, chaplains, officers—think of it!' Julia did, and very improbable it seemed that any of them might be interested in her.

'We cannot hope for a title, of course, just a comfortably circumstanced gentleman, but even so, it will be worth the effort.' Mrs Tresilian gave a happy sigh. 'You are a good girl, Julia, you deserve some enjoyment and the opportunity to find a husband worthy of you.'

Julia sat down on the hard horsehair sofa and tried to imagine being part of that social whirl. But it would be a huge responsibility, and a gamble. If Mama spent their precious savings on gowns, then she *must* find a husband. It had been so long since she had come to accept that without dowry or connections she was never likely to marry, that the idea of setting out in cold blood to find a husband was daunting.

'You are quite right, Mama.' Julia managed a smile. This was her duty and she must try, however diffident or awkward she felt. 'It is a wonderful opportunity and I will do my best to attach a respectable gentleman.' It was disconcerting to find that despite this worthy resolution, the only feature she could imagine that this unknown paragon should possess was a pair of stormy blue-grey eyes.

Hal sauntered into Lady Fanshawe's reception on the stroke of eleven with every intention of enjoying himself and no particular scruples about how. He had spent a hard day drilling with his troop at their base near Ninove, ten miles from the city. It had meant a long gallop to get back to bathe and for his valet to insinuate his long limbs into his skin-tight dress uniform. After that, he had been ready for supper and a bottle of claret with friends in one of the little bistros that had sprung up to serve the influx of officers.

Now, refreshed and relaxed, he smiled at the prospect of an evening surrounded by beautiful, intelligent and, above all, sophisticated women. He would drink champagne, find a willing partner and arrange an assignation for later. He greeted his hostess and turned to view the throng: heated, chattering, animated with the heady mix of alcohol, gossip and sexual intrigue.

And *there* was a woman who might have been designed for exactly what he had in mind: Lady Horton. Her husband, as always, was nowhere to be seen. Hal strolled across, amused by the way in which she pretended she had not seen him, posing and laughing to show off face and figure to best advantage.

And what a figure, he thought appreciatively—lush, graceful and provocatively displayed in shell-pink satin silk that clung to every curve. And if she was wearing a stitch of underwear beneath it, he was a French general. Hal made himself a small bet that he would discover the truth of that by sun-up.

'Lady Horton. Barbara—' he lowered his voice '—you look edible.'

She turned, laughing up at him, every line of her body confirming the wanton message in her big brown eyes. If he wanted her, she was his.

'Edible?' She pouted and his body tightened as the tip of her tongue touched her full lower lip.

'A perfect bonbon. Sweet strawberry cream encased in wicked dark chocolate,' Hal murmured, reaching out to flick one glossy curl over her shoulder. 'It makes me want to bite. And lick. Very slowly.' She moved close so the scent of her skin—warm woman, musky perfume, desire—filled his nostrils.

'How will you keep your elegant figure,' she murmured back, reaching up to brush an imaginary fleck from the braid on his chest, 'if you eat such naughty sweet things?'

'I will have to exercise it off.' Hal held her eyes. 'Hard.'

Barbara's lips parted and her lids drooped heavy over those insolently beautiful eyes. She adored this, lived for it—the compliments, the suggestion, the intrigue. And by reputation she was magnificent in bed: skilled, demanding and tireless. 'We should discuss that at our leisure. You know where I live. The side door will be open,' she said, husky promise in every syllable. 'Until later.'

'Later,' he agreed, lifting her hand to kiss her fingertips. Then as he straightened up, he found his gaze captured by another pair of fine brown eyes, only these were wide, clear and, he could tell from right across the room, shocked.

Hell. Miss Tresilian, here, looking like a snowdrop in a hothouse, all simple purity against glaring colour and elaboration. And with an expression akin to a nun who had walked into a brothel. What was she doing here? His assessment of her as outside Society must have been adrift. Hal was conscious of the tingling along his nerves, a sharpening of his attention that signalled the urge to flirt, to hunt, to… No, this one was an innocent.

By his side, Lady Horton had turned to another guest. She would flit through the rooms, garnering compliments and outrageous offers, laughing and teasing, becoming heated and excited. Becoming ready for him.

Hal bowed slightly towards Miss Tresilian, and her chin went up, infinitesimally. She inclined her head and turned back to speak to the young lady at her side. A display that would not have shamed a duchess acknowledging a distant, and not very desirable acquaintance—if it were not for the fact that she had blushed like a peony.

And now he felt uncomfortable to have been under that clear-eyed scrutiny while he set up his liaison. *Damn it, is she judging me? She knows what I am, I told her.* The fact that he had just told himself off for wanting to pursue her made him feel irrationally indignant. He was trying to behave himself and she was giving him the cold shoulder. The urge to hunt resurfaced, and this time he did not attempt to control it.

Hal walked straight across the floor towards the chattering group of single young ladies gathered under the eyes of the seated chaperones while they waited for suitable, approved gentlemen to come over. He was not a suitable, approved gentleman of course. This could be amusing. It would certainly teach his virtuous new acquaintance not to send him disapproving looks.

'He's coming over,' Miss Marriott hissed.

'Who?' Julia enquired, fanning herself, her shoulder turned to the room. She knew perfectly well who, and she had seen clearly the way Hal Carlow's eyes had narrowed and his chin had come up when he had found her staring. He had not relished her scrutiny, it seemed. Well, he should not flirt like that with provocatively clad ladies in public. If flirting was the word: they had looked as though they were mentally undressing each other. She put a hand to her cheek, dismayed at her own blushes.

'Major Carlow of course! Do you think he will talk to us? He is quite shocking you know—did you see him just now with Lady Horton? Mama will be furious if he does come over. Only he is *so* good looking.' She pouted as Major Carlow was stopped by an artillery officer. 'Oh. Anyway, even he would not talk to us without an introduction, I suppose.'

Julia had known Felicity Marriott for some time. Her father was a baronet and he and his family were visiting Belgian relatives by marriage, not living in exile to save money. Miss Marriott was used to parties of this kind, and her mother had assured Mrs Tresilian that she was more than happy to keep an eye on Julia as well as Felicity. Lady Geraldine might be kind enough to obtain invitations, but Julia must not expect her to play the chaperone the entire evening, her mother had warned.

'I have met Major Carlow,' she admitted. Her pulse was beating erratically; it had been from the moment she saw who it was talking to Lady Horton in her utterly indecent gown.

The conversation had been indecent too, she was certain. They had stood so close together, the eye-contact had been so intense, that Julia felt scorched by it. And he had seen her staring at him again and now he was coming over and she was probably going to sink through the floor with shame.

'Really? How?' Felicity broke off, simpering. Here he was. How he had got into that uniform, which was skin tight and blatantly showed off his quite excellent physique, she could not imagine. Perhaps he was sewn into it. Thinking about that made her decidedly flustered and cross with both of them. He should not wear such shockingly tight trousers and she should not notice.

'Miss Tresilian. Miss Marriott, I believe? A charming affair, do you not think?'

'Delightful, such fun, such lovely flowers,' Felicity babbled, beaming at him in a way that was going to earn her a severe word from her mother later.

'And do you think it delightful too, Miss Tresilian?'

Julia made herself meet his eyes, very blue in the candlelight. The dark smudges were still beneath them, making him look faintly dissipated. There was colour on his high cheekbones, but it was certainly not from shame or confusion. The thrill of pursuit, no doubt, although that woman had hardly needed chasing.

'Utterly delightful, Major Carlow. But this is a rare treat for me, so my opinion is not the equal of Miss Marriott's on the subject.' Over his shoulder, she could see the lady he had been talking to, her pink satin gown clinging to her long limbs as she prowled around the room. 'I have been admiring the gowns,' she said, coming out with the first subject that came into her mind.

'Indeed? And I am sure many will have been admiring yours, Miss Tresilian. A model of chaste simplicity, if I may say so.' His eyes ran over it as though they could penetrate the modest neckline and the layers of petticoats.

Dull, he means. Prudish compared to the other gowns. Why even Felicity's bodice is cut lower, and her mama is very strict. She had been pleased with the primrose silk underskirt and Mama's idea of buying two lengths of gauze—one cream the other amber—when they saw it at a bargain price. It would be an easy task to sew alternative overskirts onto the silk gown and give the illusion of her having a more extensive wardrobe than she did.

But *chaste simplicity,* when it was the result of having no money for lace or flounces, was not the fashion. Nor were home-made gowns a match for shell-pink satin. He had no need to patronise her, she thought, maintaining her expression of polite interest with some effort. Although how he managed to be both patronising and make her feel he was simultaneously undressing her, she had no idea.

'Felicity!' Lady Marriott swept her daughter away, leaving Julia stranded with Major Carlow. Apparently, in her haste, it did not occur to her to rescue her other charge. Julia realized she was unable to think of a single syllable of conversation to break the silence.

'What did I say to make you poker up so?' he enquired, placing her hand on his arm and strolling towards the buffet. Julia followed, chiding herself for being so meek. But just how did one snub a rake? 'Have a glass of champagne, Miss Tresilian, and explain how I have offended you.'

'You haven't,' Julia lied.

'Nonsense, you were looking highly disapproving, like one of the chaperones. You must tell me or I will not let you go and ten minutes in my company is all your reputation will bear.'

'You are outrageous,' Julia said, alarmed, annoyed and illogically inclined to laugh.

'I know. I did warn you.' They halted by the buffet where footmen were pouring wine from bottles standing in long ice troughs.

'You remarked on my gown,' she admitted, twitching the gauze as though that would transform it into a creation from the pages of *La Belle Assemblée.*

'I complimented you upon it,' Major Carlow corrected her, handing her a flute of sparkling wine.

'Sarcastically.' Julia took a sip and sneezed. 'Oh dear, I do not usually drink this.'

'Then you must have some more and become accustomed.' He took a bottle and topped up both their glasses. 'You thought me sarcastic? I meant nothing but honest admiration. That style suits you.'

'It would seem that your appreciation of gowns encompasses a wide range of styles, Major Carlow.' Julia glanced down at her wine glass in alarm. It was empty, which could be the only excuse for such a remark. He was silent. Julia risked a glance up through her lashes. He was smiling, although whether that made it better or worse she had no idea.

'Horses for courses, Miss Tresilian. Or in this case, gowns to suit personalities. You represent virtue most charmingly. Another lady may better represent…freedom.' He reached for her wine glass; she held tight to it, but his fingers lingered.

'Even when that lady is married?' she asked, suddenly reckless, goaded by his touch. And jealous, she realized, appalled at herself. Which was insanity. The other day this man had yielded to a gallant impulse and saved her from annoyance. That did not change the fact that he was nothing but trouble for any virtuous woman. He was probably deliberately provoking her.

Major Carlow shrugged, still amused. Presumably cross and indiscreet virgins were an entertaining novelty for him. 'If her husband does not build good fences, he must expect poachers in his coverts.'

'Really, Major! Ladies are not game birds for you to bag,' she snapped.

'I am sorry to disillusion you, Miss Tresilian, but for some, it is always open season.'

'Well, I am sorry for you then,' she declared roundly. 'For when you are married, you will have to spend all your time building your own fences and worrying about poachers. Poor woman,' she added with feeling.

'But I have no intention of marrying, Miss Tresilian. I have an elder brother already doing his duty by the family name, so your sympathy for my imaginary bride is quite unnecessary.'

'I am certain she would do you a great deal of good.' For a moment, she thought she saw a flicker of bitterness in the mocking eyes.

Julia found she wanted to cry. Here she was at her very first *ton* party and not one of the respectable men of easy circumstances her mother dreamed of had exchanged so much as a sentence with her. And what was she doing? Bandying words with Hal Carlow, who was the last man in Brussels she should be seen with. No-one respectable was going to talk to her now, and she had lowered herself to discuss quite shocking subjects with him.

'You disappoint me, Miss Tresilian.' And indeed, the amusement had gone from his eyes and there was a distinct hint of storm clouds back again. 'I did not think you one of those ladies who believes that all rakes are capable of redemption and that it is their duty to try to accomplish that.'

'Redeem you?' Did he mean what she thought he meant: that she expected him to fall for her? That she wanted to reform his wicked ways, to have him run tame at her command? 'You, Major Carlow, may drink yourself under the table, fall off horses and break your limbs, gamble until your pockets are to let and dally with married ladies until an enraged husband shoots you, for all I care.' She thrust her wine glass back into his hand. 'And, should you survive all that, I will pity you, because you will end up a lonely man, realizing just how empty your rakehell life is.'

That was a magnificent parting line, she told herself, sweeping round and stalking off without the slightest idea where she was going. It would have been rather more effective without the crack of laughter from behind her.

The reception room had been thrown open into a gallery

running the length of the rear of the house with views south out over the ramparts towards the Fôret de Soignes. Now, late at night, a few lights twinkled from amidst the dark blanket of trees.

'A splendid position, is it not?' a voice beside her asked. 'Of course, it is not good for security. The Capel household were burgled the other day by rogues with a ladder from the ramparts.'

'Oh, how unfortunate.' Julia pulled herself together and turned to find a sombrely dressed man of medium height and with mouse-brown hair standing at her side. 'But the walks on the ramparts are very charming unless it is windy.'

'I beg your pardon for addressing you without an introduction,' the man continued. 'Only there seem to be none of the chaperones within sight, and it does seem so awkward, standing here pretending we cannot see each other. I should leave.'

'I am sure we can pretend we have been introduced,' Julia said. How refreshing, a respectable gentleman who was worried about polite form. 'I am Julia Tresilian.'

'Thomas Smyth.' He bowed, Julia inclined her head. 'Are you a resident of Brussels, Miss Tresilian?'

'My mother and I have been here for some months, Mr Smyth.'

'A charming city. I am touring and had hoped to visit Paris, but that is out of the question now. I shall have to return home without that treat, I fear.'

'Wellington will defeat Bonaparte,' Julia said, mentally crossing her fingers, 'and then you may return.'

'I doubt I will be at liberty. In August, I take up a living in a parish in Suffolk.' As Mr Smyth turned to face her, she saw he had calm hazel eyes and nondescript features. With his unassuming manner, he exuded a feeling of tranquil commonsense.

'You are a clergyman, sir?'

'A most fortunate one. I was a scholar, with little hope of advancement, then my godfather secured me the patronage of an old friend of his and I find myself with the most delightful country parish. It will be lonely at first, I have no doubt, to be a bachelor rattling around in a large vicarage.'

Julia murmured something polite, her mind racing. Was Mr Smyth, on the strength of two minutes' conversation, telling her that he was *available?* Surely not.

'Perhaps, if I were to find your chaperone, we could be properly introduced?' he asked. 'I have hired a horse and curricle for the duration of my stay: you might care to take a drive one afternoon?'

He is! Oh my goodness, one party and I have already met a respectable gentleman who is interested in me! Mama will be so pleased.

'That would be most pleasant,' she said, smiling. 'Thank you. Lady Geraldine Masters or, if she is not free, Lady Marriott.'

She watched his well-tailored back as he left the gallery, contrasting his restrained neatness with a certain flamboyant gentleman. There was no comparison, of course, and no doubt which a respectable young lady of modest means should be associating with, she thought with a certain wistfulness.

Chapter Three

Hal had the reputation of never losing his temper. It was a valuable characteristic, whether on a battlefield, in a gaming hell or looking down the barrel of a duelling pistol. He reminded himself of it, while his friends ragged him about his assignation with Mrs Horton.

'So you can't describe her boudoir?' Captain Grey said, pushing the bottle across the table to Jameson.

The major caught it as it rocked perilously. 'Too caught up in the toils of passion to notice, old chap?'

'You must recall something,' Will wheedled. 'Don't be a spoilsport, Carlow. Mirrors on the ceiling? Silken drapes? Golden cords? A bath with swan-headed taps?'

'I cannot describe it, because I have not been in it,' Hal said, taking a swig of claret.

'What?' The captain's chair legs hit the ground with a thump. 'But we saw you, last night. Damn it, the way you were looking at each other, you might as well have called the town crier in to announce what you'd be doing later.'

'I changed my mind.' Hal stretched out and took hold of the bottle, just as Major Jameson reached for it again.

'You changed your mind? Bloody hell.' Grey stared at him. 'Are you sickening for something?'

'No. Are we going to the Literary Institute, or not?'

'We're not moving until we hear why you didn't stagger out of the luscious Barbara's bedroom, weak at the knees after a night of passion,' Jameson said, obviously fascinated. 'Cards can wait.'

'I never stagger weak at the knees after a night of passion,' Hal said. 'I stride. Last night I changed my mind and, no, I do not intend telling you why.'

'My God,' said Grey, awed. 'She'll be hissing like a cat this morning.'

'You are welcome to go and try putting butter on her paws, if you like,' Hal suggested, making his friend blush and grin. 'But naturally, I sent a note of apology.'

'Citing what reason, exactly?'

'Pressing military duties.'

They subsided, agreeing that even Lady Horton would be placated by such an irrefutable excuse under the present circumstances. Lieutenant Hayden, silent up to this point while he demolished the remains of the fruit tart and cream, looked up, his chubby face serious. 'Turning over a new leaf, Carlow? New Year's resolution or something?' The others laughed at him, but he just grinned amiably. 'I know, it's May. Thought you might be getting into fighting trim—early nights, clean living.' He sighed. 'It'll be the betting next and then we'll all be in the suds. How will we know what to back if you give it up?'

'I am not giving up gambling or betting and I am not giving up women,' Hal said, trying to ignore the strange sensation inside his chest. It felt unpleasantly like apprehension. Or the threat of coming change.

He had watched Julia Tresilian walk away from him in her modest little home-made gown, her nose in the air, her words ringing in his ears, and he had laughed. It was funny, it genuinely was, that a notorious rake should give his head for a washing by a prim nobody who had about as much clue about the things she was lecturing him on as the canary in a spinster's parlour.

And then he saw her cross diagonally in front of Barbara Horton and felt suddenly as though he had eaten too much rich dessert: faintly queasy and with no inclination to dip his spoon in the dish for another mouthful. What he wanted was a draught of sharp, honest lemonade.

He wanted Miss Julia Tresilian. As he stood there staring blindly at the chattering crowd, it hit him like a thunderbolt. *He wanted Julia Tresilian.*

It was impossible. It had sent him back to the hotel last night with his head spinning, and it woke him up at hourly intervals all night with waves of panic flooding through him. He was losing his mind, he told himself at breakfast, washing mouthfuls of dry toast down with cup after cup of strong black coffee. He never spent nights tossing and turning—not before battle, not before a duel. He, Hal Carlow, did not lose sleep over some prudish little chit.

She was an innocent, respectable young woman. A gentleman did not toy with such a woman—not unless he meant marriage. Hal did not want to marry, and he most certainly could not marry a girl like that. Not with his reputation, all of which had been hard-earned and was entirely justified.

He was not fit to touch her hand, he knew that. She might be almost on the shelf, she might be dowerless and of no particular family. But decency and integrity shone out of those expressive brown eyes and all he had was his honour as a gentleman—and that was telling him to run a mile before he touched her, physically or emotionally.

Hal drained his glass. If he had fallen in love with her, he could understand it. But he had not. He hardly knew the girl.

Men he knew who had fallen in love mooned about writing poetry, or lost weight, or likened their beloved to a moonbeam or a zephyr.

Not his brother Marcus, of course, Marcus had spent most of his courtship in a state of violent antagonism to Nell, but they were obviously the exception. Marcus was the sort of virtuous son and heir who did things properly, took his pleasures discreetly and then settled down, married and produced heirs. But a second son did not have that obligation, although that did not stop family disapproval when he acted on his freedom.

Hal shrugged away memories of tight-lipped arguments, sighs and youthful disgrace. He wasn't a youth any more, he didn't feel like mooning, he couldn't think of a line of poetry, and Julia was neither a moonbeam nor a zephyr. She was innocent, sharp-tongued, painfully honest, intelligent and pleasant to look at. He was not in lust either. In fact he shocked himself even thinking about physical passion in the same sentence as Julia's name. And he could not recall the last time he had shocked himself. And yet, he wanted her. Ached for her.

This is a passing infatuation, an inner voice lectured him, *or you've been overdoing things. Just keep out of her way and you'll get over it.*

'Right.' He grounded the empty bottle with a thump. 'The Literary Institute it is.'

The eminently respectable Institute was where the gentlemen of the British community retreated daily to use the library, write their letters, read the London papers and argue about the best way to deal with Napoleon.

It was also a front for a gaming hell. How their sharp-nosed wives had not discovered this was a mystery to Hal. Men whom he knew were living in Brussels on the economic plan, necessitated by excessive gaming, could be found cheerfully losing hundreds of pounds a night, often to him. It just went to prove, he thought, handing his cloak, hat and sabre to the attendant, that men were incapable of reform, whatever women believed.

'I'll see you down there, just need to look something up,' he called, turning into the library as they clattered off down the stairs into the candlelit fug of the gaming rooms. The *Landed Gentry* was on the shelves and he began to thumb through until he found Tresilian.

Here they were: her father David, younger brother of the present baronet. Hal cross-checked Sir Alfred Tresilian, Bt. A modest marriage, a quiverful of children, so presumably uncle had no great resources himself. David had married Amelia Henry, there were two children—Julia Claire and Phillip David—and he was marked as deceased 1810.

What had that achieved? Hal asked himself, as he walked into the card room and chose a table. Nothing, except to feed this ridiculous obsession.

Julia had been correct about her mother's reaction to the Reverend Mr Smyth. After checking with the vicar of the English church in Brussels she pronounced him eminently suitable. 'Not that we must put all our eggs in one basket,' she warned Julia. 'There is nothing wrong with meeting more eligible gentlemen.'

'No, Mama,' Julia agreed. She allowed herself the pleasure of a ride in Mr Smyth's smart curricle and then, in the space of three days, was gratified by introductions to Mr Fordyce, the confidential secretary to Lord Ellsworth, a diplomat dealing with British relations for the new King of the Netherlands, and Colonel Williams, a widower in his forties with a fifteen-year-old daughter. She attended a small dance, a musicale and a charity luncheon.

At none of these events did she see Major Carlow, which

was, of course, a relief. At frequent intervals she recalled
the way she had spoken to him and his laughter as she had
stalked off, and her cheeks burned afresh. Frequently she saw
the blue uniform of the Light Dragoons amongst the scarlet
and the green of other regiments and her heart would behave
oddly for a beat: but it was never Hal.

She did see Major Fellowes at the musicale, and whispered
to Lady Geraldine that the slimy dragon was there. Her ladyship kept her close and raised her eyeglass when she saw him
watching. His retreat was highly gratifying.

Julia was becoming accustomed to her new life. In the
course of one week her world had been turned on its head
and she felt as she had after that glass of champagne: slightly
dizzy and surprisingly confident. Mrs Tresilian, receiving
every detail with great interest, was delighted.

On the last Saturday in May Julia got up early, dressed
in one of her new gowns, picked at her breakfast and then
fidgeted, waiting to be collected for an all-day picnic in the
Fôret de Soignes.

It was the most talked-about event for weeks and now, as
she looked out at a cloudless sky, she could hardly believe
she was attending. Her gown was more than suitable, thank
goodness. Madame Gervais, the elegant *modiste* that Mama
had discovered in the Lower Town, had shown them the illustration in the *Journal des Dames et des Modes*.

'The hat composed of white and lilac satin,' Julia had
translated from the French. 'Ornamented with bows of ribbon
and a cluster of flowers. *Robe de satin lilas*…lilac satin—I
suppose I had better have muslin—trimmed entirely round
the bosom and at the bottom with a large quilling of blonde
lace. Gloves, pale tan, shoes of lilac kid.' She studied the
drawing. 'I like the way the hat brim turns up and the detail
of the sleeve.'

And now she was tying the thick, smooth ribbons under

her chin while Mama fluffed up the sleeves and the specially dyed lilac kid slippers peeped out from under the blonde lace—not quite as lavishly applied as in the illustration, but a positive snip at three shillings and six pence the yard. Would Major Carlow think this gown a model of *chaste simplicity?* But he was unlikely to be at something as staid as a picnic, she supposed.

'Now, be sure not sit down on the ground until the blankets are spread,' Mrs Tresilian fussed. 'I do not know what it is about picnics, but the most tidy young ladies always come back looking complete romps.' She frowned. 'And I worry a little about it being in the woods—do not go wandering off alone, dearest, or with a gentleman, even Mr Smyth.'

'Why not?' Phillip enquired. He was watching all this early morning prinking with close attention. 'What's in the woods?'

'Er…wolves,' Julia explained, earning a chuckle from her mother and sending Phillip off on a new game of Hunt the Wolf that the landlady's kittens found highly entertaining.

Lady Geraldine's barouche arrived on the stroke of nine. Mr Masters had gratified his wife by accompanying her, and they had already taken up Miss Marriott, a picture in lemon muslin and scalloped lace with a cottager hat trimmed with artificial primroses.

Felicity chattered; Julia simply sat drinking it all in. Around them, the cream of Brussels Society streamed out through the Namur Gate on the road south through the forest to Ixcelles and its lake, the site of the picnic. Mr Smyth waved from his curricle, a friend beside him. She saw groups of officers on horseback and numerous carriages like their own. This was going to be a picnic on an epic scale and someone had organised it with military precision.

'Miss Tresilian?' Mr Masters was looking at her in concern. 'Are you chilled? You shivered.'

'No, sir, thank you. I am not cold. A goose just walked over my grave,' she said with a smile. It would not do to spoil everyone else's enjoyment with foolish premonitions. But the sight of all those brave scarlet coats, the sound of masculine laughter and shouts, the clatter of hooves and the rumble of wheels reminded her vividly of why all these men were here. Soon, within weeks perhaps, troops would be streaming south out of this gate, down towards the French border. Towards war.

But no-one spoke of it in so many words. Not of the death and destruction to come, only of the politics, the tactics, as though they all just happened to be gathered in Brussels as an extension of the Congress in Vienna. And the balls and the parties must go on and everyone must pretend—on the surface at least—that the storm was not coming.

Her nerves were still jumping when they reached the picnic site on a rise of ground overlooking the lake. Tents had been set out for refreshments, for sitting in the shade, for the ladies to retire to. The band of the 52nd Foot played by kind permission of its colonel. It was, Lady Geraldine remarked, as though a Hyde Park review had been dropped into the midst of a garden party.

Mr Smyth was there to help her down from the barouche, Colonel Williams strolled past with his daughter and stopped to talk, his eyes appreciative when he looked at her, and then both gentlemen were cut out by Mr Fordyce who swept her off to the breakfast tent with the aplomb of the seasoned diplomat.

It was all very glamorous and rather unreal. Her gloomy visions of battles evaporated in the face of sunshine and tables with floral arrangements and Charles Fordyce fetching her hot chocolate and tiny pastries.

Only Julia could not be easy. Someone was watching her. She could feel it like the touch of a finger on her spine, the merest pressure. She scanned the sweep of meadow in front of her, but everyone was sitting or strolling and not paying her the slightest attention. She shifted in her seat and looked into the refreshment tent. But there were only bustling waiters and assiduous gentlemen fetching laden plates of delicacies for their parties.

'The woods are so pretty.' She turned in the other direction, hoping Mr Fordyce would not think her both fidgety and inane—and there he was. Major Carlow leaned against the trunk of a beech tree on the edge of the wood, his eyes steady on her.

Julia turned back, her pulse spiking all over the place, and picked up her cup. 'Is Lord Ellsworth at the picnic?' she enquired, almost at random. *He* is *here,* she thought, realizing how much she had secretly hoped he would be. And she had sensed him, had felt that sultry gaze on her. What did it mean, that she was so aware of him?

'His lordship is afflicted with the gout. He bit my head off when I brought in his post, then relented and told me he did not want to see my face again until tomorrow and I should go and fritter the day away. I was not, he informed me, to give a thought to him, alone, in pain and having to manage without his secretary.'

'Thus ensuring you felt thoroughly guilty?' Julia said sympathetically. She had learned that Charles Fordyce was set on a political career and his post with Lord Ellsworth was considered to be a useful first step. It sounded a very trying position.

'I soon learned not to take any notice of his megrims,' Charles said cheerfully. 'He will be fine once his gout subsides.'

Julia set herself to make conversation. It should be very pleasant in the sunshine, nibbling cinnamon curls and listening to the band. Only, the touch of Hal Carlow's regard did not leave her and she had to fight the urge to turn round and stare back. Her stomach tightened with nerves, not unpleasantly. She could feel her colour rising and her pulse quickening at the thought of another exchange of words with him. Why was he watching her? Surely not to give her the opportunity to throw any more ill-considered and outrageous remarks at his head?

With the last crumb consumed, Charles Fordyce stood. 'Shall we stroll down to the lake, Miss Tresilian?'

Julia opened her new parasol and took his arm. It gave her the chance to look up towards the trees, but the lean figure in blue had gone. Had she imagined him?

Julia made herself attend to the man with whom she was walking. He was pleasant, intelligent, cheerful and well-connected and although Mama thought his current circumstances not as comfortable as Mr Smyth's, Julia found him better company. But it was a very cool and calculating matter, this husband-hunting, she decided, thinking of the little rituals, the formal games, the pretences that one was expected to go through on the route to the altar.

What did the men make of it? Or perhaps they did not mind very much, provided their bride brought what they required to the match, whether it was connections, or breeding or money. *Or, in my case,* Julia thought, waving to Mr Smyth and his friend, *none of the first, a touch of the second, none of the third but an unblemished reputation to sweeten the bargain if a gentleman is attracted enough to overlook what was lacking.* Falling in love was out of the question. Respectable couples only did that in novels and a realistic young lady did not think of it.

'Mr Fordyce!' A lady was gesturing imperiously.

'Oh lord,' he muttered. 'Lord Ellsworth's sister, Lady Margery.'

'You must go and speak to her, of course.' It would not do

for him to antagonise his employer's relative. 'Look, there is Miss Marriott, feeding the ducks. I will join her.'

'Bless you. Lady M will want a blow by blow account of the gout and what medicines he is taking.' Charles rolled his eyes and strode off. 'Ma'am?'

Underfoot, something squelched. Julia looked down and saw the ground was marshy. For the first time she realized that Felicity was standing on a low wooden jetty; to join her she would have to go up the slope to the path. She reached the fringe of the wood and rested a hand on a tree to look at her new kid slippers.

'Botheration!' There were traces of mud along the sides and the ladies' retiring tent with its attendant maids was right across the far side of the site. By the time she got there the moisture could have soaked in, taking the dirt with it.

But she could hardly remove her shoes here, baring her stockinged feet in full view: only the fastest young lady would do such a thing. Julia slipped between the trees and into the wood. It did not take long to be completely out of sight of the open meadow, although the music was still clearly audible. The trees parted onto a sunlit glade with not only a fallen tree to sit upon but soft long grass to wipe her shoes with.

Julia perched on the trunk and untied the ribbons around her ankles, slipped off the shoes and regarded them critically. The water had not soaked through and a careful dab with the grass took off the mud almost entirely. A careful wash with soapwort when she got home and they would be as good as new.

She wriggled her stockinged toes and leaned back, staring up through the leaves to the cloudless sky above. This was perfectly lovely. She must persuade Mama to hire a gig one day and they could bring Phillip for a picnic by the lake.

'Why, Julia! Tying your garter in public? How very dashing of you.' Major Fellowes strolled out of the trees, an almost lurid figure in his scarlet uniform against the fresh greens.

'I am wiping my shoes,' she said coldly. There was nothing to be afraid of, she told herself. She was only yards from a crowd of people. 'And a gentleman would leave me in privacy.'

'Let me tie up your ribbons for you,' he said, his voice suggestively husky. 'Or untie some others.'

But of course, as he very well knew, she might be within yards of safety but if she ran she was going to burst out of the woods, barefoot and dishevelled—and he had only to let his vivid uniform be glimpsed through the trees for it to appear that she had been involved in a most disreputable tryst.

Julia jammed her feet into the slippers, tying the ribbons with a hasty knot. 'Go away.' She got to her feet, the fallen tree trunk massive behind her: no escape that way. She began to edge around the glade, but he was faster. With two long strides he had her, his hand fastening around her wrist to jerk her to him. Julia landed with a thump against his very solid chest, the braid and buttons of his uniform imprinting themselves painfully through spencer, gown and camisole.

'Now then, stop being difficult—' Fellowes wrapped his left arm around her, imprisoning her as she struggled to lift her free hand.

'Stop it!' Julia ducked her head to find some bare skin to bite. She wouldn't win, she knew that, he was too big and too strong, but if she could just get him off balance she might have a chance to run.

'Let her go.' The words dropped into the still air of the clearing like three strokes on a bell. *Hal.*

Chapter Four

'**Y**ou are developing a bad habit of spoiling my fun, Carlow.' Fellowes did not release her, but against her breast Julia felt his heartbeat quicken. He was not as unmoved as his drawl might suggest.

'I do not think Miss Tresilian shares your idea of *fun*.' Hal was behind her, but she could hear from his voice that he was coming closer. 'Let her go.'

'I don't come interfering with your bits of muslin, Carlow, though by all accounts, the town is littered with them. I suggest you leave mine alone and get back to that opera dancer you're chasing.'

'Oh dear.' Hal sounded vaguely regretful. By tipping her head back Julia could see Fellowes's jaw clench. He was no more fooled by the mild tone than she was. He began to edge backwards, keeping her between himself and the other man.

'You know,' Hal continued, close now, 'I was ready to settle this with just your grovelling apology to Miss Tresilian and your word that you would not trouble her again. But now I am going to have to hurt you.' Fellowes went very still. 'Of course, if I am to do that, you will have to let Miss Tresilian go and stop skulking behind her like a coward. But perhaps you are that, as well as being no gentleman?'

'Be damned to you, Carlow.' Fellowes spun Julia round and pushed her towards Hal. For the second time, she landed painfully against braid, buttons and solid man, but this time it took an effort of will not to cling on for dear life.

'Miss Tresilian, are you unhurt?'

Except for frogging imprinted all over my bosom, she thought wildly. 'Yes, thank you, Major.'

'If you would care to sit on the fallen tree, ma'am? Just while I deal with this—' He waved a hand towards the other officer.

'Of course. Thank you.' Julia suppressed the urge to curtsey—Hal's manner was better suited to the ballroom than to a brawl in a woodland glade—and retreated to the log. 'You won't kill him, will you?'

'I would remind you, sir, that duelling between serving officers is forbidden,' Fellowes cut in.

Julia sat down and tried to tug her clothing into order while keeping her eyes riveted on Hal. Fellowes was right. If Hal fought a duel he could be in serious trouble with the military authorities. If he assaulted a fellow officer without the benefit of a duel's formalities and killed him, then things would be even worse.

'He is a blackguard,' she said, controlling the shake in her voice. 'But Wellington will not thank you for killing any officer of his just now.'

'Exactly,' Fellowes blustered.

'Thank you both for your flattering, and quite accurate, assumption that I would best Major Fellowes,' Hal remarked, and despite everything, Julia felt her lips curve at the arrogance in his voice. 'What would you like me to do with him, Miss Tresilian?'

A well-bred lady should have fainted by now. Or, if conscious, she might say, in a forgiving and dignified manner, *Send him on his way with a warning.* Julia smoothed down her skirt, straightened her bonnet and said, 'Hit him, please.'

'With pleasure.' Hal took two long strides, doubled his right fist and hit Major Fellowes squarely on the point of the jaw. The taller man went down on his back, scrambled to his feet and launched himself at Hal, meeting a solid left hook that threw him back against a tree. Hal closed in, hit him in the stomach, took a blow to the side of the head, countered with another left, and Fellowes slid ungracefully to the ground, legs sprawling.

Hal took him by the lapels, hauled him to his feet and gave him a push that sent him staggering out of the clearing. 'And if I ever find you have been bothering Miss Tresilian again, I really will hurt you.'

He turned back to her, blowing on his grazed knuckles. 'Are you all right?'

There did not appear to be much breath left in her lungs. Julia collected what little she could find. 'Yes. Thank you. I feel a little…odd.' He frowned, as he came towards her. 'He didn't hurt me; I am just not used to violence.'

'You did say to hit him,' Hal pointed out, not unreasonably. 'Running him through would have been—'

'Messier,' she finished faintly, then got a grip on herself. 'Thank you, Major Carlow. That is the second time you have rescued me from Major Fellowes. You must think I have been encouraging him, but really, I have not.'

'I know.' He stopped, perhaps six feet from her, and grinned. Her stomach swooped in a most disconcerting manner. Really, the wretched man had far too much charm to be allowed out. As for the effect on her of the way he had dealt with Fellowes—that was too shamefully primitive to contemplate. 'But I am surprised you didn't give him a lecture on his morals. It worked with me,' he continued, managing to look penitent.

Julia bit back a gurgle of laughter. It was the shock, it was making her positively hysterical. 'Indeed, Major Carlow? Are you telling me that you have reformed?'

'I am working on the gaming, ineffectually so far I am afraid, and I am not making much progress with the fighting or the drinking either, but otherwise, yes, I am completely reformed.' He looked convincingly serious.

'Gaming, fighting, drinking—what does that leave?' Julia asked and then realized: women! Opera dancers. Lady Horton. 'Oh! Major Carlow, you should not mention such things to me!' *As if he is going to give up womanising because I do not approve!*

'I very carefully did not,' he said, his lips twitching in the way that made her want to smile back. 'I am afraid you have just revealed a surprising indelicacy of mind, Miss Tresilian.'

'You—' Julia bit back the words, seeing the wickedness in the blue-grey eyes. 'I know what you are doing: you are teasing me to take my mind off Fellowes.'

'Did it work?'

'Admirably,' she acknowledged. 'Do I look respectable enough to go back to the meadow?'

'Yes.' He studied her, frowning. 'Although one of the flowers in your bonnet has come unpinned. I can fix it well enough for you to get to the retiring tent.'

'Thank you.' Julia got up and took a step towards him, rather too hastily she realized as her feet tangled in her trailing shoe ties. 'Ah!' She pitched forward and was neatly caught. Hal did not seem inclined to release her, and she found she had no will to step away either. 'Major, I have to say that, however magnificent officers' uniforms are, they are not comfortable if one is propelled into them…'

Her voice trailed off. Hal was looking down at her, all the laughter gone from his eyes. And all the blue, too. Stormy grey stared down into her wide gaze and her breath caught up as though in that storm. His hands curled lightly around her upper arms, holding her away from his chest where she had landed, but not so far that she could not see the pulse beating hard in his throat above the rigid neck cloth or the way his lips had parted fractionally.

He is going to kiss me, she realized, heart pounding. Her first kiss. She had imagined it would be a chaste and respectful salute by a gentleman who, once they were betrothed, would only commit such an intimacy in the presence of a chaperone.

Only Hal's kisses would not be chaste, or respectful or subject to the dictates of a chaperone. His would be exciting and dangerous and she had no vocabulary to even fantasize about them. But she wanted them. Mouth dry, Julia stared back into the troubled, stormy eyes above her and became very still, waiting.

Julia was waiting for him to kiss her. Hal could see it in her wide, trusting eyes, in the softly parted lips, in the way her breathing had become faster as he held her. Had she ever been kissed before? Kissed, as a man like him would kiss her? Of course not. And he wanted to take that first kiss, that first taste of innocence. He wanted to mould her lips with his, to open them and explore with his tongue, plunder the sweet, moist secrets of her mouth. Taste her, teach her his taste. Teach her to know his body and her own.

Wanted? Hell, he *needed* to kiss her, ached to do it. He was iron-hard with arousal as he stood there.

She would let him because, madly, she seemed to trust him, despite his warnings, despite what she must have heard about him. She would let him kiss her, because she had no idea what it would be like or what fire she would be playing with. She thought kisses were sweetly romantic, that one brush of the lips was all that would be exchanged here.

He stared down at the heart-shaped face, the absurdly determined little chin, the tip-tilted nose, the intelligent eyes, all shadowed by the upturned brim of that fancy new hat. She was his to take. She was all he wanted. And he had no idea why.

Hell, why not? He had always felt denying temptation was over-rated. He wanted her, she wanted him—and afterwards, he would be cured of this ridiculous desire. Hal swallowed. It wasn't like that with Julia; he couldn't be that calculating, it was wrong…

But if he kissed her, made love to her skilfully so he did not alarm her, if he was careful and made certain she wanted him as much as he wanted her—was that so very wrong?

As though of their own volition, his hands came up to untie the thick silk of the bonnet ribbons, slithering like a warm caress over the backs of his hands. He tossed the hat aside, and her eyes widened so he could see his own reflection in them, but she made no sound of protest, only parted those soft, infinitely tempting lips in a little gasp.

Hal bent his head and skimmed his lips over her temple, feathering the delicate skin with tiny kisses. Julia tipped her head like a cat, and he moved lower, down her cheek, nipping lightly at the earlobe. She caught her breath, and he stopped, waiting for her to accept the different sensation. It was intriguing to discover her untutored responses, to lead with an inexperienced partner and not to expect her to reciprocate.

His fingers moved up to cup her head and encountered pins. One by one, he pulled them free and her hair came down, transforming her into the image of a wood nymph in the green glade.

'Ah yes,' Hal murmured and bent to kiss her. Her mouth

was so sweet, tasting blamelessly of sugar and spice and lemonade. She smelled so fresh, so good, and, when he pulled her to him she came with a yielding that part of his mind, the part that was quite deliberately using all his skill to seduce her, recognized as innocence.

How long was it since he had tasted innocence? He recoiled from the memory of youthful passion, of naïve intentions made to seem impure and wrong. He wanted that purity again, even though all he could bring to it was the soiled expertise of experience.

Under his, her lips softened, parted without resistance when he probed with his tongue, feeling the sensual delight overwhelm his lingering scruples. *Ah yes.* Her response was total and trusting; it told him he could move further, and, when he slid one hand to her breast, rubbed his palm against it as if by accident, he felt the nipple peaking, rising for him.

Julia could hear her own voice, even though words were beyond her. She had expected Hal to kiss her on the mouth, and he had. But he seemed as fascinated by her throat, her ears, her cheek, her temple… *'Aah,'* she whispered as his lips found the swell of her breasts above the froth of lace.

She wanted to pull him back to her mouth, which ought to feel safer than these mysterious sensations that were sending shivers down her spine, making her breasts ache, creating that strange sensation in the pit of her stomach and the embarrassing heat where her thighs… She couldn't think about it, only feel.

Julia lifted her hands and ran them into the thick gold-brown hair, tugging gently until he lifted his head, his eyes bright and intent. 'What do you want?' he asked, his voice husky.

'I don't know,' she whispered. 'I want something and I don't know what it is.'

* * *

'We will find it,' Hal promised, capturing her mouth again, one hand cupping her breast, the thumb stroking through the flimsy fabric, tormenting the hard nub. It would take very little, he thought hazily, to bring her to the peak, to tip her into ecstasy, to give her pleasure and be satisfied with that himself. But his usual control seemed to be slipping, his breathing was all over the place, and it was an effort not to crush her to him, grind his hips against her yielding body. She smelled so sweet, felt so soft, yielded so passionately.

He was drowning in her as much as she in him, swept away by emotions he had had not felt in years. He had to have her, he realized, his sophisticated control shattered.

There was fabric and fastenings between him and his goal now. Without lifting his mouth, Hal went to his knees, taking Julia with him, down into the long, soft grass spangled with flowers, their scent as innocent as she was. Then he was stretched above her, his fingers finding their own wicked way around buttons and tapes; she quivered as they brushed her skin.

His booted feet shifted, crushing the lush grass, filling the air around them with the smell of it, bringing with it a swirl of memories and emotions long buried. Confused, Hal opened his eyes. The sunlight through the branches sifted shadows over her spread hair, and he was shaken out of the present, back to another wood, another time—with a girl as innocent and sweetly generous as Julia.

The suppressed memory surged back: shouting and discovery and a rural idyll exposed as adolescent desire that had got out of hand. *Whoreson rakehell…* The voices filled his head, stabbed at his conscience, killed his desire.

Hal rolled away from Julia and sat up, raking his hands through his hair, breathing hard through clenched teeth. Damn it, he had learned expertise and with it, control, so that a whoreson rakehell he might be, but he was a skilful one, utterly in command of himself. *So command yourself now.*

'I am sorry.' He made himself look at Julia as she sat up, her mouth swollen with his kisses, her eyes wide and confused by his assault on her senses and his withdrawal. 'Did I hurt you? I'm as bad as he is. Hell…'

'No,' she said, her hands fumbling blindly with the bodice of her gown. 'No. You would have stopped if I had asked you, wouldn't you?'

'Yes.' *Please God that is true.* He rested his head on his knees for a moment, fighting the dread that he might not have listened. 'I'm sorry, I warned you what I am, but I should not expect you to understand.'

Julia was silent. He made himself look at her and found she had fastened her gown and was standing up, brushing at her skirts, her hair still tumbled around her shoulders. Just the sight of it sent a spear of lust through his groin. Hal got to his feet and went to pick up her bonnet, holding it while she twisted her hair up, fixing it with the pins that remained, then trapping it under the hat.

'No, I do not understand,' she murmured at last. 'I do not understand what I felt just now, why I…when I know I should not.'

He had no answers for her, no excuses. 'If you take that path there, you will find you come out very close to the tents.' Hal pointed back to the way he had entered the clearing, just wanting her gone, safe, away from him.

He made himself stand still while she smiled a little uncertainly and walked away, vanishing in seconds into the green foliage. Then he went to sit on the tree trunk, clasped his hands, leaned his forearms on his thighs and stared at the crushed grass. He must stay away from her. There were a number of perfectly pleasant men—worthy men, he had no doubt—who were taking a respectable interest in her. She would marry one of them. And then she would be safe from men like Fellowes. Men like himself.

There was a small scrap of blonde lace lying by his boot. Hal bent and picked it up, smoothing it between his fingers for a long time—until he thought he could master his expression—then he slid it into the breast of his jacket and walked out of the clearing.

'Have you ever been kissed, Felicity?' Julia asked without preamble as they sat side by side on a rug, under their parasols, waiting for Mr Smyth and Mr Fordyce to fetch them ices. Half an hour in the ladies' retiring tent, and she was tidy and composed enough to make the grass stains on her skirts plausibly the result of a trip.

'Kissed?' Felicity simpered, blushed, then asked, 'Properly kissed?'

Julia nodded.

'Yes, once.'

'What was it like?'

'Oh, wonderful…' She smirked, glanced sideways at Julia, then admitted, 'No, actually it was horrid.'

'Horrid?' No, Hal's kiss had not been that. It had been wonderful, terrifying, puzzling.

'It was *wet*. He wanted me to open my mouth and—' Felicity lowered her voice even further '—he tried to put his tongue into it.'

'What did you do?' Julia fought the blush rising to her cheeks at the memory of that shocking intimacy.

'I kicked him,' Felicity said, smug. 'And told him he was a beast. And so he slunk off.'

'Well done,' Julia said weakly. Her nerves were tingling, her pulse still erratic; a strange, unfamiliar restlessness was making it very difficult to sit demurely on the rug as a lady should; and her conscience was struggling to make itself heard against those novel physical messages.

'Why do you ask? Has someone tried to kiss you?'

'Well, er, yes,' Julia confessed. Was that all it had been: a kiss? It had seemed more somehow.

'Mr Fordyce?' Felicity hazarded. 'I think he is very nice. So is Mr Smyth, but he's a clergyman, so I don't expect it was him.'

'No, neither of them. Ssh, here they come.'

Julia ate her ice and talked and strolled around and was introduced to people, drank lemonade and joined in the applause at an impromptu cricket match. The sun began to dip in the sky, and the restless, nameless yearning became stronger, harder to ignore, no easier to control and her eyes searched fruitlessly amongst the crowd, seeking Hal's face.

Whatever these feelings were, they had everything to do with a lean, hard body against hers making her feel, at one and the same time, both recklessly abandoned and utterly insecure. *I must not see him again. I must not.*

When stumps were pulled and the company began to wander towards the tents for tea, Lady Geraldine said, 'There is talk of a torch-lit carriage drive through the forest after dark. Do you think your mamas would object if we kept you out so late?'

'Why no, I do not think Mama would mind; she said that as I was with you, Lady Geraldine, she was not at all concerned what time I was home.' Felicity nodded energetic agreement.

'Well then, we will all take part. And, Julia, if one of your beaux should ask, you may ride with him in his carriage—provided that it stays close to ours at all times.'

Both Mr Smyth and Mr Fordyce had their sporting carriages with them, it was just a question which of them asked her first. A drive through the forest would be exciting and romantic in the most innocent and respectable of ways, she was sure. Only it was not one of her respectable potential suitors she wanted to be with. In the darkness the only man she yearned to be beside was Hal Carlow, her pulse beating wildly, her breath catching in her throat, as they galloped through the night, his hands strong on the reins.

A Gothic romance in fact, she scolded herself. She was obviously reading too many of them, if she found the idea of being alone with *him,* racketing through the darkness at a potentially lethal pace, romantic. In reality, it would be thoroughly alarming, just as that kiss had been.

That bracing thought supported her through tea and the flattering experience of having not just Mr Fordyce but Mr Smyth and Colonel Williams solicit her company for the torchlight drive. Mr Fordyce was first, so good manners dictated that she accept his offer, although if she had a free choice she could not have said which gentleman she preferred. They all seemed pleasant, intelligent, worthy—and rather dull. Just what she should be hoping for in a potential husband in fact. Excitement in a husband would be very wearing.

As the sun dropped below the trees a cool breeze set in. Julia wrapped her cloak snugly around herself while the men set about organising the carriages into a line. Someone had anticipated the drive and had brought a wagon filled with torches to light at the brazier, and the horsemen were drafted into acting as outriders to carry the burning brands.

At last, all was ready and the cavalcade set off at a decorous trot. Julia wondered if someone staid had been put at the front, then decided not as the trot became a canter. From in front and behind there were whoops of delight, but Mr Fordyce kept his pair well in hand.

On either side, riders holding up the torches were cantering on the wide grassy verges. 'It is like a scene from fairyland,'

Julia gasped, entranced by the wild shadows thrown on the trees, the thunder of hooves, the echoes of laughter.

'That's a fine animal,' Charles Fordyce observed, glancing to his right.

Julia leaned back so she could look around him and gasped. It was, indeed, magnificent. A huge grey, so pale as to be almost white in the torchlight, its mane and tail dark charcoal. Its rider, quite still in the saddle, was watching her, his face garishly highlighted by the flaming brand he held. *Hal.* Everything that she had been trying to forget about the day came flooding back, and she gave thanks for the darkness hiding her face.

'A Light Dragoon.' Fordyce gave his own team more rein. The grey lengthened its stride to stay alongside.

'It is Major Carlow,' Julia said without thinking, and the pair pecked as though the reins had been jerked, just as her heartbeat seemed to jolt in her chest.

'Carlow? You know him?' Fordyce's normally pleasant voice was cool.

Hal's wretched reputation, he did warn me about that too…'He rescued me from a man who accosted me in the Parc,' she said. 'And he introduced me to Lady Geraldine at once; that is how I met her.' She managed what she hoped was a light laugh. 'I understand he is the most terrible rake, but on that occasion, I would have welcomed the assistance of Bonaparte himself.'

'Who would have been rather less detrimental to your reputation, I imagine,' Charles said, sounding intolerably stuffy.

'I am sure that would be the case, if I had continued round the Parc in Major Carlow's company,' she said stiffly. 'As it was, he took pains to limit any damage that might arise from sanctimonious persons getting the wrong idea.' *Oh dear, now that sounds as though I have accused him of being a prig. And if only he knew it, he is right: Hal is dangerous.*

Mr Fordyce obviously thought so too. 'An unmarried lady cannot be too careful,' he snapped. 'One can only speculate upon why he has chosen to ride beside *this* carriage.' He turned more obviously and stared at Hal. 'I've a mind to call the fellow out—'

'No! My goodness, please do not do any such thing!' Julia grasped his forearm. 'He is said to be lethal.'

'—but I will not, lest your name were to be linked to the affair,' Charles said, as if she had not spoken. 'You will not, naturally, have anything more to do with him.'

'What?' Julia gasped. 'I have no intention of doing so, but you have no business telling me with whom I may, or may not, associate, Mr Fordyce!'

'I most certainly have, unless you have been playing fast and loose with me, Miss Tresilian.' It was not easy, quarrelling in a moving carriage behind a team cantering through near darkness, but Charles Fordyce was obviously set on it.

'You, sir, have been leaping to quite unwarranted conclusions,' Julia snapped.

The big grey suddenly surged ahead of them, crossed between their team and the rear of the Masters' carriage in front and was brought round to canter close beside Julia.

'What the devil!' Fordyce exclaimed.

'Miss Tresilian, do you need assistance? You sounded distressed.'

Julia glared up at Hal, suddenly completely out of charity with the entire male sex. 'I am perfectly fine, thank you, Major Carlow. Will you please *go away?*' *I would be as calm as a millpond, if it were not for you,* she wanted to throw at him, confused at her own anger.

'Ma'am.' He spurred the horse ahead without looking back, leaving Julia fulminating beside an equally furious driver.

'He has the nerve to ask if you are all right when you are

driving with *me?'* Charles Fordyce demanded. 'That hell-born blood thinks you need protection from *me?'*

'Mr Fordyce!' Julia grabbed the side rail as the carriage lurched. 'Will you kindly look to your horses and stop lecturing me and ranting about Major Carlow?'

'Certainly, ma'am,' he said between gritted teeth. 'I apologise for boring you.'

'Not at all,' she replied, equally stiffly as they drove on in seething silence.

Well, at least I know he has an unpleasant jealous streak. Better to know now than after I have agreed to marry him, Julia thought, wondering how she was going to explain the disappearance of one of her handful of suitors to her mother and Lady Geraldine.

Chapter Five

$\mathcal{H}$al woke with a thundering hangover. He lay flat on his back trying to work out why, when he could recall no party. He was still in shirt and trousers and was wearing one boot; his mouth felt as though a flock of pigeons had been roosting in it overnight and his head was splitting.

When he sat up with a groan, keeping his stomach in its right place with some difficulty, he saw the bottles on the floor and realized why. There had been no party. He had been drinking brandy—his foot knocked against a black bottle that rolled away and crashed into the others with nerve-jangling effect—and claret, all by himself.

'What the hell?' he enquired of the empty room as he squinted at the clock. Ten. He wasn't on duty until the afternoon, thank God.

Julia. He had kissed her. Oh God, he had more than kissed her. He had almost debauched her, right there in that glade.

Hal got to his feet and lurched for the bell pull. Trying to think was damnably painful, and he didn't seem to be doing very well. *Keep going,* he told himself. *It will make sense eventually. But why? What came over me?* There was only one answer to that: lust. Then he had seen Julia in the carriage with that smug secretary of Ellsworth's so he had ridden alongside, just to keep an eye on her. And she had been upset, he could hear it in her tone as she talked to the man, even if he could not hear her words. So he had asked her if she was all right, because no-one was going to distress Julia while he could help it—except, obviously himself—and something had gone wrong...

And then he'd been angry and... He couldn't recall anything else. But whatever had happened, it had not involved either Julia or any other sort of satisfaction, otherwise he would not be ankle-deep in bottles.

'*M'sieu?*' The waiter flung the door back with his usual enthusiasm.

'*Silence!*' Hal started to shout, then dropped his voice to a hiss. 'Coffee. Strong, black. Lots of it. Toast. Dry. And is Captain Grey in his room?' The man nodded nervously. 'Then ask him if he will come here, will you? *Quietly.*'

'Headache?' Grey asked with a cheerful lack of sympathy five minutes later, picking his way through discarded bottles and clothing.

'You might say that.' Hal sat on the edge of the bed and waited for the room to stop moving.

'I thought you had the hardest head of any man I know,' Grey observed with a grin. 'How gratifying to find you are human after all.'

'I do have the hardest head. And just now, the most painful. Will, did I challenge anyone last night?'

'What? To a duel? No.'

'Thank God for small mercies.' So, he had ridden away, not challenged Fordyce for whatever quarrel he and Julia had been having. Such restraint surprised him.

It was not until he had drunk three cups of coffee, forced down two rolls and stuck his head into cold water that he remembered that Julia had told him to go away in a voice icy with anger, and he had gone, because, much though he wanted to quarrel with her companion, he wanted her to forgive him. And she was angry with him, not just with Fordyce.

'There's post.' Will Grey strolled back in and poured himself some coffee from the second pot that Hal was working his way through. He tossed the heap onto the table, ignored Hal's wince, and sorted through it.

'Who's that?' Hal pulled the top one in his pile towards him. 'Don't recognize the writing.'

'Open it,' Grey suggested as he broke the seal on one of his, scattering wax shards all over the table. A waft of heavy perfume filled the air, revolting Hal's stomach. 'Ah, the divine Susannah.'

Hal opened it and glanced at the signature. *Your obedient servant, Mildenhall,* the strong black signature said. What the devil was Monty, Viscount Mildenhall, doing writing to him? He'd been at Monty's wedding to Midge Hebden, back in February, but they were hardly regular correspondents, despite having both served together before Monty left the Army.

Despite his aching head, he grinned at the memory of the most chaotic wedding he had ever attended. The groom had dragged his bride up the aisle of St George's, Hanover Square, and demanded that the vicar marry them, the vicar had protested that the bride was obviously unwilling, her relatives were swooning from mortification or glowering like thunderclouds, depending on their sex, and the bride was arguing with almost everyone. At this point Hal had been forced to stuff his handkerchief into his mouth and duck under cover of the pew in order to stifle his laughter.

Monty, a man of quiet determination, had not been an effective officer for nothing. He overcame both bride and cleric, and the couple were duly wed. It was not until Hal and his brother Marcus were back at the wedding breakfast that Rick Bredon, Midge's step-brother, drew them to one side to explain the chaos.

Hal's reminiscent grin faded. Midge had been stopped on the steps of the church by a man claiming to be her half-brother, Stephen Hebden. Midge, affectionate and impulsive as ever, had wanted him to come into the church, only for him to be violently rejected by her uncle until Monty, marching out to find his bride, had stopped the argument. By which time the man had gone.

Rick, whose father had tried to find Midge's half-brother for years and believed him dead, was adamant that the man was an impostor, but Hal had known better. Stephen Hebden, also known as Stephano Beshaley, was the illegitimate son of Midge's father and his Gypsy lover and a sworn enemy of the Carlow family, and of the family of Marcus Carlow's wife, Nell Wardale.

The reason for his hatred was a mystery that they were only slowly unravelling. All they really knew was that it reached back twenty years to the days when Hal's father, the Earl of Narborough, Nell's father, William Wardale, the Earl of Leybourne and Midge and Stephan's father, Kit Hebden, Baron Framlingham, had worked together to unmask a French spy at the heart of government.

Hebden, the code breaker, had been murdered, apparently by Wardale, who went to the gallows for the crime while his best friend George Carlow, Lord Narborough, stood by, convinced of his culpability. His father, Hal knew, had never recovered from his sense of guilt over that. With their title and their lands attaindered, the Wardale family had slipped into poverty and lost contact with each other. Midge's mother had remarried.

And then, for some reason no-one could fathom, the old scandal had resurfaced last year in a series of attacks on the three families that all seemed to centre on Stephen Hebden. Hal felt the cold anger sweep over him again as he recalled the nightmare.

But the more they had discovered, the more people who were drawn into the mess, the less they understood, even with the assistance of old family friend Robert Veryan, Lord Keddinton. Although Veryan was high in government circles, even he could not explain it.

When Hal was last home on leave, Marcus had said that he suspected someone else must be involved, that it could not just be Stephano Beshaley, ruthlessly fulfilling his mother's dying curse on the three families.

Hal shook his head, winced and focused on the letter.

My dear Carlow,

I have been in some trouble to decide what best to do in this matter, but, given that I know you better than your brother, I have decided to write to you.

You will recall the events that disturbed my wedding in February. Despite my best efforts, my wife continues to associate with her half-brother, Beshaley. Midge, bless her, would believe the best of Beelzebub.

Damn it, this was what he feared. Had another of Beshaley's calling cards—silken ropes that recalled the execution of a peer—been found? If it had, danger at worst, scandal and ruined reputations at best, were to be expected.

You will forgive me, I hope, for referring to the gossip that arose when your sister-in-law resumed her place in Society. That, and the other incidents affecting the three families, have been well-managed by those concerned. But now murmurings have come to my ears from busy-bodies who delight in telling me gossip affecting Midge. Speculation is resurfacing about the old scandal.

To be frank, there is doubt thrown on Wardale's guilt as the murderer. Hebden died in your father's arms, outside your father's own study. I will tell you this bluntly, as in your shoes I would prefer to be told—there are whispers at the highest level that it is suspicious that Lord Narborough did nothing to help clear Wardale's name, despite the fact that they were close friends.

I have tried, discreetly, to find the source of these rumours, for the respect I have for you from our days fighting together, and for the friendship Midge has for your sister Verity. But it is like chasing a wisp of smoke.

Nothing is spoken of that links your father's name with the spy's treachery—that aspect of the original murder is still not common knowledge. But whispers about Wardale's liaison with Midge's mother are circulating, along with comments that your father is known to hold the strongest of views on marital infidelity. Without an understanding of the work the three men were engaged on, a puritanical aversion to adultery is no motive to be taken seriously for murder. But once spying is added to the mix, at this time when the whole country is in uproar over the renewed French menace, God knows what stories will be spun.

I hope this warning will suffice to put you on your guard to protect your father and your family. I imagine you could well do without this news, just when the great confrontation with Napoleon is looming. I envy you the opportunity to take part in that fight.

For myself, with a happy event expected in the autumn, I only want to keep Midge safe from the poisonous webs her half-brother weaves.

Believe me, my dear Carlow,
Your obedient servant,
Mildenhall

'Hell and damnation.' Hal tossed the letter onto the table and tried to think. He had two conflicting duties, but the priority was clear. He must not follow his immediate instinct and go home: Napoleon could make his move at any moment, this was no time to take leave. All he could do was to write to warn Marcus.

'Problems?' Grey raised a languid eyebrow. 'I'll swap you for my mail; it is all bills—and Susannah wanting a new gown. Could I have spent so much at my snyder when I was last in town? Hard to believe.'

'You don't want this,' Hal said casually. 'Legal problems with some tiresome old family legacy. And yes, I can believe your tailor's bill is astronomical.' He stood up, letter in hand. 'I'd better write to my brother, I suppose.'

'I'll leave you to it.' Grey ambled out, coffee cup in hand. 'See you at luncheon?'

Hal shuddered at the thought of food, although he knew he was going to have to eat. 'Yes.' As the door shut, he flipped open his writing desk and unscrewed the top of the ink pot. Best to send Monty's letter as an enclosure, save rewriting the lot.

> *Marcus,* he scrawled.
> *Read this. What the hell is going on? Can't someone put a bullet in the bastard?*
> *Say the pretty to the parents and my love to Nell and the girls,*
> *Yr. affect. brother,*
> *Hal*

Not his greatest literary work, but the best he could do with this headache. Hal folded Mildenhall's letter inside his own, sealed it in four places and wrote the country address on it, adding *To be forwarded,* just in case Marcus had taken it into his head to travel. He doubted it. His sister-in-law was increasing again and Marcus, deeply protective, was certain to have her tucked away in deepest Hertfordshire.

Monty about to be a father, Marcus with a little son already and another child on the way. People no sooner got married than they were fathering brats, he thought irritably, despite the fact he was fond of young William George Carlow. He was half way to the bell pull to have the letter taken down, when a mental picture of Julia with one hand resting protectively on the swell of her belly hit him like a blow.

He made a sharp gesture of shocked repudiation. First he had almost ravished her, now his imagination had made the wild leap to her carrying his child. Which she might well be, if some shreds of self-control hadn't saved them both yesterday. He tried to recall what had stopped him, but he couldn't, it was all too confused. But one thing was clear: this could go no further. There was no way he could allow himself to see her again.

Julia tried hard to look regretful while Mama and Lady Geraldine regarded her with expressions of deep disappointment over their tea cups. She was not used to disappointing anyone and it was an unpleasant novelty.

'You *quarrelled* with Mr Fordyce?' Mrs Tresilian said in tones of disbelief. 'But you never quarrel with anyone, Julia. You would never do anything so unladylike, surely?'

'He was priggish and jealous beyond bearing,' she said, setting her cup down with a rattle. So much for making a clean breast of it—*of some of it*, she corrected herself—you got lectured. Being a fast and disobedient young lady was beginning to have its attractions. 'I was sharp with him.'

'Jealous of whom?' Lady Geraldine enquired. 'Mr Smyth or the colonel?'

'Major Carlow,' Julia said, hurling oil on flames.

'Hal Carlow!'

'But you said he was a rake, Julia,' Mrs Tresilian said into the silence that followed Lady Geraldine's exclamation. 'What could you possibly have done with him to make Mr Fordyce jealous?'

'Nothing,' she denied vehemently, managing to blush rosily at the same time. She had done nothing that Charles Fordyce knew about, that was true. But she had done more than enough with Hal Carlow to send her mother into fits of the vapours.

'Julia,' her mother began as Lady Geraldine's eyebrows arched in surprise.

'I let slip that I know him. So Mr Fordyce treated me to a lecture on the danger to my reputation. Which he had no call to do,' she added hotly, guilt making her protest too much. 'Anyone would think he had made me an offer.'

'Who?' Mrs Tresilian gasped. 'Which of them? What kind of offer?'

'Mr Fordyce. Marriage,' Julia said, hanging on to her temper with difficulty. 'But he has not.' What was the matter with her? She never lost her temper, never answered Mama back. And now listen to her!

Her mother subsided, fanning herself. 'Oh dear, oh dear.'

'Mama, I do not want to marry a man who could exhibit such jealousy when I have done nothing to deserve it,' Julia said, trying for a more moderate tone. 'Mr Fordyce has no reason to suspect Major Carlow of anything.'

Lady Geraldine smiled. 'The day that one did not suspect Major Carlow of something, the moon will be made of green cheese.'

Julia smiled tightly and poured more tea. This promised to be a long afternoon, and all she had to distract herself was the guilty knowledge that she had lost one suitor and had lost her temper with Hal.

But to her surprise, and relief, their guest turned the conversation. 'Have you been to hear Madame Catalani at the Opera yet, Mrs Tresilian?'

'No, I am afraid not.' Tickets for the opera were not within the household budget. 'I believe she is very good.'

'Oh, stupendous! Her *Semiramide* has such passion, such dramatic range,' Lady Geraldine enthused. 'I have written to ask her to perform at the reception I am giving in honour of the duke.' There was no need to ask which duke. In a city full of the aristocrats of half a dozen nations, 'the duke' could only mean Wellington.

To Julia's relief the conversation turned to plans for the reception and her mother's attention to what she should wear for it. All she had to do was to behave herself and not alienate either of her remaining suitors. That was her duty, especially now that Mama had spent so much money on her gowns. But it all sounded rather dull. It was not until several minutes later that Julia realized what she was thinking. Two weeks ago, she would have been stunned with delighted disbelief to have a pair of eligible gentlemen showing an interest in her. But then, two weeks ago, she had not met Hal Carlow. *I must not think of him. I* must *marry.*

The next morning there was a note with her post.

My dear Julia,
 Madame C. has refused my request that she sing at the reception!! And I am laid on my bed with a putrid sore throat and am thus unable to go and reason with the creature face to face. Imagine refusing the Duke!!
 Julia, my reliance is entirely upon you utterly—go

*and reason with her—my dear Masters is from town
and will not return soon enough to press the matter.
Offer her whatever is necessary to secure her agreement.*

G.M.

Julia passed it across the table, trying to imagine herself
confronting a demanding *prima donna* and insisting upon
her performing.

'My goodness,' Mrs Tresilian said faintly. 'How alarming.
But you cannot refuse to oblige Lady Geraldine, not after her
kindness to you. You must take Maria and go at once.'

'But, Mama, the marketing…'

'Do it at the same time, dear. The shops in the Lower Town
are acceptable, and cheaper.'

'Yes, Mama.' At least she could not get into any scrapes
at the Opera.

Chapter Six

Julia stared at the imposing portico of the building in front of her. Did one go through the public entrance at the front, or around to the stage door? Beside her, Maria shifted the weight of the basket from one hand to the other and sighed.

Julia put back her shoulders and marched up the front steps. She was, after all, the representative of one of the leading figures of Brussels' Society, calling on a singer of international renown. 'Wait there.' She gestured to some niches along the walls of the heavily gilded entrance hall. 'And hide the basket underneath the bench.'

A bored looking porter approached as Maria sat down. '*Oui?*'

'I am here to see *Madame* Catalani,' Julia said in French with a faint smile, trying for the sort of confident and commanding charm that Lady Geraldine appeared to find so easy. 'On behalf of Lady Geraldine Masters.' She produced one of Lady Geraldine's cards. He glanced at it.

'*Madame* is expecting you?'

'Of course,' she said. She was going to look foolish if the porter informed her that the singer was not here.

'*Madame* is in consultation with the leader of the orchestra. She will not be free for at least an hour.'

'In that case, I will wait. Kindly show me to her dressing room.' Julia decided she was definitely more afraid of Lady Geraldine's displeasure than she was of bored porters or even temperamental *prima donnas*.

The porter, on the other hand, appeared distinctly unimpressed with her. Presumably, he spent his life fending off demanding members of the public—mostly gentlemen—all wanting access to the singers, dancers and actresses. 'Through there, *mam'zelle*.' He pointed to a door. 'Right along to the end, turn left.'

'You had better go back to Place de Leuvan,' Julia told the maid. She could hardly accompany Julia and sit in the singer's dressing room, not with a basket containing fish. 'I do not want that herring hanging around in the heat. I will take a cab back.' The cabs in Brussels were clean and respectable; even Mama could not disapprove of her taking one.

The crimson-flocked wallpaper and gilt and mirrors vanished as soon as she was through the door which opened onto a narrow white-washed corridor leading deep into the backstage area. At one point, she heard a magnificent voice penetrating faintly through the walls. It broke off abruptly, to be replaced by a shriek of displeasure. *Madame* was obviously not in a good mood. Julia's steps slowed. She really was not looking forward to this.

Men and women passed her, all incurious, all hastening along on their own business. She could see the end of the corridor ahead and made herself think positive thoughts.

Then she heard Hal's laugh. That rich, wicked chuckle could not belong to anyone else. There was no-one in sight: Julia applied her ear to the panelling of the nearest door. 'I look a complete fool,' he said, his voice becoming fainter as though he was moving away. 'And I'm bloody uncomfortable in this rig.'

'Suits you,' another man said, sounding as though he was choking back laughter. 'You look remarkably—' His voice was cut off abruptly as though an inner door had closed. Silence.

Frustrated, Julia stared at the door. It was not as though she wanted to see Hal Carlow again. *Liar,* an inner voice said. Very well, it was not as though she prudently *should* see him again. Or dared. She knew she should not trust him. So why was she standing here mooning outside a dressing room door at the Opera?

'Dressing room,' Julia muttered. Of course, he was probably in there, with his friend, waiting for a dancer or a member of the chorus. She felt unaccountably miserable.

There was a shout of laughter from around the corner in the corridor ahead of her. Men, several of them by the sound of it, and not the incurious stagehands. They sounded English, boisterous, out for fun, and it was a long way back the way she had come. Then one of them came into sight, talking over his shoulder to the men behind him, and she saw his scarlet uniform. Officers—and here she was, backstage and without her maid.

Julia opened the door and stepped inside, realizing as she did so that she was acting on instinct, going to Hal. The room was empty, but an inner door was ajar and there were sounds of movement from beyond it. Outside, the laughter came closer, stopped. She whisked through the other door, closed it behind her and leant on it. There were two people in the room, but there was no sign of Hal.

Neither occupant had noticed her presence. A broad-shouldered, dark-haired officer with magnificent side-whiskers had a woman with tumbling golden hair bent back over his arm and was embracing her with fervour. The woman flailed her arms, then caught the man a resounding blow on the side of the head that made Julia flinch. The man dropped the blonde with ungallant promptness and she sat on the floor with a thump.

'Get up, damn it!' The man was very big and, in his blue uniform, extremely imposing. But Julia could hardly stand by while he assaulted an unwilling female. 'And don't look at me like that,' he added to his victim, hauling her to her feet as Julia reached out to tap his shoulder. 'You're enough to put a man off sex for life.'

'And you, sir, are no gentleman,' Julia said hotly, prodding his broad back instead of politely tapping as she had intended. 'Is it not enough that you assault an unwilling female, without insulting her into the bargain?'

The woman gasped, rather hoarsely, but then, she had just had a most unpleasant experience. The big man turned round, grinning. 'You have the advantage of me, madam.'

'I most sincerely hope so. Now, kindly leave, sir. Major Carlow is close by and, I can assure you, he does not stand for such behaviour.' He turned away, his shoulders heaving. 'Are you laughing at me, sir?' Julia demanded.

'Oh God forgive me, yes,' he gasped, staggering to the nearest chair and sinking onto it. The unwilling object of his affections was left face to face with Julia.

'You poor…thing.' Her voice trailed off. Large blue-grey eyes swimming with tears of mirth regarded her. Turbulent blonde curls cascaded onto broad shoulders and over an start-lingly opulent bosom clad in shiny pink satin that seemed under considerable strain. Bright lip stain was smeared over a tanned cheek. A large hand came up and pushed the hair back and it came off and fell to the floor. A wig.

'Hal?' Julia gaped as the tears began to pour down his cheeks and he collapsed onto the bench next to the big man, holding his sides as he laughed.

'Hell! These corsets!'

'Hal Carlow! What the…the *devil* do you think you are doing?'

Behind her the door opened and another six large men spilled into the room. 'Gentlemen!' Hal stood up, his appearance, without the wig, beyond incongruous. 'There is a lady present.'

'You can't call yourself a… Ah, sorry, ma'am.' They sobered immediately, and stood regarding her with barely concealed interest.

'This lady has kindly offered to help with the female costumes and *macquillage*,' Hal said smoothly. 'It is extremely kind of her and, as you may imagine, her presence here is not something to be mentioned outside this room.' The look he directed at the big man who had been embracing him held a definite warning, but the other officer grinned back and nodded as he got to his feet, joining the others in a chorus of thanks.

Julia found herself being introduced to all of them, including one plump young man who nervously confided that he was the other female character in the entertainment. 'We're putting it on for a regimental dinner in ten days' time,' he explained. 'Lieutenant Hayden, ma'am. I can't walk properly wearing those, er, am I allowed to say *corsets?*'

'Yes, of course, Lieutenant, but only inside this room,' Julia assured him gravely, suppressing her own giggles. 'Why don't you go and get changed, and I will see what I can do with your deportment—and Major Carlow's.' She turned to look at Hal. 'Are we trying for humorous effect or realism?'

There should be awkwardness between them, but despite the quivering sense of awareness, as though her skin was bare, she was managing to keep up a bland façade in front of these men. She supposed Hal was too. Or perhaps that kiss was simply not of importance to him.

'Humour,' he said gravely; she wondered how he managed to look so very masculine despite his attire.

'Thank goodness for that,' she said, making the others laugh. Lieutenant Hayden stumbled in after a few minutes, red in the face and making a ludicrous woman. 'Now, *ladies,* stand up straight, shoulders back—no, not like that, Lieutenant, you are not on parade. Like this.'

She walked up and down while they studied her. 'Small steps, you see? And hold your skirts up, just a very little. You do not want to show your ankles.'

'They aren't swaying much,' the big man remarked, regarding the rear view of his colleagues as they minced up and down the room.

'What kind of ladies are they, Captain Grey? Respectable ones?'

'Yes, ma'am.'

'Then they need to glide, not sway,' she said repressively. 'Like this.'

Half an hour later, neither man was clomping any more and Hal, at least, could unfurl a fan with dextrous grace. Julia considered that he showed altogether too good a facility with a fan—learned, no doubt, in dubious circumstances. 'I must go,' she said, hearing the clock strike twelve. 'I had quite lost track of time.'

'Let me show you out.' Hal emerged from the other room, dressed as a man again.

'Thank you. Gentlemen, good luck with your entertainment.'

They bowed and thanked her and she left, feeling happily that she had made friends.

'What are you doing here?' Hal demanded, when they were out in the corridor again. 'They will not talk about seeing you, by the way; you have my word on it.'

'I know.' She smiled, finding that, after all, it was possible to be alone with him without embarrassment. 'I liked them all very much. Do you often do this sort of thing?'

'Dress up as a woman? No, I am happy to say. Although we are in the habit of regimental entertainments from our days in the Peninsula. But what are you doing here?'

'Lady Geraldine asked me to persuade Madame Catalani to sing at her reception for the duke. She wrote to her and received a refusal, and now Lady Geraldine is unwell and cannot deal with it herself.'

'Come along then. Where's her dressing room?'

'It is just down here. You will help me?' Julia looked up at him, 'Oh, thank you. I was so nervous.' *And I should be nervous of you,* she thought as Hal smiled back and her heart skipped a beat. There was a shadow behind those smiling eyes: he had not forgotten the forest glade.

'Of course I will help you.' He stopped, just as they turned the corner, and took her hand. 'Julia, am I forgiven for...for the picnic?'

'When you *kissed* me,' she managed to say without stumbling over the word, 'I should have told you not to. But I kissed you back. I do not know why, but it was very wrong of me.' He started to protest, but she shook her head. 'No, I should have known better, especially when you warned me that you are a rake. As for the carriage drive, it is I who should beg your pardon,' she murmured, looking down so that she was not staring up into those troubling eyes. Then she found that she was looking at his big brown hand enveloping hers, and that was equally troubling. 'I should not have spoken so sharply when you were only trying to help me.'

'You had experienced a long and rather difficult day,' Hal said, the bitter edge to the words making her flinch.

'Parts of it were difficult,' Julia agreed. 'I enjoyed others.' She could feel herself blushing. 'The picnic and the forest and the views were all delightful,' she added hastily, in case he thought she was referring to that shattering embrace.

'I enjoyed parts too,' Hal said. Her fingers were still in his grasp and, although he was not holding her tightly, somehow they had become meshed with his.

'We had better find the right door,' Julia said, a little breathless.

'Mm,' Hal agreed, not moving. 'May I ask you something?' He began to play with her fingers.

'Yes.' Then Julia thought about it. 'But I will not promise to answer.'

He laughed, and she looked up and smiled in return. 'Wise woman. I just wanted to know: is it very tiresome, being so well-behaved?' Julia stared. 'My younger sister, Verity, is good because her spirits are crushed if everyone does not think well of her. And she is very, very innocent and trusting, so it does not occur to her to get into scrapes. My elder sister, Honoria, was extremely fast—' He broke off, perhaps reading Julia's thoughts on her face. 'Yes, like me, but not as wicked. She's married now—happily, I believe—to a man as wild and unconventional as she is.

'But you, I think, are good, because you know you should be and it is your duty to be well-behaved.'

'You sound as though that makes me an exotic creature, difficult to understand,' Julia said, puzzled.

'For a scapegrace such as myself, yes, you are.' He was still smiling, but something changed in his expression as he asked, 'Do you never want to rebel?'

'Society is full of well-behaved, unmarried girls,' Julia protested, avoiding the question. 'To be anything else is to be considered fast, and that is a definite handicap to one's marriage prospects. Look what happened the other day.'

It was his turn to flinch, but he let the comment pass. 'Yes, but you are not one of those just-out, fluffy-brained little things, are you?' Hal leaned a shoulder against the wall, her hand still in his, and frowned at her. The theatre seemed to have gone quiet, perhaps for the noon meal, and they were quite alone.

'Are you politely telling me I am on the shelf, Major Carlow? At my last prayers?'

'No.' He shook his head. 'No, I am trying to understand you, and you have avoided answering my question, just as you warned me you might.'

Julia felt the warmth of his hand enveloping hers and the stillness that surrounded them. He had used a cologne that morning, or perhaps it was his soap: just a faint hint of sandalwood teased her nostrils.

'Yes, I do want to rebel sometimes,' she said finally. 'I should not have entered that dressing room just now, I should not be standing here with you. I should have run from that clearing the moment you made Fellowes release me. And I should not snap at gentlemen who give me well-meaning warnings about my conduct.'

'Is that what he did? Pompous idiot,' Hal said. 'I should have called him out.'

'You cannot call someone out for being pompous.' Her little finger had found the signet ring on Hal's hand and she realized she was fiddling with it. She stopped abruptly.

'How did he find anything to criticise, anyway?' Hal asked.

'I admitted I knew you,' Julia confessed.

'Ah.' Hal released her hand and stood up straight. 'Well, in that case, I forgive him. He was quite right to warn you.'

'Major Carlow! You cannot spend time alone with me now, er, chatting and then lecture me on the *unwisdom* of such behaviour.'

'Why not? I am dangerous; you know it and you should be avoiding me, for you have the evidence now. You are correct,

I'm afraid: Society being what it is, the responsibility is down to the lady.' He moved away and began opening doors and looking in.

'Oh, so the responsibility is mine, is it? And what are you doing?'

'You are supposed to be the virtuous one,' Hal pointed out with exasperating logic, closing another door. 'Here we are, just the thing.' He ducked into the room and emerged with a large bouquet, ribbons trailing.

'For *La Catalani?* But you cannot just steal flowers!'

'It is only theft if I remove them from the premises with the intent to permanently deprive the owner of them,' Hal said, revealing a worrying familiarity with law-breaking. 'Now, let me do the talking; this is her room.'

He knocked on the door with a name-card thumb-tacked to it. 'Major Carlow and Miss Tresilian for *Madame,*' he announced to the elderly maid who answered, sweeping in on the words, then stopping dead so abruptly that Julia bumped into his back. '*Madame!* Your very humble servant and admirer. I had to come: I could not stay away when I heard the dreadful news that you were unwell.'

'Unwell?' A heavily accented, rich voice demanded in tones of outrage. 'Unwell? Me?'

'But yes, *Madame*. When I heard that you had declined the most prestigious, most historic event ever to take place in Brussels, I knew there could be but one explanation. Do please accept this humble token.' He was presenting the flowers, Julia assumed, unable to see around him. She contented herself with admiring the elegance of his back and the width of his shoulders.

'Lovely,' Madame said vaguely. 'Emily, find a vase. What event?'

At last, Hal moved far enough in for Julia to see. The singer reclined on a couch, eyeing her visitor with interest. And it was not the event that she was concerned with, Julia could tell. It was the handsome man standing in front of her. She glanced at Julia, dismissed her of no importance, and fixed her large dark eyes on Hal again.

'Why, Lady Geraldine Master's reception in honour of the Duke of Wellington,' he said. 'The greatest living general, the man who will defeat Napoleon in the defining battle of our time. The man who will save Europe. Everyone will be there, their children will talk of it—and they will not be able to say, *Madame Catalani graced it with the power and beauty of her singing and the glamour of her presence.*'

You have to admire his technique, Julia thought, struggling to keep a straight face. The *prima donna* was almost certainly old enough to be his mother, her high-piled hair was an improbable shade of brown and her figure was, to be kind, voluptuous—and she was regarding Hal with the air of a cat who has just seen her next meal. It occurred to Julia that it was her responsibility to get Hal out of there with what remained of *his* virtue intact. She avoided thinking about the implications of the fierce feelings the other woman's scrutiny aroused.

'I had no idea it was an event of such magnitude,' the singer said slowly. 'You describe it with such…passion.'

'How can one fail to be passionate in the presence of such high art and great beauty?' Hal said in throbbing tones. Julia raised her hands to her mouth and bit hard on one knuckle to suppress her giggles. 'And when that passion meets the power of a man such as Wellington—history will be made.'

'Tell me the date again. You will be there?'

'The eighteenth of June. If I have to walk over hot coals, *Madame,* I will be there.'

Julia choked as quietly as she could. The dresser produced a diary; it was consulted, and Madame agreed she was free to attend.

'The fee,' Julia murmured.

'It may be that there is no fee,' Madame purred, her eyes on Hal. 'If the event lives up to…expectation.'

'*Madame.*' Hal went forward, dropped to one knee and saluted the heavily be-ringed hand that was held out to him. 'Lady Geraldine will confirm all the details in writing. I cannot tell you my relief at finding that you are well.'

'Foolish boy.' She petted his hair for a fleeting moment, then Hal was on his feet and backing out of the room as though from the presence of royalty. Julia followed with what grace she could muster, bobbing curtseys as she went.

She pursued him down the corridor and into the dressing room he had been using before. 'Of all the shocking things! She expects *you* for the fee! It is outrageous, disgusting! What on earth are you going to do, Hal?' Julia demanded as soon as the door was closed behind them. Then she realized she had called him by his first name.

'Run like hell,' he said with feeling. 'But she will be all over the duke, there's no need to fear for my virtue, Julia.'

'You went in there,' she said, still so aghast at what had happened that she could not stop talking. 'You went in, *intending* to flirt with her, *intending* to seduce her!'

'Seduce? Hell's teeth,' he said with feeling. 'I didn't have to do any seducing. The woman's ravenous.' He frowned at her. '*You* lecturing *me?* I used the weapons I have, and I got what you wanted—possibly at no cost to Lady Geraldine.'

'Weapons? Your looks, your charm I suppose. You, Hal Carlow, are utterly unscrupulous. I am shocked.' Julia found that she was, indeed, scandalised.

The animation drained out of Hal's face leaving him expressionless. 'Me? You find me unscrupulous?'

Julia caught her breath. If she did not know better, she would have thought she had hurt his feelings. But this was the man who freely confessed to being a rake, who admitted the ploys he had just used to get what he wanted from a woman. How could her words, or her poor opinion, hurt Hal Carlow?

Chapter Seven

Unscrupulous? That hurt, Hal realized, hurt more than he could have imagined. Even as he thought it, even as he saw the look of alarm in Julia's face at his sudden coldness, he knew he was being unreasonable. How could she have any idea what he was going through? She had no inkling of how he was having to control himself not to do any of the unscrupulous things he was perfectly capable of to seduce a woman.

In the wood, he had simply let his passion have full rein, but now, he wanted her so much it hurt physically and it required conscious discipline not to flirt, not to cajole, not to seduce her into his arms. And mentally, it was an effort to concentrate on anything else except the conundrum of why he was obsessed with her.

Laughing with her and his friends had been blissfully dangerous. Holding her hand, alone in the corridor, had been self-inflicted torture. And it was perilous, not only to her virtue, but to her heart. He had no intention of having her fall in love with him, but he knew, without vanity, there was that risk.

'I am sorry,' she said, her voice faltering. God knows what she had seen in his face.

'No, I am.' Hal smiled, rueful. 'Was I looking so fierce? It is only that you are quite right: I am unscrupulous. But I am trying very hard not to be so with you.'

'No, not fierce.' She smiled, happier, and something stabbed under his breastbone like a sharp finger, warning him. 'But your eyes change colour when you are angry. They go completely grey, all the blue vanishes. I know you would never harm me, Hal. I trust you.'

Oh God, it needs only that. If she had any idea of the fantasies I have about her, of the things I want to do with her... The acute physical desire for her had gripped him from the moment when she had stumbled into his arms in the forest. Now, to his shame, he wanted her in his bed, under him, around him. He wanted her innocence.

Hal was not used to feeling guilty about anything. He did his military duty with passion and integrity, because that was his life and his responsibility and his honour would not allow him to do anything else. The women he associated with were all at least as experienced as he—nothing to feel guilty about there—and all his other sins harmed no-one but himself.

But now he felt guilt, not for what he had almost done, but for what he wanted to do. A sense of utter unworthiness swept through him. Julia was standing there, trusting and friendly. How would the look in those clear brown eyes change if she saw what he knew was the real Hal Carlow and not the fiction he had created for her?

She was an innocent who believed he was her friend, a rake who had momentarily lost control of himself. Hal tried to find the strength to snub her, drive her away, and he failed utterly. He must, if nothing else, distance himself from her after today. *I am not worthy of her.*

'Are you going to the cavalry review next week?' he asked, aghast to hear the words coming out of his own mouth.

'No, we are not asked. I believe Lady Geraldine has been invited to the banquet afterwards, so I could not go with her.' She sounded regretful, despite her smile. 'And in any case, it is at Ninove, is it not? That is miles away.'

There, she had handed him the opportunity to negate that reckless enquiry. All he had to do was agree that it was a pity she would not be there. With an escape route clear before him, Hal promptly dug himself in deeper. 'I have an acquaintance, an older gentleman native to Brussels, who will be driving there in his barouche. He would be delighted to take you and Mrs Tresilian and young Phillip along with him. I know he was planning a picnic. He is most respectable—not at all like me.'

'Then how do you know him?' she asked wickedly, making him laugh.

He comes regularly to the Literary Institute.' In fact the Baron van der Helvig came solely for the high-stakes card play, but other than that, he was a respectable and sober widower in his sixties. He was wealthy, sociable and amiable, and Hal had conceived the plan of asking him to keep an eye on the Tresilian household when the situation with Bonaparte came to a head. They might need to leave Brussels in a hurry, and the baron had a large stable.

The review would be an admirable opportunity to introduce Mrs Tresilian to him, and the baron was enough in Hal's debt—quite literally—to be obliging, although he suspected that the sociable Belgian would agree anyway. He tried to tell himself that this was his reason for persuading Julia to come to the review. It was not, he knew perfectly well. His newly awakened conscience was pointing out to him that he wanted to parade in front of her in his uniform, on his big horse, at the head of his men, to prove himself worthy in his profession, if nothing else. *Cockscomb,* he told himself.

'Mama would not wish to impose upon him,' Julia said doubtfully.

'He would enjoy it. He's a sociable man, but rather lonely since his wife died, I suspect. And he was going in any case.'

'You must not tell him you have mentioned it to me,' Julia said. 'If he thinks we know, then he will feel obligated.'

'Very well. I will be tact itself,' Hal assured her, opening the door. 'Now, I had better find you a cab.'

They stood under the portico, surveying the street. 'There's one.' Hal took a step forward and then backed into the shadow. 'And here comes the Reverend Mr Smyth. I think I will make myself scarce, before I am the cause of you losing yet another of your worthy suitors, Julia.' He allowed himself the indulgence of lifting her gloved hand to his lips. 'I hope to see you at the review.'

Julia felt suddenly bereft as Hal vanished back into the theatre. He was so vivid, so alive that when she was with him she felt more alive too. Mr Smyth was making his way past the theatre, heading perhaps for the cathedral. Julia walked out into the sunlight and down the steps. 'Mr Smyth!'

'Miss Tresilian.' He stopped and doffed his hat. 'You appear to have lost your maid.'

'I had to send her home with the fish,' Julia said vaguely, hoping that housekeeping details would distract him from her unchaperoned state. 'I had an errand for Lady Geraldine, but I would be most grateful if you would call me a cab.'

'Of course.' He looked happier now she was relying on him. Julia repressed a sigh. He was a very nice, decent man, but no-one, however charitable, could call him *vivid.*

However he was excellent husband material, she reminded

herself as she got into the cab he most efficiently found for her. She waved to him as he stood on the pavement—solid, patient, kind. She must remember that. It would make all the difference in the world to Mama and Philip if she were to be respectably married. The obligation, the realization that she could do something to help them should make her happy—proud even. She felt miserably aware of her own lack of dutifulness: it was beginning to seem like an intolerable burden.

As the cab rattled up the hill to the Upper Town she sighed. It was her duty to marry, even if it were to a man who could most charitably be termed *mousy*.

What had Hal said about his sister? That she was *fast* and had found a man as wild and unconventional as she was. It sounded exciting and passionate and dangerous. Would life with Hal Carlow be like that? She must not think about it, even in her dreams.

'Julia.'

She started, feeling unaccountably guilty, and put down her slice of bread and butter. 'Mama?'

Mrs Tresilian waved a sheet of thick cream paper. 'I have just received this letter from a Baron van der Helvig, who introduces himself as a friend of Major Carlow and an acquaintance of Lady Geraldine. What do you know about him?'

Julia smiled brightly. 'I have never met the baron, Mama.'

'That is not what I asked you.'

'Major Carlow mentioned him. He is a widower, I believe. In his sixties.'

'He is inviting all three of us to accompany him in his barouche to the cavalry review near Ninove. He *says* he was mentioning to Major Carlow that he was without company for the event and the major suggested we might like to go. What do you know about that?'

'Er…Major Carlow did suggest it, but I asked him not to mention to the baron that we had any idea, so he did not feel obligated.'

'*We* certainly had no idea.'

Julia shifted uneasily as her mother looked at her. 'Phillip would love it,' she suggested, 'and you would enjoy the spectacle and the opportunity of getting out of the city, Mama.'

'Julia,' Mrs Tresilian said carefully. 'You are not *meeting* Major Carlow, are you?'

'Only accidentally,' Julia said, her conscience clear on that at least. 'I came across him when I was calling on Madame Catalani for Lady Geraldine. But then I met Mr Smyth and he got me a cab home from the Lower Town.' That was, she knew perfectly well, an outrageous editing of the events. Julia wondered uneasily if association with Hal Carlow was as dangerous as he had warned her it could be. Her moral standards seemed to be slipping; she could feel it almost as though the ground were moving slightly below her feet. But the thought of never seeing him again made her feel positively unwell. It was very hard to understand.

Mrs Tresilian re-read the letter. 'I will ask Lady Geraldine's advice,' she said after an agonising few moments of suspense. 'I would not like to deprive any of us of a day's harmless entertainment, and this could be a spectacle of historic significance.'

'Wake up, Phillip.' Julia shook her brother's shoulder as he lay curled up on the carriage seat beside her. 'Look, we are almost there.'

Phillip wriggled upright, scrubbing at his eyes. 'Ooh! Is that for us?' *That* was the decoration of leafy branches that covered every upright pole or surface and drooped from ropes and frameworks. Ahead was a great triumphal arch, topped with what looked like laurel wreaths. Even Mrs Tresilian leaned out of the open carriage to see.

'I think it is to honour the duke and Marshal Blücher,' Julia explained.

'And the Prince of Orange,' the baron added, smiling at the small boy. Rotund, jovial and expressing himself delighted to have two 'lovely ladies' in his carriage, Baron van der Helvig had made the journey pass with an inexhaustible flow of good-natured gossip, enquiries about London and stories about life in the Low Countries under Napoleon.

'What time will it begin?' Mrs Tresilian asked as the baron checked his pocket watch.

'Not until noon at least, ma'am, and it is half past eleven now. I have a place reserved in the meadow which is just a little way beyond the town.' The carriage turned down from the main street amidst crowds on foot, horseback and in carriages, all heading in the same direction into the countryside.

Then Mrs Tresilian gasped, and Julia craned round to look. Ahead was nothing but a sea of colour and a milling mass of horses and riders covering the wide meadows that stretched along the River Dender, up to the sharp slope of the woods.

'There must be thousands of them,' Julia murmured in awe as the coachman manoeuvred the barouche into position.

'Six or seven thousand,' he agreed. 'Forty six squadrons, so Major Carlow tells me. There, you see: the heavy dragoons, then the light dragoons.'

Julia craned her neck: Hal would be there, impossible to distinguish in the mass of horsemen.

'And the batteries-howitzers as well,' the baron explained. 'And I believe they have the Rocket Brigade in there somewhere.'

'It is like a wall of red brick,' Mrs Tresilian murmured,

gazing at the heavy dragoons, but Julia was searching the lines of blue, distracted by the shifting pattern of broad lapels in at least four colours. And then she saw the big horse, ghostly grey amongst the darker bays, blacks and chestnuts. There were other greys, but none as big and pale as that one. She had found Hal. Julia sat back against the squabs, her eyes fixed on the distant figure, happy.

The sun shone and the troops manoeuvred, wheeled, reformed. The inspecting dignitaries came down over a temporary bridge and then passed up and down the ranks; the picnic was unpacked and consumed; and Julia nearly spilled her lemonade down her new walking dress when the twenty-one gun salute was fired.

Phillip was struck almost dumb with excitement, his eyes wide, fixed on the shifting pattern of horsemen, the displays of artillery drill, the glitter of weapons and orders.

Then the duke and his guests left, heading—so the baron informed them—for a grand dinner at Lord Uxbridge's head-quarters. Julia took a deep breath, half dazzled by the spectacle, half disappointed that it had all been at a distance.

'Ah, they are beginning to break up,' the baron said. 'Many of them have a distance to go back to their quarters. If we stay here, young Philip will see some of them closer. You would like that? Eh?'

Julia kept a firm hand on her brother's shoulder as they stood by the carriage watching the troops clatter past in small groups. And then Phillip gave an excited squeak and Julia turned. A big grey horse was approaching from behind them.

'Baron.' Hal touched his hand to his shako. 'Mrs Tresilian, Miss Tresilian. And Master Phillip, are you enjoying yourself?'

Julia could only be thankful he was talking to her brother. If he had asked her a question, she doubted she could have made a sensible remark. It was ridiculous, she told herself. She was a mature woman, not some silly chit to be dazzled by a uniform. But here she was, her heart pounding, wanting to smile like a looby, all because one man was there looking like a statue of valour come to life.

'What's your horse called, Major?' Phillip asked. He was standing, at a cautious distance from the big hooves, hands behind his back.

'Max.' The horse turned his head and looked down at the small boy who stood his ground and stared back.

'He's very big.'

'Seventeen hands. Would you like a ride?'

'Me?'

'If your mama permits.'

'Major—'

'He will be quite safe, ma'am. Phillip, hold up your hands.' Hal leaned down, caught the boy's wrists and swung him up onto the saddle before him. 'There you are. Perhaps Miss Tresilian should walk with us, just in case he wants to get down?'

'Yes, of course.' Julia kept pace as Hal turned the horse down towards the river, through the long, untrampled grass and away from the bustle of people leaving the review ground.

Hal spoke quietly to the child. 'I bred Max from one of my big hunters and a mare belonging to my brother, but he's bigger than both of them. He is five years old, just a bit older than you.'

Julia saw her brother relax and begin to grin. He leaned back trustingly against the man holding him and started to ask questions, all of which Hal answered with patience, speaking to the child as though to an equal. He seemed to understand the little boy and be prepared to take any amount of trouble with him. Julia looked up and saw the two of them, chatting away like old friends as the horse wandered down towards the river. Then she stumbled as realization hit her like a blow.

She was falling in love with Hal Carlow. She hadn't seen it when she had looked at the dashing, dazzling cavalry officer, then, she had simply admired and desired him. It was this quiet man, absorbed in amusing a small boy he hardly knew, who had snatched her heart.

'Yes please, sir!' Phillip said and she stared, realizing she had missed something.

Hal swung down, leaving Phillip perched up alone in the saddle. 'Hold the reins like I showed you,' Hal said, walking round to run the stirrups right up the leathers so the child could put his feet in them. 'Sit up straight. There you go.' He bent and whispered, 'It is all right, Max will just walk with me. Come on, Mr Tresilian! At the walk. Forward!'

He took Julia's hand and tucked it under his elbow. 'Did you enjoy the review?' Max plodded after them.

'It was wonderful, thank you so much for arranging it. The baron has been kindness itself.' She hoped she was sounding normal; it was difficult to tell.

'Go to him if you and your mother need to leave Brussels in a hurry,' Hal said. 'He will put a carriage at your disposal for you to go to Antwerp.'

'Might we have to?' It seemed impossible that any army, even one commanded by Napoleon, could get past the wall of men she had seen today. And none of the infantry had been there.

'You never know.' He squeezed her arm against his side. 'And I don't want to be worrying about you.'

'You would worry?' The question came out sounding curiously breathless. Julia kept her eyes fixed on the waving grasses in front of them.

'Oh yes,' Hal said softly. 'I would worry.'

'May I trot?' Phillip demanded, peering down from his perch.

'No, but we can gallop together,' Hal said, letting down the stirrups again. 'Sit up a bit.' He swung into the saddle and looked down at Julia as he pushed his feet into the stirrups, his hands closing over Phillip's on the reins. His mouth smiled, but his eyes were serious. 'I need you to be safe. Hold tight,' he added to Phillip and dug in his spurs to send the grey thundering along the river edge.

Julia walked slowly back up to the carriage, her head spinning. She was falling in love with him and he worried about her. He wanted her safe. She watched as Hal brought them back at a flat-out gallop, the little boy in front of him shrieking with excitement. He wanted her safe—did that mean he wanted her safe from him?

Chapter Eight

The first of the month was an excellent day for good resolutions. Julia strolled down the wide central path of the Parc, her maid at her heels, her most sensible bonnet equipped with a modest veil which hid the fact that her eyes had dark shadows beneath them from lack of sleep.

Any hope that she would recover her senses once away from the glamour of Major Carlow in full uniform on horseback in the sunshine had fled after three nights of dreaming about him and a third day when she just could not get him out of her head.

On Tuesday, she made a list of the admirable qualities possessed by Mr Smyth and promptly burst into tears. On Wednesday, she deliberately instigated a discussion of who were the most dangerous men in Brussels amongst a group of young ladies at a party. Heading the list of those agreed to be incorrigible flirts, not to be trusted on the terrace after dark and incapable of sincere attachment or commitment was, as she had expected, Major the Honourable Hal Carlow.

Then today, Thursday the first of June, she startled her mother by insisting on attending Matins before taking Phillip to play in the Parc. Efforts to set her thoughts on higher things, or even on her duty to encourage Mr Smyth, evaporated before the sight of a stained-glass window showing the fall of Lucifer. Hal Carlow might have acted as the model for the renegade angel in all his arrogant, defiant, beauty.

Even Phillip seemed to have caught her mood and trudged along kicking gravel, leaving the pigeons unchased.

'Miss Tresilian, good day.' It was, inevitably, the Reverend Smyth, doffing his broad-brimmed hat.

Julia put back her veil and forced a smile. She had asked for strength to do the right thing, now she must try. It felt as though her cheek muscles were cracking. 'What a lovely day, Mr Smyth.'

'Indeed it is, we are enjoying a most clement summer. May I walk with you a little?'

'Of course, sir.' Julia took his proffered arm and immediately adjusted her gait to the slow stroll he obviously thought fitting for a lady. 'We had a great treat on Monday: the Baron van der Helvig was kind enough to take us to see the cavalry review.'

'Baron van der Helvig? I do not have the pleasure of his acquaintance.' He sounded so put out that Julia rushed to reassure him, realizing as she spoke that she was only encouraging him. *As I must, I need a declaration.*

'An elderly gentleman. He was very charming to Mama,' she added. 'And it was such a treat for Phillip.'

'But hardly the sort of entertainment for ladies, I would have thought. However, those of us expecting to find a quiet retreat in Brussels are now finding ourselves in the midst of stirring events,' Mr Smyth commented. 'No doubt, Mrs Tresilian is making plans to return to England before the menace from France becomes any greater.'

'Why no, we had no plans to do so,' Julia said.

'Because when you do, it would be my pleasure to offer

you my escort. I will be travelling to take up my new living shortly.'

'Oh yes, in Suffolk, is it not?' She tried not to feel annoyance that he had simply ignored her own statement.

'You remembered?' He sounded delighted. 'Perhaps you would all come and visit me once I am settled.'

'I… Oh, thank you, but our plans are not to return…'

'Let us sit here and young Phillip can play with his ball.' He took out his pocket handkerchief and brushed some dust off a seat for her, then gestured to the grass before them. 'There you are, young man.'

Phillip stared stolidly back, the ball clutched to his stomach. 'I rode a big grey horse the other day and I galloped.'

'What an imagination,' Mr Smyth chuckled. 'He needs a steady male presence in his life, of course. A boy that age, before the influence of tutor or school, requires firm but tender guidance.'

He needs someone like Hal who would take him on adventures and who listens to him, Julia thought mutinously as Phillip walked off and began to kick his ball. He did not appear to like the clergyman very much.

'…of course, we poor males all need a steadying influence in our lives.' Mr Smyth was saying something; Julia hastened to murmur agreement. 'I am glad you think so,' he said warmly, as her brain caught up with his last few sentences.

He is going to make a declaration at any moment. He is perfect, really he is. Mama would be so pleased. I ought to say Yes *if he asks.* She met his eyes and saw the intent in them. *Oh dear, not* if, *but* when.

She should either say something encouraging, and precipitate matters, or snub him now, before this got any further.

'Disgraceful!'

'What?' Julia thought for a startled moment that he was

reading her thoughts, then saw his gaze was fixed on a group of blue-jacketed officers on one of the paths crossing at right angles to where they sat. Her heart sank as she recognized them. They were Hal's friends from the theatre, and in the middle, laughing as the others slapped him on the back and teased him loudly about something, was Hal.

She pulled her veil down without thinking, then saw Phillip. Hal would recognize him and look for her and then…

'Do not worry,' Mr Smyth said. 'Should one of those young bucks so much as glance in your direction, I will know what to do.'

'Oh good,' Julia said faintly, imagining the clergyman squaring up to the group who looked as though they had all breakfasted from the brandy bottle. But they were almost at the end of the path now, their backs to Phillip who was running over to her.

'Drunk, I have no doubt—and at this hour!'

'Perhaps not drunk exactly—they seemed to be celebrating,' Julia ventured, scooping up the ball and throwing it for Phillip before he said anything about Major Carlow and his big horse. 'It is only eleven in the morning.'

'They will have been at the Literary Institute all night,' the reverend said in a tone of voice that would not have been unsuitable if he had said they had been in Sodom and Gomorrah.

'I thought that was a very respectable club,' Julia said, tearing her gaze from the retreating group.

'It is, upstairs. Downstairs is a gaming hell. Those rakeshames will have been playing cards and drinking all night.'

'Shocking.' And of course it was. But they had all looked and sounded so happy and cheerful. Was it really doing any harm if they did not gamble more than they could afford to lose, or so long as they did not win money from someone who would then be ruined? Hal said he rarely lost: perhaps those he played with stumbled out of the card rooms destitute and desperate. She *had* to stop thinking about him, wanting him.

Julia put up her veil again and turned a bright, determined smile on Mr Smyth. He was a kind, decent man. She must do the right thing, even if it broke her heart. 'Do tell me more about your living. Is it in a pretty part of the county?'

Hal walked into his hotel room and let the door bang behind him. He'd been feeling good. Better than good. His men had turned out so well at the review that both the duke and Marshal Blücher had stopped to comment favourably. The atmosphere back at their quarters had been better than he could ever remember it, the men itching for the fight, morale sky-high.

And then there were those few moments in the meadow with Julia, her voice soft and breathless when she had asked him if he would worry about her. Moments like clear, still waters in the midst of a maelstrom. He did not dare think about what her emotions might be, because he was not sure he could live with his conscience if he broke her heart, even if all she felt was an illusion of first love.

And young Phillip. Hal grinned as he thought of the boy's excitement, of his courage when he found himself alone on top of the mountain that was Max. The smile faded as he recalled him moments ago in the Parc. The child had not seen him, thank God, and neither, he thought, had Julia.

Those officers who were off duty had got back from their bases in the small hours, too stimulated after the day's hard work to sleep. And there, in the Institute's card rooms, had been a Prussian count whom they all suspected at fuzzing the cards. It had been too much of a temptation not to take him for every franc in his pockets, matching Hal's skill against the count's sleight of hand, and all too natural to drink solidly while he was doing it.

Julia had been sitting demurely with her clergyman as they'd passed, high as kites on success and wine. He had been almost past them when he first recognized Phillip and then saw her. For her sake, he dared not risk scandalising another of her worthy suitors: he was sober enough to remember his good resolutions—just.

There were letters on the table with one in Marcus's hand on top. Hal slit the seal and opened it one handed while reaching for the decanter with the other. He did not want to sober up. Sober, he thought too much about Julia Tresilian.

The news started soothingly enough. Marcus had an idea about an ideal man for their younger sister, Verity. Mama had sprained her ankle, but only mildly and she was on the mend. Nell, his wife, was six months gone with child. Half a sheet was filled with domestic details by a man in love with his wife, besotted with his baby son and torn between anxiety and joy over the next arrival.

Hal dropped the letter, hating the twist of jealousy that he felt for his brother. He had burned his own boats. Married bliss—with its ties and terrors—was not for him. He was a career soldier and, of his free choice, had made himself unfit for any decent girl. He had decided his own fate, and it was too late to regret it now, just because of one brown-eyed girl who was too good for him.

Cursing his sentimental weakness, he picked up the letter and made himself focus.

I could wish this French business over and you safely home, Marcus wrote. *The letter from Mildenhall confirmed the rumours I have been hearing. Someone is stirring matters and, although I have no proof, I cannot believe that this time it is entirely down to Hebden,*

*or Beshaley, or whatever the damned man is calling
himself this week. Or not him alone, at any rate. He
was certainly to blame for the attack on Nell, for that
appalling episode with Honoria. And I could wring his
neck, the bastard, for the anxiety he put Nell through
so recently, worrying about her sister Rosalind. But
this feels different, not like his direct attacks or the
confounded silken ropes he leaves to alarm us.*

*The rumours are at too high a level in government.
Men of our father's generation stop me to have a quiet
word in my ear. They do not believe something is seriously amiss, of course, but they are uneasy.*

*You recall that three pages were torn from Father's
journal for '94 when we finally got it back? I still
cannot get Father to talk about what is in them. He
says he does not recall, that there can be nothing he
has not told us. Sooner or later he is going to hear these
rumours too, and then the rats will be out of the bag
with a vengeance.*

*Take care of yourself. I am oppressed by a feeling of
danger for you—which is a damn fool thing to worry
about with a soldier, I know!*

Nell sends her love…

Nell was free with her love, Hal thought with a smile,
generous with it even for her brother in law who had enjoyed
teasing Marcus by flirting with her. Perhaps that had helped
his brother realize he loved her.

But Marcus was the sensible one, the steady son. He would
know how to deal with the rumours in government circles—
just so long as they did not reach their father's ears.

And he sensed danger, did he? So did Hal, but it was not
coming from the muzzle of a French gun.

* * *

'Oh, for some real news!' Mrs Tresilian exclaimed on the eighth of June as the last of her Thursday afternoon guests departed, sustained by tea, pastries and gossip. 'No-one seems to know what is happening, but everyone has a theory,' she added irritably. 'First we hear Napoleon is still in Paris, and then he is on the borders, and then the duke is going to invade. And then he is not.'

'The Harringtons have packed up and left for Ostend,' Julia said. 'But the Wingfields—you recall they moved to Antwerp ten days ago?—they have come back. I do believe they are rather ashamed of their jittery nerves.'

'I might be jittery myself, if it were not for the dear baron,' her mother confided, sinking down in the most comfortable chair and putting her feet up. 'The knowledge that we can get away when we want to is so reassuring.'

Thank you, Hal, Julia thought, breaking, yet again, her resolution to put him out of her mind. *And what am I going to do about Mr Smyth?* She could not convince herself that she was not in love with Hal, so was she wrong to encourage the clergyman's advances? Many people married who were not in love with their spouses; she knew that. But it was different to agree to marry when one's affections were already engaged, or so it seemed to her.

She sighed. If he did make an offer, then she was going to have to confess that she loved another. If Thomas Smyth still wanted her on those terms, then so be it. The prospect of possibly forty years of marriage to a nice, kind, dull man she did not love made her heart sink. Somehow she would have to learn to keep Hal locked away in her heart and not think about him, for to do that would be wrong. At least he would not be affected: she had fallen for an experienced man, not some youngster with a heart as vulnerable as her own.

'Is something wrong, dear?'

'I was just thinking about Mr Smyth,' Julia admitted.

'I am sure he is about to make you an offer any day,' her mother said, plunging her deeper into gloom. 'Which is why I asked the baron if he might offer Mr Smyth a place in his carriage when we go to the races on Tuesday.'

'You did?'

'Did I not tell you, dear?' Mrs Tresilian said. Her attempt to look innocent would, under other circumstances, have been amusing. Julia had been looking forward to that trip as a distraction from the increasing intensity of Mr Smyth's conversations as they took their daily walks in the Parc. *If he would only get on with it!* she found herself thinking in exasperation one moment and then dreading the inevitable proposal the next.

'No, Mama, you did not,' she said with a smile. 'What a good idea.'

'And I have been thinking,' Mrs Tresilian added, looking a trifle uncomfortable, 'that perhaps you should have a new outfit for the race day. And there is Lady Conynham's party on the forteenth and the Duchess of Richmond's ball the night after and I really feel a new gown would be best for that.'

'But, Mama—the money,' Julia protested. More expenditure, another link in the heavy chain of duty and expectation around her neck.

'It is an investment; we have said so all along. And if it helps bring Mr Smyth up to the mark, it will have been well worth while.'

'Even if I am fortunate enough to be invited to the ball,' Julia pointed out, 'Mr Smyth will not be.' She did not want a man who needed the stimulus of a new gown or bonnet to be prompted to declare himself.

'But the colonel will, and other gentlemen you have not yet met. It is as well not to neglect any opportunity, just in case Mr Smyth proves a disappointment.'

'Yes, but the cost—'

'That had been concerning me a little, I confess. But I received a note yesterday from a dealer in jewellery. Here.' She took a letter from the table by her side and handed it across. Julia spread it open. The heavy cream paper had an impressive engraved heading: *Hebden. Jewellery of Quality bought and sold.* 'He sounds most respectful—but you read it, dear, see what you think.'

...in Brussels for a short visit acquiring gems and jewellery for the London market...venture to approach ladies of quality as those most likely to have trifles of the nature in which I am interested...willing to give a fair price in sterling cash with the utmost discretion...

'It seems straightforward enough,' Julia said, fingering the reassuringly thick paper. 'And we have a good idea of the value of what we have, because of the valuation when Papa passed away.'

'Obviously we would not wish to dispose of anything your dear father gave us, or family pieces,' Mrs Tresilian mused. 'But there are those ugly brooches old Miss Anderson left me and the chains from Cousin Maria. We never wear those.'

'And that hideous tie pin that Papa never wore. I suppose there is no harm in seeing what this man would offer us, and making sure the money is paid at the bank so it can be checked,' Julia added.

'I will write to him at once,' Mrs Tresilian decided. 'It occurs to me that if Bonaparte does advance sooner than expected, there may be a flood of people trying to realize assets for cash. And the banks have closed at least twice in the past month in a panic.'

Mr Hebden called the next day. Julia sat demurely beside her mother, the pieces they had selected laid out on the table and her notes from the valuation folded under her hand. She was surprised and unwillingly impressed by him.

He was much younger than she had expected—not yet thirty she guessed—and quite uncomfortably attractive in a very physical way. *Italian,* she told herself, attempting to rationalise away the frisson of awareness that ran through her whenever he turned those dark, hypnotic eyes in her direction.

To her surprise, considering how very attractive he was, he made no attempt to flirt or to charm the two ladies. His manner was serious, his tone respectful, but there was something in the way he handled the jewellery with his long fingers, the way he used his voice with its lilting accent, that left her in no doubt that he was utterly aware of her as a woman and knew that she was looking at him, assessing him as a man.

'These would need reworking.' He touched the three heavy brooches in turn. 'The stones are good, but the settings are quite out of fashion. These chains are heavy for the current taste, but saleable in some quarters.' He let them run from one hand into the other. 'The pin is a trifle ornate, but saleable.' He lifted his loupe to his eye and studied the enamelled centre of the pin. 'French. I would be interested in making you an offer, Mrs Tresilian.

'None of this is jewellery for a young lady about to marry,' he added, slanting a look at Julia. 'I am sure it will be better converted to some other use.'

'Marry?' Julia said sharply. 'What do you know of my circumstances, if you please?'

'I have offended you.' The accent was stronger now as he turned fully to face her, the dark eyes smiling, his sensual mouth serious. 'No dealer would do business without making a few discreet enquiries about those he hopes to buy from. It helps judge provenance, the likely quality of a collection, that is all. No-one would have any idea that I was intending to do business with you.'

'And the rumour is that I am about to marry?' Julia resisted the urge to smile back into his eyes.

'Yes, although who the lucky man is, now *that* is undecided by the gossips. The reverend gentleman? The widower? Or the rake?'

'Rake?' Mrs Tresilian said sharply. 'Which rake?'

'The gossip must simply be the result of Major Carlow giving Phillip a ride on his horse after the review, Mama,' Julia said coolly. 'People *will* talk so.'

'Oh yes.' Mrs Tresilian fanned herself, and Julia cast a suspicious look at Mr Hebden. Was he deliberately flustering Mama to take her mind off the price he was about to offer?

He met her look with one of limpid innocence. The man was a rogue. 'Well, sir? Are you able to give us a price?' she asked.

The amount he named was squarely in the middle of the range Julia had calculated. Less than she had hoped, more than she had feared. So, an honest rogue. 'It is twenty guineas too little, sir.'

'I can offer five more, ma'am.'

'Fifteen, sir.' She had to bite the inside of her lip so as not to smile. He really was outrageous with that wounded look.

'Ten more, ma'am and that is the highest I can go.'

Julia glanced at her mother. 'We accept, sir. Shall we go to the bank now?'

'But of course.' He put the items back into their cases and stacked them for her.

The walk to the bank was not a long one, and Mr Hebden made no attempt to carry the small valise with the jewel cases in it. Julia had been prepared to contest the point if he had offered, her suspicious nature envisioning him escaping with them once outside the house.

But the transaction passed off smoothly: the bank approved the guinea coins and transferred them to Mrs Tresilian's account, and the three of them were outside again within half an hour.

'Ladies. A pleasure to meet you.' He raised his hat and was gone, vanishing into the crowd on the pavement like a fish slipping into the current of a river.

Julia raised her parasol. 'Well, Mama. That was very satisfactory, do you not think?'

'Perfectly, I—'

'Miss Tresilian!' Hal Carlow skidded to a halt in front of them from a flat-out run. 'What the devil were you doing with that man?'

Chapter Nine

'Major Carlow,' Mrs Tresilian said in freezing tones. 'What conceivable business is it of yours with whom we associate?'

'Ma'am, I apologise.' Hal was frowning in frustration as he craned to see where Hebden had gone. 'But the man is known to me. He is dangerous.' He glanced up to see they were standing beneath the bank's engraved sign. 'Have you done any business with him?'

'Well, really, Major—'

'Yes,' Julia cut across her mother's indignant words. 'We have just sold him some items of jewellery and have had the money he paid us checked by the bank before parting with them.'

'Thank God for that.' He jammed his shako back on his head. 'Do you have an address for him?'

'Of course,' Mrs Carlow said, still thoroughly affronted. 'I do not do business with someone off the street.'

'Ma'am, I am sure you do not. But he is not to be trusted and has done my family a great deal of harm.'

'The Hôtel de la Poste,' Julia said. 'He was very charming and gave us what I know to be an honest price.'

Hal's face was set, his jaw formidable. 'Yes, his *charm* is part of his stock in trade. If you will excuse me, I will go to that hotel, although I doubt he will return there. The man is like mist. Have nothing more to do with him, do you understand me, Julia?' She nodded. '*Nothing.*' And then he was gone, cutting through the crowd, heading for the steeply sloping streets down to the Lower Town.

'Well really!' Mrs Tresilian fumed. 'Of all the abrupt, outrageous—and he called you by your given name!'

'I think only to emphasise the importance of the matter, Mama,' Julia soothed. Trying to sound calm was an effort. She felt flustered and…aroused. There was no other word for it. Hal, urgent and forceful and powerful. *Oh my,* she thought faintly. It made her feel so…Julia groped for the right word. *Female.* 'I am sure Major Carlow's judgment is to be trusted. We should have nothing more to do with Mr Hebden.'

'You will have nothing more to do with Major Carlow, my girl! That is rather more to the point. Nothing—do you hear me?'

'Yes, Mama.' As Julia said it, she meant it. Whatever the mystery behind Hal's vehement attack on the gem dealer, she was never going to find out what it was. By the end of the month, she was going to be another man's affianced wife, she was certain of that.

'There's a lot of money on you,' Captain Grey remarked as Hal ran his hand down the bay gelding's fetlock. 'Most of it mine.'

'Is that a plea or a threat?' Hal enquired, straightening up. 'Put fifty on for me, will you?' The animal fidgeted, tossed its head and rolled its eyes. 'Stand still you daft lump,' Hal murmured, and the twitching ears swivelled to listen. 'You are big and you are beautiful and no-one is going to beat you, do you hear me?'

'Understands every word you say, does he, sir?' the lanky trooper holding the gelding's reins enquired.

'Every word.' Hal narrowed his eyes at the man who stared back. The pockmarked face was unfamiliar. 'Where's Trooper Godfrey?'

'Saw 'im over by that tent, sir.' The man jerked his head towards one of the beer tents that was doing a roaring trade in half a dozen varieties of Belgian beer. 'Castin' up 'is accounts. Sick as a cat he was, said to come over here and 'old the 'orse, sir.' He shifted under Hal's stare. 'Trooper 'arris, sir. Just transferred from the Ninth.'

'Right.' Hal told himself he was being jumpy, but the fleeting appearance of Stephen Hebden had him checking every shadow. And the damn man had been with Julia. He was gone from the hotel when Hal reached it, of course, and there had been no sign of him since. He tried to tell himself it was coincidence; after all, the man genuinely was a gem dealer when he wasn't pursuing his vendetta against those he blamed for his father's death. And just now, Brussels was full of people with debts to pay and jewellery to dispose of.

Hal turned his attention back to the gelding, his second-string horse. Too young and nervy for battle yet, it had a turn of speed that was breathtaking. He'd hoped to keep that a secret, but word seemed to have got around, unless of course they were simply betting on him as a rider, which was flattering.

'Carry on, Trooper Harris. Walk him slowly, and keep the flies off him. The start's in half an hour.'

'Sir.'

'Drink?' Will suggested.

'No.'

'Given it up for Lent?' his friend enquired.

'It isn't Lent.' Hal strolled through the crowd, studying it as he might scan a hillside for enemy snipers. The consciousness that he was being watched had him turning, but there was only Trooper Harris, leading Chiltern Lad towards a clump of shade trees.

The truth was, he wasn't sure whether it was Hebden or the fact that he hadn't touched anything stronger than ale since Friday that was jangling his nerves. And he wasn't even sure why he had stopped drinking, other than a vague feeling that Julia would prefer it if he didn't. Which was absurd, as he had promised himself to stay away from her and if ever there was a reason to drown his sorrows, that was it.

'Major Carlow. Captain Grey.' A feminine voice.

Hal stopped so suddenly that Will ran into the back of him. 'Miss Tresilian.'

'Good morning, Major. Captain.' She stood there with Miss Marriott, pretty and poised, twirling her parasol, and tricked out in a gown so frivolously delightful it should have been illegal anywhere near susceptible bachelors. She did not look particularly pleased to see him. In fact, her face in the shade of her bonnet brim was a trifle pale.

'We were wondering where the best place was to watch,' her friend said.

Will, at least, appeared to have the power of speech. 'To watch the start or the finish, ladies?'

'All of it, I suppose.' Miss Marriott was batting her eyelashes at Will. 'I suppose we *ought* to go and watch from the carriages.'

'You are with the baron?' Hal managed to get his brain and his vocal cords under some sort of control.

'I am,' Julia replied. For a moment, he thought she was going to turn on her heel and walk away, then she sighed, as though in resignation and added, 'With Mama and Mr Smyth. Did you say something, Major?'

Hal unclenched his teeth. 'No, Miss Tresilian.'

'Do you have a suggestion for us to place a bet,' she persisted, her brown eyes just hinting at a smile at last.

'You can't do better than to put it on Carlow, ladies,' Will Grey said before he could answer. 'Chiltern Lad in the third race.'

'You are riding? Then of course.' Julia dug into her reticule. 'Will you put it on for me, Captain?' She handed over a half sovereign and beamed at Will, the long Pomona green ribbons on her bonnet fluttering in the light breeze.

'May I beg a token for the race?' Hal asked, the words out before he could stop them. Miss Marriott's eyes widened in delighted horror.

'A token?'

'The major means a favour, like a knight had on his lance. His lady's handkerchief,' her friend said, giggling.

He might as well be hanged for a sheep as a lamb. 'One of those green ribbons?' Hal suggested.

'Very well.' The tip of her tongue just brushed her lower lip in fleeting uncertainty. Hal swallowed, hard. 'Miss Marriott, can you find one of the long ones attached to the crown? I think they are only lightly tacked on.'

Amid much giggling on Felicity's part, a ribbon was detached. Julia held it out.

'You must tie it around my arm, I believe, ma'am,' Hal said. Anything to have her touch him.

She was blushing now, delightfully, her cheeks pink as she stepped forward and tied the long ribbon around his right biceps leaving streamers floating in the breeze. 'You will ride in uniform, Major?' Julia asked as she stepped back.

'Yes. Without my sword and shako and in lighter boots. I will not need to disturb your handiwork.' He touched the knot and she blushed more deeply. *As though I had touched her,* he thought. What was the matter with him? How long was this infatuation going to last?

'Good luck then. Felicity, we should get back.'

Hal watched her retreating back, the ruched hem of the Pomona green gown flirting away over the deeper hue of the grass, the dainty white parasol twirling as she fidgeted with the handle. It seemed he had no willpower as far as Julia Tresilian was concerned, whether he was drunk or sober.

'When are you going to ask her?' Will enquired. 'You might as well carry a placard, the pair of you. She blushes, you are tongue-tied—'

'Never, damn it! And don't suggest such a thing when anyone else can hear either.' He swung round and glared at his friend, his hand tightening instinctively on his sword hilt.

'Hey!' Will took a step backwards, hands raised in a fencer's gesture of surrender. 'I won't say another word. I'll just go and get this money on.'

Aware he had revealed far more than he wanted, Hal strode back to Chiltern Lad. Horses, at least, were straightforward. Unlike emotions.

The baron knew just where to place his barouche, Julia realized. They had only a distant view of the start, but by standing up in the carriage they could see clearly the main part of the track running across a broad meadow, looping around a spinny of trees and then finishing with a short straight right in front of them. The men, perched on the driver's box and the footman's stand at the back, had an even better view.

The baron had placed money for both Mrs Tresilian and Julia, answering their protests with the airy explanation that it was no fun at all watching races when you had no interest in the outcome.

His choices were placed first and second in the first race and nowhere in the second, but the excitement of jumping up and down and cheering on your favourite in a most unladylike manner infected even her mama, much to Julia's amusement.

But she had an unpleasantly hollow feeling of guilt in her stomach when she contemplated the next race. She really should not have allowed Captain Grey to place a bet for her, and she most certainly should not have given Hal her ribbon. Her first instinct when she and Felicity had virtually run into him was to turn and walk away, to put an end to this by cutting him dead.

But she had found that she could not, whatever her mother had decreed, whatever her common sense was telling her. She needed to be near him. It was extraordinarily fast of her to have given him her favour, and Mama would be horrified if she found out. But her heart was still pounding from seeing him so unexpectedly and the day, already enjoyable, had become vibrant with excitement.

'May I see the list of runners?' she asked, and the baron did his best to point out which was which in the jostling, distant, mass of horses.

'That's yours, Miss Tresilian, the grey. And yours, ma'am, the black to the right.'

Chiltern Lad, bay, three years old. Owned and ridden by Major the Hon. Hal Carlow, the list read. Julia put her thumb firmly over the entry and scanned the distant horses for a bay with a rider in a blue jacket. *There he is. Good luck, Hal.*

The starting pistol fired and they were off, bunched into a tight knot at first and then, as the field opened out, she could make out individual horses.

'Come on, Black Knight,' Mrs Tresilian called in a ladylike voice that would hardly reach outside the carriage.

'Saturn!' the baron was bellowing, jumping up and down on the box.

Even Mr Smyth was throwing himself into the mood. 'Ajax, come on Ajax!' he shouted, waving his hat.

Chiltern Lad, Julia repeated over and over in her head, *Come on, Hal, come on, Chiltern Lad!*

As the first horses came out from behind the spinny turn, Black Knight was in the lead, a small grey second and Chiltern Lad was neck and neck in third with Mr Smyth's favourite.

Surely there was not enough time now? They swung round the shallow curve towards the finishing straight, and she saw Hal clearly, the ribbon streaming behind him as he leant forward. The bay responded, stretched out its neck and they left Ajax trailing, then they were past the grey. 'Come on, Chiltern Lad!' Julia screamed, forgetting where she was. 'Come on!'

Black Knight responded, pulled away for a second, and then it was as if the bay had only been cantering. With Hal flat on its neck it lengthened its stride and took the black, crossing the finishing line with a length to spare.

Hal sat back and punched the air with his right fist, the Pomona green ribbons fluttering incongruously against the masculine cut of his uniform. Julia subsided onto the carriage seat, breathless and triumphant.

And then she looked up and saw Thomas Smyth's face as he stared from the winning rider to the trailing ribbons on her frivolous bonnet. 'The winner,' he remarked, his mouth hard, 'appears to have a lady supporter.'

'What was that, Mr Smyth?' Mrs Tresilian said, fanning herself. 'I did not quite catch your words.'

'Nothing important, ma'am,' he said. 'Merely my commiserations. We have several losers in this carriage today.'

Julia felt sick. He had seen the favour on Hal's arm and he had drawn the correct conclusion and now…now she had one suitor left, and that the most lukewarm of the three. She closed her eyes, wondering if she was going to faint. It was her duty to marry respectably. Mama had spent a great deal of money on her and invested much hope and worry, and she had not even been able to control her wicked, wayward heart sufficiently to live up to her obligations to her family.

She had thrown away security and respectability and upbringing, not just by falling in love with a rake—a man who had no sense of responsibility except to a regiment of troops, who had no intention of marrying and who lived a dissolute lifestyle—but by publicly displaying her feelings for him.

The carriage shifted as people moved about in it. Julia opened her eyes, braced for accusations, but her mother was climbing down and taking the baron's arm and Mr Smyth was getting in.

'I gave Major Carlow a ribbon as a token for good luck,' she said bluntly, as he sat down opposite her and the others moved away out of earshot. 'I met him by chance just now. I owe him a great deal for rescuing me from a man who accosted me in the Parc, but it was indiscreet—fast, indeed— of me to have done what I just have.'

'Indeed.' Smyth frowned. 'You cannot be unaware of my feelings towards you, Miss Tresilian?'

'You have been most kind, sir.'

'I meant more than kindness, Julia.'

Past tense. She forced a smile. 'Yes.'

'Have you an understanding with this man?' He was staring at the floor, his clasped hands between his knees.

Julia stared at his bent head. At least he was not shouting at her. 'No. I have a sense of obligation and of liking. You see, I wish to be honest with you. He can be very charming. I am also aware that he is not a man that it is right for an unmarried lady to associate with. My conduct has been…unwise.'

'Unwise?' He did raise his head at that, his brows drawn hard together. 'The swine has not—'

'No! No,' Julia repeated more softly. 'The major has not

seduced me if that is what concerns you.' *Only stolen my heart.*

'Oh.' Mr Smyth sat back. 'I see. You greatly relieve my mind. It is your natural amiability and innocence that has led you astray, allowed an unwise friendship, I can see that now.'

Julia felt faint with relief and then queasy with realization of where this confession had taken her. If Thomas Smyth proposed and she accepted him, but confessed she loved another, then he would be certain it was Hal. And would he believe her protestations of innocence then?

'Thank you,' she murmured.

'Julia, this is not the time or the place, but I would speak with you, most earnestly, about the future.' He leaned forward and took her hands in his. 'May I do that?'

'Yes. Yes, of course,' she managed. 'But…next week? When this is behind us?' Somehow, she would work through this moral conundrum. Duty and loveless security on one hand. Hopeless, one-sided love on the other. It ought to be an easy choice: she just had to summon up the strength to be able to put Hal out of her heart and mind and to tell Thomas Smyth that with a clear conscience.

'Of course.' Smyth patted her hands. 'And I will speak to your mother first, of course. Shall we say I may call on the twentieth? In the morning?'

'Yes.' Julia smiled, summoning up all her courage. 'Yes. That would be delightful.'

Mr Smyth glanced around, but there was no-one in their vicinity and the nearest spectators were looking down the course to where the next race was being marshalled at the starting line.

'Miss Tresilian—Julia.'

'Yes?' she said, braced for further difficult questions.

'Forgive me, but my ardour—' He leaned forward, caught

her hands in his and pulled her to him. 'You look so enchanting.' And then he kissed her.

Ever since the moment when Hal had made love to her
in the woodland glade, Julia had been dreaming about his
kiss, the touch of his hands. It had never occurred to her that
another man, one on the brink of proposing to her, would
expect to kiss her, but obviously he would. She fought her
instinctive recoil and closed her eyes.

Thomas Smyth's lips were warm and dry and pressed
lightly on hers. Was that it? Did he expect her to do something? With Hal, her instincts had taken over; now, she felt
nothing. Julia pressed back tentatively, and he put his hands
on her shoulders and held her. The pressure continued. Julia
opened her eyes and found that his were closed. It was difficult to see properly at such close range, but he appeared to
be enjoying the sensation.

She ought to concentrate. It was going to be her duty to
kiss this man—and more. Her mind skittered away from the
thought of any greater intimacy. He smelt quite nice, of plain
soap and starch. He tasted of toothpowder and tea, neither of
which were very exciting. It was all most respectful and not
at all alarming.

Julia realized that what she wanted was not something
respectful. She wanted Hal's thoroughly shocking kiss, she
wanted to be held forcefully in strong arms, she wanted to be
excited and alarmed and…ravished. Well, perhaps not that,
exactly. She wanted the illusion of ravishment, to experience
again the sensation that the man holding her was barely in
control of his emotions, he was so excited by what he was
doing. She wanted Hal, wicked and experienced and intoxi-
cated by her.

'Forgive me.'

She was placed carefully back in her seat and Thomas was
sitting looking at her, his eyes faintly glazed. Julia supposed

that was flattering, although what they had done hardly seemed sufficient to glaze any man's eyes.

'Of course.' She should be exhibiting maidenly confusion at what he would think was her first kiss: Julia dropped her gaze and managed a faint smile. She could not force a blush. Then she thought about Hal and felt her cheeks glow.

'I was overcome by your beauty.'

She nearly looked up, incredulous. That really was coming it too strong! She looked well enough but she was no beauty either. Perhaps the poor man really was in love with her. How awful if he was. Her conscience gave her a painful nudge.

'Oh look, here comes Mama.' Julia had the lowering suspicion that her mother had left the carriage just so Thomas could kiss her.

'Perhaps it is as well,' he said, his voice thrumming with a passion that his kiss had most certainly not held.

'Yes,' Julia agreed. 'Perhaps it is.'

Chapter Ten

Julia studied the guests mingling in the large salon at Lady Conynham's party the next night. She had furbished up her ball gown with new ribbons, keeping the brand new one for Lady Richmond's ball the following evening, and she felt she did not cut too poor a figure amongst the guests. All of the Ladies of the Parc were there of course, many of the diplomats and dozens of officers.

It was rumoured that the duke would be late, and that fact, in its turn, fostered even more rumours. Napoleon was on the march, some whispered. The French had crossed the frontier, or perhaps they were poised to do so. The Duchess of Richmond, it was said, had asked the duke if she should go ahead with her plans, and he had replied, 'Duchess, you may give your ball with the greatest safety, without fear of interruption.' So surely there was no need for concern?

'Miss Tresilian, I was hoping to see you here.' It was Captain Grey, smiling down at her, a comforting figure despite his height and fearsome whiskers. 'I have something for you.' He delved in his pocket and produced a tight roll of paper, handing it over under cover of a flower-filled urn. 'Your winnings on Chiltern Lad.'

'Thank you!' It felt like quite a lot. Julia tucked it into her reticule, wishing she could count it. But she must not be seen taking money from a man.

'Thank Carlow and that horse of his,' he said with a grin. 'May I fetch you some refreshments?'

'I would like a glass of lemonade, but I will walk over to the buffet with you.' She slipped her hand through the crook of his arm, comfortable to be with a man for whom all she felt was mild liking. 'Major Carlow rides very well.'

'He has no nerves, the devil's own courage and the lightest hands I ever saw,' his friend said warmly. 'And so long as I can keep putting money on him, I am never going to be in need of funds.'

'He said he was a lucky gambler,' she observed, fanning herself as they made their way through the hot, crowded room. It was a sinful luxury to be able to talk about Hal.

'He is. Lucky with cards, lucky in er… Just generally lucky,' the captain finished lamely.

'In love?' Julia could not resist teasing him even if the thought was painful. But of course Hal was involved with women. Lots of them, she was sure. And love would not come into those liaisons. They would be relationships of pure passion. She felt quite strange inside, even thinking about it.

Captain Grey made an uncomfortable, throat-clearing noise and covered it by hailing a waiter. Julia sipped her lemonade and wondered if Hal was there.

'Miss Tresilian,' said a voice behind her. She took such a sharp breath that the lemonade went up her nose, leaving her coughing and spluttering.

'Lord, I am sorry! Here, take my handkerchief.' Through streaming eyes, she saw Hal produce an immaculate white square and shake it out.

'Thank you.' She buried her face in it, certain that half the guests would be staring at the exhibition she was making of herself. One of the men took her elbow. She looked over the edge of the linen and saw it was Hal.

'Come on, I'll take you across to the retiring room.' Blind, she let him guide her across the room while she sneezed and coughed. Then the noise dropped and she realized they were out of the doors. 'Here, it is just down that corridor.'

Julia emerged from the handkerchief and managed a sticky, watery smile. 'Oh dear. Did I make a total exhibition of myself?'

'Not at all. I could hear Will saying something about you being attacked by a wasp. I am sorry.' His lips were twitching and she could hardly blame him: she must look a sight. 'I made you jump.'

'We were just talking about you.' She should go and make herself presentable, but somehow she could not make her feet obey her.

'You were?' He was smiling now and his eyes were almost blue. Julia smiled back, warm and happy just to be with him when he was so obviously glad to be with her. He looked well, less drawn than she recalled. The dark shadows had gone from under his eyes.

'Captain Grey gave me my winnings,' she explained. 'Are you…were you ill? Only you look different, as though you had been unwell and are better now.' He went still and she cursed herself for tactlessness.

'I have not been drinking brandy for a few days,' he said. 'I had not realized it made a difference to how I look.'

'Not drinking? Why? Oh, I beg your pardon, it is none of my business.' Why did she feel she could say anything to him? And why did she forget her manners and do so?

'No, of course you may ask.' He looked rueful. 'I thought

perhaps you would prefer it if I gave it up. I did tell you, at the picnic, that I was attempting to reform, did I not?'

'So, that means you have given up strong liquor and, I believe you implied, bits of um…muslin,' she said, very daring. He nodded, his eyes laughing at her. 'Which leaves gaming and fighting, does it not?'

'It does.'

'And so long as you remain lucky with the gaming, I suppose that is not so bad.'

'Have you no opinion on fighting?' He had moved very close now. She could see the grain of his close-shaven beard and the tiny details of the gold braid of the frogging on his jacket. The corridor seemed suddenly short of air. Her head began to spin.

'I found it exciting, when you hit Major Fellowes,' she admitted, shocking herself and startling him.

'Oh, Julia.' His eyes were very definitely blue now and she had a disturbing mental image of that stained-glass window of the falling archangel. A tempter. His voice had become husky. 'You say such provoking things.'

She could feel the blush sweeping up from her toes, even as she spun round and ran, down the corridor and through the door into the ladies' retiring room. Two matrons looked up from the sofa, their stares congealing into disapproval at her precipitate entry and her flushed and streaked face.

'Excuse me,' she blurted out. 'Wasp,' and hurried into the inner room to splash cool water on her face.

Exciting. Of all the things to say! And it was true, that is what is so awful. And he found my reaction arousing. There had been no mistaking the look in those wicked blue eyes, even for someone as sheltered and inexperienced as she was. They burned with the heat and the focus of a hunting cat. And she had been the mouse, foolishly playing between the cat's paws.

Julia stared at her flushed face in the mirror and tried for some semblance of calm. Her pupils were wide, her cheeks still pink, and her mouth, for some reason, seemed swollen. As though he had kissed it and not just looked as though he wanted to ravage it.

After careful work with rice powder and ten minutes sitting out, Julia felt strong enough to go back. The room was full of uniforms now, and there was a strange atmosphere, as though everyone was listening, taut, for a clap of thunder.

She wove her way through the talking groups, trying to find someone she knew, or catch a hint of what was causing the tension. The officers seemed more alert, taller—which was absurd. Shaking her head at her own foolishness, Julia found herself facing a sober suit of black, immaculate but plain white linen and the rounded and stubborn jaw of the Reverend Thomas Smyth.

'Mr Smyth.' Julia managed a creditable smile, despite her surprise. 'I had no idea you were here.' He frowned. 'Why is everyone so strange? I was sitting out for a while, and when I got back, the atmosphere had quite changed.'

'Napoleon is at the border,' he said.

'They've been saying that for weeks,' Julia shrugged, tired of rumour and false alarms.

'No, this is from a military despatch. We must assume it is accurate. That is why I am here, to find you.'

'You mean you were not invited?' He shook his head impatiently. 'And why the urgency? Napoleon can hardly reach Brussels so very fast, surely?'

'Within days,' he said tersely, drawing her into a curtained alcove at the side of the room. 'I would wish to make your status as my affianced wife official, to be in a position where I may organise the travel arrangements for your family. We must leave tomorrow.'

'My status?' Something very like panic swept through her,

the urge to turn and run was so great she had to grip the back of a chair to steady herself. 'But you have not asked me. Mr Smyth—Thomas—you are presuming a great deal.'

'Then I will ask you now.' He took both her hands in his and stood staring down with an expression she could only describe as grim. This was hardly the romantic proposal a girl dreamed of. 'Will you do me the honour, Julia, of becoming my wife? Naturally, I will ask Mrs Tresilian formally as you have no male relative here.'

'I…well…'

'You can hardly protest that this is sudden,' he said. 'Not after our conversation at the races. I am not given to kissing young ladies to whom I am not about to declare myself, believe me.'

That was obvious, Julia thought, recalling that lukewarm caress. 'No, of course not,' she agreed.

'I have made up my mind and fixed my intention upon you, Julia,' he said with the air of a man about to embark upon a well-conned speech. 'I am convinced that the occasional irregularity of moral purpose, the impulsive lack of discretion that was obvious at the races and that I observed tonight is something that can be overcome and that you will make an excellent wife for a man of the cloth.'

For a moment, she was so taken aback that she gaped at him. 'Lack of discretion? Tonight? What do you mean?' True, she had inhaled lemonade and spluttered and choked, but that was hardly indicative of—*what did he say?*—irregularity of moral purpose.

'I saw you, Julia,' Thomas said, more in sorrow than in anger. 'First you were flirting with the large officer with the whiskers and then you left the room with that rake Carlow.'

'If you thought that I was engaged in an amorous encounter with Major Carlow,' she said coldly, 'then I am surprised you did not come to confront us. I told you that he and I are not…

have not… Oh!' She glared at him. 'I am not conducting any sort of flirtation with Major Carlow or anyone else, and let that be the end of it. Either you believe me or you do not. And if you do not—'

'Yes, I believe you,' Thomas said hastily. 'But, dearest Julia, it is incumbent upon you to learn discretion. You will be the example to all the ladies of the parish, you must be above reproach in your behaviour.'

'I have not yet said *Yes*,' she pointed out. This was even worse than Charles Fordyce's jealousy. Thomas would lecture her, would disapprove and would then forgive her for every little slip. Julia was suddenly utterly convinced that she could not bear to be constantly forgiven.

'Yes, my dear, but you must see—'

'I see only that we will not suit, Mr Smyth,' she said firmly. 'I thank you for your most flattering offer and your most Christian forgiveness, but I will not marry you.'

'Julia!' He took her arm as she lifted the curtain to step out. 'Have you been toying with me? I did not think it of you.'

'My intentions were most certainly not to toy with your affections, sir.' She winced inwardly at the jolt to her conscience. She should have been stronger, clearer in her mind. She should have run every time she saw Hal Carlow, and erased him from her head and her heart. But it seemed she was not that strong. 'I had thought that we would suit, but I thought I knew you better than it seems I do, and you have an image of me that is, perhaps, inaccurate. It is better that we find these things out now, is it not?'

'I am sure it is.' He bowed stiffly. 'And it will be a lesson to me to be more careful in the future.'

Thomas thought her a flirt and a tease, she could see he did. And his crime had been to be dull and worthy and a little sanctimonious. Perhaps he was right about her. Julia pulled her arm free, pushed the curtain aside and almost ran from the alcove.

The buzz of conversation was louder in the room. As she hurried towards the exit, she heard snatches of conversation: *…cross the Sambre, I have no doubt… Prussians will have to hold them…best to go to Antwerp now, by canal boat… God, I'm looking forward to this.*

The last speaker stopped her in her tracks. He was one of a group of young infantry officers, their eyes alight with excitement as they argued and talked.

They want this fight, they want this great battle and the death and the glory and the bloodshed, she thought, turning away, sick at heart. *Thank goodness, there is the door, and no-one I know standing there.* And instead of Mama being able to leave Brussels with the support of a future son-in-law, they must rely on the baron and their own wits. And somewhere to the south, Hal would be fighting. He could be wounded, killed perhaps. And somehow that would all be her fault too.

Julia ducked though the knot of people into the front hall. She could ask a footman to take a note to Lady Geraldine and call her a cab. If she stayed here a minute longer—

'Yes, you'll get your battle, Bredon, I'm sure of it.' It was Hal talking to a slightly younger man in the scarlet coat and yellow reveres of one of the infantry regiments. There was a black mourning ribbon around his left arm. Brown haired, his face seemed made for laughter. Something about him reminded Julia of an eager hound.

They were all going to be killed, all the young men…

'Miss Tresilian, what is wrong?' Hal had seen her. Had the man eyes in the back of his head? Julia forced back the threatening tears and shook her head, unable to speak.

'Rick.' Hal turned to the young man. 'Go and find Lady Geraldine Masters. Take her aside and tell her Miss

Tresilian is unwell and I am putting her in a cab home. Discreetly now.'

'Sir. As if it were my sister's reputation.' He flashed a smile at Julia and walked briskly off.

Julia took a deep breath and told herself she must be calm. Her nerves were in tatters, that was all. Her refusal of Thomas Smyth was a disaster, but there was nothing that would be helped by tears or the vapours or panic. At least she had the money Captain Grey had won for her at the races. That might pay for a few gowns, but it was no substitute for a husband. She managed to walk with composure to retrieve her wrap. When she turned back, Hal was at the door.

'I have a cab. Come along, no-one is watching, just round this corner.'

'Thank you.' She let him help her in, then stared as he joined her and closed the door. 'What are you doing?' The horse set off at a walk in the opposite direction to home. 'And where are we going?'

'I am abducting you.' Hal sat back, crossed one long leg over the other and regarded her gravely in the borrowed light from the street. Her alarm must have shown, for he relented and explained. 'I have told the driver to walk round and round the Parc until told otherwise.'

'Oh. Thank you.' *Abducting me indeed. If only he would! At least I would not have to make any decisions.* 'I suppose I ought not to go home until I have worked out what to say.' Her mind felt curiously blank and rather bruised.

'What has happened?' Hal asked, his voice deep and soft in the shadows. 'Who has upset you?'

'At least you do not ask me what *I* have done, which is what Mama will ask, and she will be quite right,' she replied wryly. 'It was all my fault. I have just lost another suitor.'

'What? That prosy bore Smyth?'

'Yes, although as you have never spoken to him, I do not know how you can be so judgmental.'

'He stalks around with a look of moral superiority on his face. Either that or he has a permanent bad smell under his nose,' Hal said with a distinct lack of charity.

'He certainly has high standards,' Julia said with a sigh. 'But although I am prone to an occasional irregularity of moral purpose and exhibit an impulsive lack of discretion, he was sure I could be set on the right path with suitable guidance and can be a model of rectitude in the parish. Only I did not think I could stand it.'

'I should think not.' Hal sounded aghast. 'What irregularities and impulsiveness, for goodness sake?'

'That favour at the races.'

He groaned.

'And he saw me leave the room with you earlier tonight.'

'So I have lost you another suitor. I am sorry, Julia. It is I who has been showing the impulsive lack of discretion.'

'Oh, he would still have taken me,' she said, realizing as she spoke how cross that patronising attitude had made her feel. 'I turned him down.'

'Good for you.'

'Mama is going to be so disappointed in me. I have had this chance to make all our lives so much more secure and I have just thrown it away.'

'Surely when she sees how you feel about him?'

She shrugged, depressed.

'Has he hurt you very much? Were you very fond of him, Julia?' Hal leaned forward and took her hand, stroking it as though to comfort her.

'Fond of him? Certainly not, how could I be when I lo—' She froze, the two betraying words trembling on the tip of her tongue. *Love you. I love you.*

Chapter Eleven

Hal went very still, while the warm pressure of his hand through the silk of her white evening gloves sent her erratic pulse wild. For an appalled moment, Julia thought she must have said the words aloud.

'Lo…*Loathe* being lectured like that,' she finished, desperately.

'I see,' he said, and she could not read the underlying emotions in his voice. 'What will you do now?'

'Keep parading myself on the Marriage Mart,' she said, beyond keeping up pretences with him. 'Before Napoleon escaped there wasn't much point—anyone who might have been interested was as hard up as we were. But with all the new arrivals, and Lady Geraldine being so kind, Mama thought it worth the investment in gowns.'

'It's a cut-throat business for a young woman, isn't it?' he asked, shifting on the seat so he was directly in front of her and could take both her hands in his. *Just like Thomas Smyth at the races,* Julia thought. But then she had felt mildly embarrassed, now she was scarcely aware of her surroundings, only of the man sitting opposite her, his hair pale in the flickering, intermittent light, his face turned down to their clasped hands.

'My sisters both had their Seasons,' he went on, as though he was thinking aloud. 'But it is easier for them, I suppose. They both have titles, dowries; their father is an earl. Not that Honoria found her husband that way.' There was amusement in his voice, not disapproval.

'Honoria is like you?' Julia asked, fighting with the urge to lean forward, kiss the sharp angle of his cheekbone that was all she could see of his face.

'Lord, yes!' he laughed. 'Hence the trouble.' For a moment she thought he would explain, but then he said, as though his words were a logical continuation of what he had just been talking about, 'Has Hebden made further contact with you?'

'The jeweller? No. It was strange though. When he was looking at the pieces he mentioned you.'

'What?' Hal sat bolt upright and released her hands. Julia just managed not to grab his back.

'He implied that he had heard gossip that made him assume I was selling the jewellery to finance my—oh, husband-hunting is what he meant, I suppose.' Hal went very still. 'He said something about the reverend, the widower and the rake. You are the only rake I know,' she said with an attempt at a laugh. 'I remarked to Mama that no doubt someone saw us at the review and gossiped.'

'So he thinks I am a suitor for your hand?' Hal sounded decidedly worried.

Julia's stomach ached with embarrassment. He thought she was trying to imply he was courting her. 'No, I think he was only...'

'If he thinks that, then you are in danger,' Hal said bluntly, and she realized his anxiety was for that, not that she might assume anything about his intentions. 'He bears a deep and savage grudge against my family and two others. He was responsible for driving my sister from Society, he kidnapped my brother's wife and tried to ruin her sister. The infantry officer you saw me with in the hall—Rick Bredon?' She nodded. 'Hebden is his step-sister's half-brother and is causing her new husband sleepless nights, believe me.'

'You think that if he mistakenly believes I am…important to you in some way, he might attack me too? Although why should he think that, beyond some foolish gossip?'

'Smyth thought it,' Hal pointed out. 'And if Hebden is watching now, he knows we are alone in circumstances that would ruin you if they became public. Damn it, if I had had any notion that he knew of a link between us, I would never have got into this confounded carriage with you. The man is obsessed.'

Julia almost asked what the Carlows had done to attract such virulent hatred, then good manners caught up with her. If Hal wanted her to know, he would tell her.

'And you *are* important to me,' he added, cutting back to her last comment.

'Then let us hope your Mr Hebden considers friends unimportant in his campaign of vengeance.'

'Is that what we are, Julia?' Hal took her hand again, apparently interested only in tracing the fine lines of sewing that shaped the back of her glove. The movement of his finger made her want to shiver.

'I hope so,' she said brightly. Then the recollection of the talk in the grand salon came back to her and a shudder ran through her. 'Hal, is it true? Is Bonaparte at the frontier?'

'Yes.' The eagerness in the single word told her all she needed to know: Hal Carlow was itching to get into battle.

'How soon will it be?'

'Before the battle? I do not know. Not very long: days not weeks, but it depends which way Bonaparte moves once he crosses the Sambre. Do you and your mother want to leave for Antwerp now?'

'If we go, it would be because we believe Wellington—all of you—will lose,' she said slowly. 'Are you telling me that is what to expect?'

'No. But you can have no concept of what a city close to a great battle would be like. I have seen it, in the Peninsula.'

'I do not want to run away,' she said, realizing as she spoke how passionately she felt it, although not why. 'I would feel a coward. You—the Army—will not run.'

'No,' he said again, and his hands on hers were stilled. 'We will not run. But this is Bonaparte, one of the greatest generals in history.'

'We have Wellington,' she protested, shaken by his words.

'Who has never met Bonaparte in the field. I want you to leave, Julia. I want you to go to the baron as soon as it is certain the French have crossed in to Belgium. Promise me that.'

'I promise I will not do anything to put Mama and Phillip in danger,' she said, not understanding why she was equivocating, but knowing that she needed to.

'Good,' he said as though she had taken a great weight off his mind. 'And now, you must go home.'

Julia watched as he lowered the window and leaned out to call up to the driver, unashamedly admiring the flexibility with which he moved and the line of his lean body. Here she was, in a closed carriage, at night, with a notorious rake, and he did not so much as flirt with her. He had held her hands as though she was one of his sisters, that was all.

If I was bolder, knew what I was doing, I could encourage him to kiss me, she thought, biting her lip as he sat down again. *With passion. But what if he does not want to again?*

I would sink with shame. He doesn't want a good girl. He wants someone with experience.

And then it was too late. The carriage drew up, Hal opened the door and jumped out to hand her down, and she thought, *I should sink for shame just thinking about it.*

'Good night, Major. And thank you for seeing me home.'

'Good night, Miss Tresilian,' he said with equal formality, raising her hand to his lips.

Through the silk, she could feel the heat of his breath, the firm pressure of his lips, and her breath caught in her throat as he released her and turned back to the waiting carriage.

'Will you be at the duchess's ball tomorrow night?' he asked, one foot on the step.

'Yes—if the enemy is not at the gates,' she managed in an attempt at lightness.

'I will see you then, I hope. And if not, remember what you promised me.' And he was gone.

Julia climbed the stairs to their apartment, her brain spinning. If Napoleon advanced, then Mama and Phillip must go to Antwerp with the baron, but she would not. There was nothing she could do, but she would not leave Brussels while Hal was fighting, in danger. To do so would feel like running away, deserting him. How she would manage to stay, she had no idea. But, she resolved as she reached the door, she was not going to tell Mama about Mr Smyth either, not until at least the day after tomorrow, after the ball, after they knew when the battle would be.

'Let me out here,' Hal called up to the driver as the carriage rattled past the duke's house opposite the Parc. He was too restless to sit in a stuffy carriage, too energised by the intimacy with Julia, not to walk.

He paid off the man and began to make his way downhill.

He did not understand what he felt for Julia Tresilian, but it was powerful, too powerful to resist without pain.

The physical yearning for her was stronger than for any woman he had ever wanted, but perhaps that was simply the result of denying himself another taste of her. The urge to protect her was as visceral as the instinct he had to shield his sisters from harm. He liked her. He liked her honesty and her intelligence and her humour. He had stopped drinking and had not looked at another woman for her, although she had not asked it of him.

He admired the dogged way she set about husband-hunting when he knew she found it distasteful. Through his carelessness he had scared off her two serious suitors. Hal's pace slowed until he stopped; he put one foot on a low wall and looked out at the lights of the Lower Town. He discovered he was examining his conscience: an unfamiliar exercise.

Was it carelessness or had he intended to drive those men off? He was not sure he wanted to know the truth about that. And he certainly did not relish telling Julia that the remaining candidate, Colonel Williams, had maintained a mistress for many years and had done so when his wife was alive. But he would do if he thought she was going to marry the man: she should know something like that.

So, now she was back where she had begun, only out of pocket, perhaps in debt, for all her gowns. Would that make him an acceptable suitor?

The idea, the very fact he was even contemplating such a thing, shook him. And yet, here he was, thinking about marriage. He had a small estate of his own, she might like that. Her mother and Phillip could live there. He could afford to bring her up to Town for the Season every year, when he was in England.

When he was in England. A group of soldiers with their whores passed him, drunk and cheerfully noisy, but Hal hardly heard them. He was a soldier, that was what he did. But what if there was no more soldiering to be done? Could he settle down like his brother, manage his land, raise a brood of children? They'd be quite handsome children, he decided, almost dreamily, putting together his features and Julia's.

Someone jostled him from behind. Hal swung round, the light dress sword sliding out of the scabbard, the hilt firm in his hand, and the man, a hulking figure in a shabby greatcoat, shambled off hurriedly.

A drunk? A thief? Or a little reminder from Hebden? Hebden, who associated Julia with him, who could have watched them tonight. It seemed difficult to realize that this elusive and implacable enemy was the same seven year old who had played with Marcus in the woods and streams for a long hot summer while Hal, two years younger, had tagged along behind, falling over his wooden sword and demanding piggyback rides.

And now their old playmate did not just want the Carlow men to suffer, but wanted to make them do it through their women as well. Was Julia Hal's woman? Would she want to be? He thrust the slim blade back into its scabbard and walked on, all his senses alert now. She was, he thought without vanity, aware of him as a man, although she was too innocent to recognize what that meant. She liked him and trusted him or she would not have gone with him tonight or confided as easily as she had.

And there had been that moment when he had asked her about her feelings for Smyth and he thought she was going to say she loved someone. Him?

If only he understood what that meant. Marcus had gone up like dry wood in the path of a forest fire when he met Nell, even though he had every reason to distrust the woman who was now his wife. Hal supposed he could write and ask how you knew when you were in love. How you knew if a woman loved you. And he could be teased for the rest of his life, he concluded, trying to imagine his brother's face if he ever got such a letter.

Unless they got the order to march between now and ten tomorrow night, he and Julia would both be at the duchess's ball, he realized, feeling rather more apprehensive than he had last time he had eyed a row of French artillery all pointed in his direction at short range.

He reached the main street leading to the Anvers Gate and had to wait while a stream of carriages and carts rumbled past, all intent, he supposed, on running for Antwerp. Julia did not seem to have the same sense of urgency about evacuating Brussels as those people did. He sent up a silent prayer of thanks for van der Helvig and his amiable agreement to look after the Tresilians.

'Carlow?' Will Grey was standing on the steps of their hotel, hands on his hips and an expression of bemused amusement on his face. 'What the devil's the matter with you? You've a damn-fool look on your face, you're muttering and that last carriage nearly ran you down.'

'Will.' Hal looked at his best friend's smiling face and found he had no idea what he wanted to say, or do.

'Bloody hell, you've done it!' Will bounded down the steps and buffeted him hard enough on the back to send him staggering.

'What?'

'Asked Miss Tresilian to marry you.' Will took him by the shoulders and stared at him. 'My God, the worst rake in the Hussars, leg-shackled. She's a brave woman if she's taking you on, I'll say that for her.'

'I haven't asked her.' Hal got a grip on the railings and fended his friend off. He really could not face being warmly embraced by Will Grey, whiskers and all, on a public street. And his friend's words ran through him like a sabre thrust.

To ask a girl like Julia to marry a man like him was not the action of a gentleman. His honour would not let him do it, and he would just have to live with the consequences.

'Why the hell not?'

'For all the reasons you said. I can't ask it of her, she's too innocent to understand what I am, the life I've lived.'

'Damn it…' Grey blundered to a halt, his face reflecting both his agreement and his regret.

'Look, Will, if I don't…if I'm not in a position to look after her, will you get her back to England? Ask my brother Stanegate to keep an eye on her?'

They knew each other too well, and knew the risks only too clearly, for Will to make any false protestations or to pretend he did not understand what Hal was alluding to. 'Yes,' he said simply. 'I'll make sure she is all right.'

Then he threw an arm around Hal's shoulders and towed him towards the front door. 'We've got deployment orders to go over, just come down the hill from the duke. I hope you weren't expecting to sleep tonight.'

Hal shook his head. After studying the papers, they'd need to ride out to their troops, get them into marching order, check on provisioning and then, if they were lucky, get back in time to change and dine before tomorrow night's ball. Excitement and a fierce focus gripped him: this was what he lived for. At the back of his mind was the nagging certainty that Julia would be appalled to know he was happy about the prospect of the next few days. He pushed the thought aside: the important thing was to make certain she was completely sheltered from the realities of what was going to happen.

'Julia!' Mrs Tresilian thrust the door open and arrived panting in their sitting room. 'There are soldiers all over town with armloads of swords, taking them to be sharpened! And the banks are closed again.' She sat down on the sofa and fanned herself with a journal.

'We should pack,' Julia said, leaning down to untie her mother's bonnet. 'And send to the baron to ask for the use of a carriage to go to Antwerp.'

'But the ball—you cannot miss the Duchess of Richmond's ball, it will one of the highlights of the month,' Mrs Tresilian lamented.

'Well, so *she* thinks,' Julia said with a smile, recalling one of Lady Geraldine's catty observations. 'Apparently the duke is teasing her Grace by referring to their house as the Wash House—because it is on the Rue de la Blanchisserie.'

'Even so,' her mother said, 'a ball given by a duchess is not to be sneered at.' They looked at the clock. The hands stood at just after two.

'If it goes ahead. We should pack. And then have our dinner at six.' Julia began to move around the room, making piles of those things which should be taken and things that could remain. It was essential that Mama and Philip were ready to leave at a moment's notice.

'Very well, dear,' Mrs Tresilian got to her feet. 'I will write a note for the baron. I just hope we can get the laundry back before we have to set out.'

Packing did not take as long as Julia had feared. Her mother, apparently prepared for headlong flight, intended to travel light with a few changes of clothing and all their items of value, which, as they largely consisted of a few pieces of jewellery, bank notes and lace, took up very little space. She went through the motions of packing her own bag, silent about the audacious idea that had come to her last night in the carriage. But she had to make sure Mama and Phillip were safe first.

They had just sat down to dinner when their landlady

knocked and announced Mrs Cairns and Mrs Templeton, two of Mrs Tresilian's closest friends.

'My dears—' Mrs Cairns waved aside offers of a glass of wine '—are you not leaving? The officers are riding around, the men are forming up all over the place-everyone is going!'

'They say the French have attacked the Prussians at Charleroi,' Mrs Templeton, a faded blonde, chipped in. 'One hundred thousand French troops!'

Charleroi, Julia guessed, was perhaps a day's march away. Or less. Her mouth went dry. Antwerp suddenly sounded very enticing.

'We will leave first thing in the morning,' Mrs Tresilian said, the sparkling prospect of the ducal ball for her daughter still over-riding rumours of the French advance in her mind. 'Julia has been invited to the Duchess of Richmond's ball.'

'Along with all those floosies the Duke of Wellington has prevailed upon her to send cards to,' Mrs Cairns said waspishly. 'Lady John Campbell, for one.'

'Julia will be under Lady Geraldine's chaperonage,' Mrs Tresilian said, her chin up. 'Do you both leave for Antwerp this evening?'

'Most certainly,' Mrs Templeton said. 'We are going together in an hour. It is almost impossible to find a team of horses now: I thank heavens that Mr Templeton bought one last week.'

'Then we will see you in Antwerp,' Julia said with a smile, wishing they would leave and not continue to over-excite Phillip who was sitting there, his eyes like saucers with all the drama. 'I will show you out, you must not linger.' She closed the door behind them and came back to the table. 'What time did the baron say he would collect us tomorrow morning?'

'I said we would be ready at eight. I am afraid you are

going to get very little sleep, my dear.' Mrs Tresilian began to carve the cooling chicken.

'That doesn't matter, Mama,' Julia said, tucking a napkin into Phillip's collar as he squirmed on his chair. 'I suspect no-one will for the next few days.'

Chapter Twelve

'I was quite expecting to receive a note from you to say that you were about to leave the city,' Lady Geraldine remarked as her footman closed the carriage door at ten o'clock. 'Did you hear the gunfire to the south?'

'I think so—it was very distant. Perhaps it was thunder. Mama has arranged with the baron for him to call at eight tomorrow morning,' Julia said, carefully smoothing down the fine tissue of her skirts. The new gown—semi-transparent white silk over jonquil yellow with a draped bodice of white lace—felt too fragile to move in. 'Will you leave the city, ma'am?'

'We will go to friends who have a chateau some ten miles to the north,' Lady Geraldine said. 'I expect we will leave a little later than you. My husband has the grooms with shotguns guarding the horses against looters. I do hope the baron is taking similar precautions.'

It was a short drive down the hill to the large house the Richmonds had taken. 'It used to be a carriage builder's establishment,' Lady Geraldine observed acidly. 'No doubt we will be accommodated in some barn.'

The barn turned out to be the former carriage showroom which seemed, to Julia's curious eyes, quite well disguised with hangings and a podium for the band. When they finally managed to reach the doors, after a long queue in the street and an even longer one in the receiving line, the noise from within was considerable but, as they moved through the doors, Julia thought she heard the sound of bugles and drums from outside.

'They are sounding the assembly,' a civilian guest remarked, and Julia strained her ears until the noise of over two hundred people and an orchestra overwhelmed any other sound.

She supposed it was really no different from any other ball that had take place in Brussels over the past month. But the atmosphere was utterly changed, as though everyone was waiting for some momentous announcement, yet were united in a great conspiracy to pretend that they were doing nothing of the kind.

There was no sign of Hal. Had she seen the last of him before the battle? *Or ever?* Julia closed her eyes against a moment of panic, then opened them to find one of the *aides de camp,* whose name had completely gone from her head, offering his hand for the next dance.

So she danced and chatted and smiled until her feet, her head and her lips ached and rehearsed over and over what she as going to do tomorrow.

The band ended the waltz they were playing and put down their instruments. The duchess stepped onto the podium and clapped her hands. 'The Gordon Highlanders!' she announced to a flurry of applause. It was drowned out in the skirl of sound as a tall pipe-major marched into the hall with four kilted sergeants magnificent behind him.

Julia had never heard pipe music before. Slightly stunned

by the effect in a crowded room, she began to make her way back through the crowd towards the chaperones' corner.

'Don't you like the pipes?' an amused voice by her left ear asked.

'Hal!' She swung round, so relieved to see him that she almost took his hands there and then. 'I thought—I thought you must have gone already. The French are advancing, are they not?'

'Yes. You are packed and ready to go?'

She nodded and saw the tension around his mouth ease into a smile. 'Good girl. Come, let's go up to supper; there will be a rush as soon as the Scottish dancing demonstration is over.'

He seemed to assume she was his partner: Julia wondered what Hal would have done if she had said she was already engaged for supper. It was rather pleasant to be so masterfully swept along, although she knew if it had been anyone else she would have resented it.

The supper room on the first floor was only partly full and the noise of the pipes penetrated even there. 'That table down there,' Hal announced, pointing to one in a deserted corner. 'I'll bring some food.' He came back to the table with a footman behind him carrying a bottle of champagne and two glasses.

'Right.' He waited until the man had gone, poured the wine and looked at her. 'We need to talk. About things.'

'Yes?' Julia enquired as his silence stretched on. Across the room, people were beginning to come in and the tables were filling up, although their gloomy little corner was ignored. A tall man with a beak of a nose strolled in, officers clustered round him. 'Look, there's the duke—'

'I am a younger son,' Hal said, ignoring Wellington's arrival and making her jump.

She nodded, puzzled, dragging her attention away from the bustle around the great man. She knew that.

'And I am a soldier. Beside that I have only a small estate in Buckinghamshire.' He picked up his glass and drained it. 'Julia—'

'Yes?' Perhaps he was going to ask her to take a message home if…if something happened to him. Her heart lurched and she felt herself go pale. Her hand trembled as she picked up her own glass and sipped, grimacing at the way the bubbles tickled.

'I ought to ask you to marry me.'

Julia stared at him across the rim of her glass. Had he really said that? She opened her mouth, found no words and closed it again. *Ought* to ask?

'I nearly ruined you, I've compromised you with two suitors,' he said, his smile a little twisted. 'I drove with you last night, after dark and unchaperoned. But I am utterly and completely unsuitable as a husband for a lady like you, Julia.'

'But—but why are you telling me this?' she stammered. This was not her dream, her fantasy. Everything was wrong. He did not want her, she should have accepted that, realized that he would have kissed her again before now, shown her how he felt, not treated her like one of his sisters, or a friend, if he did.

'I realized last night that the idea rather appealed to me, but that I must not give in to such a whim.' For all his sophistication, he looked suddenly both younger and bitterly uncertain.

'*Rather appealed? Whim?*' At least Mr Smyth had managed a proposal, however unromantic. She realized the glass was still in her hand and tossed back the wine recklessly. 'You mean you have a guilty conscience because you have lost me two suitors and you are worried about Hebden so you thought you ought to propose! But then you realized that your reputation makes you unsuitable. How very convenient!

'Do you know something, Hal Carlow?' She grounded the glass with enough force to crack the stem. 'I would rather you had not made this confession. I can do without a catalogue of the reasons why you are not about to make me an offer.'

Julia found she had lost her temper, rather comprehensively, and that under the anger, what she was feeling was disappointment. Bitter disappointment for the shattering of the fantasy that, because she loved him, he loved her too and only had to realize it.

'I am sorry,' he fired back. 'But you don't want to marry me, do you?'

'How do you know? You haven't asked me what *I* want. You have produced this confession to quieten your conscience, that is all.'

'I know I want you, I know I want to keep you safe. And that means keeping you safe from me,' he fired back, the hardness and the edge back in his voice and his face. 'That's the best apology I can come up with. Won't that do?'

'No, it won't *do!*' Julia grabbed her fan and reticule and jumped to her feet leaving Hal to catch her wildly rocking chair. She swept across the room, weaving between tables, and came up hard against a solid figure. 'Oh. I am—Your Grace.'

The duke looked down at her, the hard, preoccupied eyes barely seeming to notice her. Then he stepped back, bowed slightly, and the hint of a smile touched his mouth. His reputation with women was terrible, Julia recollected hazily, and she could quite see why. He was formidably attractive.

'Please—' she gestured to the corridor ahead of them '—I am in no hurry.'

He bowed again and strode off trailing his retinue. Julia

followed more slowly. Hal, it appeared, was willing to let her go.

Blank with confused misery and the acid seething of her anger, she passed a dust-covered soldier, incongruous as he slumped back against the wall to make way for the gorgeously dressed guests. A messenger perhaps.

The duke had vanished when she reached the ballroom, but there were eddies of movement all around, cutting across the grain of the dancing couples, the groups in conversation. Something was happening; her already painful stomach cramped. The Duke of Brunswick was sitting to one side, the young Prince of Ligne on his knee. An officer bent and spoke in his ear, and he leapt to his feet, sending the child sprawling.

'Julia.' Hal had followed her after all. He took her arm, pulling her behind one of the long tapestries that draped the walls hiding recesses and doorways. 'The Prussians have been defeated at Ligny,' he said without preliminaries. 'I must go now, we all must. Find Lady Geraldine and leave with her. When you get home, tell your mother to send to the baron at once. You must leave at first light.'

'Hal.' Julia found she was clinging to his arm, the anger melting into something else in her fear for him. 'I don't want to part with you feeling like this, so angry.'

'I know.' He smiled and ran his fingers down her cheek. 'I didn't know you could be, I thought you were always quiet and ladylike. It is quite a stimulating revelation.'

'Well, after the picnic, nothing about me has ever seemed to stimulate you,' she retorted, not sure whether it was the memory of his excuses for not proposing or her fear for him making her so snappish.

'Were my efforts at self-control so successful then?' he asked, his hand slipping round to cup the back of her head.

'Extremely. I might have been your sister.'

'Hardly,' he said dryly. 'But I am not used to good girls, Julia. I am not fit for them, you know that.'

'I am not a girl.' His eyes crinkled as he smiled at her. Very close, very big. Very, very dear. 'And I am so tired of being good.'

It seemed he needed no other encouragement. Julia had yearned for a kiss, now, as his mouth closed over hers in expert possession, she was receiving one that fulfilled all her dreams.

One hand held her head still while his mouth moved over her lips, the other was at the small of her back, pressing her to him. His body was hard and hot, and her own arched into him without her having to even think, which was good, for thinking was becoming difficult. His mouth demanded something, and then she remembered and her lips opened for him.

Without hesitation he filled her, took everything she offered and showed her more, so that her tongue tangled with his and her breasts ached and tightened as she was crushed to him and her hands knew just where to touch the nape of his neck and make him moan into her mouth.

And then he released her, stood her away from him with his hands firm on her waist, and just stared at her. 'My God, Julia.'

'Oh.' There did not seem much more to say, and besides, she was shaking.

She looked down at her trembling hands and so did he. 'That is why you must not marry me. You see again that I am not to be trusted with virgins,' he said bitterly.

'Don't you think the virgins might have a point of view?' Julia said.

'No. Not while I've the strength to behave like a gentleman.' The dark, smouldering grey of his eyes showed the intensity of his emotion just as well as it hid what he was feeling.

'Damn it, Julia, there are more decent men out there, not just Smyth or Fordyce or Williams—who has a mistress, by the way, don't have him. Find another one and marry him.'

'No. No, I realise now what was wrong with Thomas and Charles…they were not important to me,' she said, watching the expression on his face in the shadowed niche.

Slowly he smiled. 'You know how to drive a knife into the wound, don't you, Julia? But this changes nothing of what I said upstairs, you know that.'

She murmured a protest, but he put two fingers against her lips. 'Take great care. If there is anything—after the battle—and I am not around, go to Captain Grey.'

'If you are killed,' she murmured, almost frightened to say the word as though speaking it brought death into the room with them.

'Yes. There is a good chance of that. I am a soldier, that is a fact of life—and death. If I do not come back, try and remember that I did what I thought was right for you.'

How can he be so matter of fact about it? How can he want to go into battle? Yes, he will do his duty because he is brave and honourable, but he is eager to fight. I wish I understood that. Desperate to stop the tears that were welling up, Julia pulled open her reticule. 'You must have another token,' she said. 'Something for a real battle, not just a ribbon for a race.'

Her fingers closed over the small notebook her father had given her. Barely two inches by three, it was covered on both sides in mother of pearl with *Julia* carved on it. She carried it everywhere, sometimes jotting a line of verse or a phrase that struck her, occasionally making a tiny pencil sketch.

'Take this, please.' She pressed it into his hands. She wanted to give him everything, give him herself.

Hal stood there holding it, tracing her name with his finger, then undid two buttons and slid it into the breast of his jacket. 'Against my heart,' he murmured. 'Such as it is. Come.'

They emerged from behind the arras, unremarked. A tall, dashing man was on the low podium, every eye turned to him. 'Lord Uxbridge,' Hal murmured in her ear. 'My cavalry commander.'

'You gentlemen who have engaged partners had better finish your dance and get to your quarters as soon as you can,' his lordship said crisply.

Distantly, Julia could hear the Duchess of Richmond, 'But those of you who do not have to join the Army need not… please, stay…'

Hal stooped, his mouth hard on hers like a brand. When he lifted his head, his eyes held hers, dark and bleak. 'Good bye.' The unspoken word *forever* hung in the air between them. Then he was gone.

They were all going, and the room emptied of colour like the face of a girl about to faint. The uniforms ebbed away out of every door, and all that was left was the white and pale colours of the gowns.

They had all stopped pretending it would never happen, Julia realized. This was reality. Tomorrow—no, today: the clock was striking two—battle would blast their world apart.

There was a chair just behind her; she sat down, her legs too weak to stand safely. Julia knew next to nothing about kissing, but it did seem that had been…heartfelt. But Hal was normally so assured, so confident so…fluent. What had made him come out with that painful explanation of why he would not ask her to marry him?

Had she said anything, done anything that had led him to think she expected a proposal? Julia searched her conscience. *No, not wittingly.*

Perhaps it was the prospect of battle and death that made

him think he must not leave any unfinished business, any uncertainties. But Hal had fought in the Peninsula, he must have faced this point of crisis countless times before. And he came back safely then, she reminded herself, her fingers tight on her reticule as though she was holding on to him. He will be safe this time. He must be. He was trying to prepare her for the worst, being cruel to be kind, that was all. And his safety was more important than her feelings.

'Julia?' It was Lady Geraldine, pale and somehow less *soignée* than she had seemed only a few hours before. 'We must go, my dear.'

'Yes, of course, ma'am.' She collected her cloak and followed the erect figure, her mind racing. This changed nothing of what she had resolved to do. 'Ma'am?'

Lady Geraldine turned at the doorway. 'Yes, dear?'

'Would you be so kind as to drop me at the Baron van der Helvig's house? I must change the arrangements for tomorrow.'

'You will want to leave at first light,' the older woman nodded. 'Very wise. Would you like me to send the carriage back for you?'

'Thank you, but I am sure he will give me an escort home, it is very close.'

Now it all depended on the baron. If he refused to help her with her plan, then she did not know what she was going to do.

'You want me to take your mother and brother to Antwerp but to leave you? My dear Miss Julia, you cannot possibly stay in Brussels alone!' The baron, roused from his usual amiable placidity, strode up and down the salon in his dressing gown. His house, like most in Brussels, was a blaze of light despite the hour, and the baron was wide awake supervising the packing of his silver.

'I am going to stay in our apartment.'

'But why should you want to?' He threw up his hands and sat down, baffled.

'I just cannot go,' she replied. 'I feel I have to stay, very strongly.' She understood better now, although she could not explain it to the baron, not without betraying her innermost feelings. Hal was going into battle, going to do his duty even though he knew the chances of death or wounding were very great. To run away would be like deserting him and once she had begun to think more clearly—with the icy clarity of terror, she supposed—she saw that there would be a need to nurse the wounded too. A shocking thing for a gently bred girl to do, but she was beyond caring about that, not with Hal's life in the balance.

'And what does your mother have to say about this?'

'She does not know,' Julia admitted. 'I am relying on you, Baron, to say nothing until we are about to leave, then to go on, whatever she says. Otherwise,' she continued as he began to splutter, 'I will get out at the first stop and do my best to get back. Or run away when we get to Antwerp.'

He stared at her, apparently marshalling arguments to counter this insanity and failing.

'And I must ask another favour, sir. Will you leave me that big English groom, George, and the gig?'

The baron's beady, intelligent eyes studied her. 'This is about one officer, is it not? I believe I could put a name to him. You want to be here, if he is wounded.'

'Yes,' she admitted. 'I cannot bring myself to leave. And if I had George armed with a shotgun, then I would be safe.' She watched his frowning face for a moment, then added, 'You see how much safer I will be if I can plan this properly and not just run back here from goodness knows where?'

'Your mother is going to be beside herself,' he said at

last, and she let out the breath she had not realized she was holding.

'Yes, but if she knows it is planned and I am guarded…'

'Very well. I believe you will do this, whether I help you or not. I would say, come here and stay. But if the French take the city, this house is too tempting a target for looters. Your more modest apartment will be safer. I will send George and the horse and gig, and he can sleep in the stables at your lodgings. And I will bear your mother away and she will probably call down curses upon my head all the way to Antwerp.'

'Thank you so much, Baron.' Julia slumped back in her chair, too tired and relieved to care about deportment. 'Might one of the footmen walk me home now?'

Chapter Thirteen

'Julia!' Mrs Tresilian's voice rose in a shriek as the carriage rolled away from the house in Place de Leuvan in the dawn light. 'Julia!'

'Mama,' she said as she ran alongside, one hand on the edge of the window. 'There is a note in your reticule that explains it all. I will be safe here with Madame and with George. Monsieur le Baron will tell you.' Then she had to let go and stand there as the coachman took the turn towards the Anvers Gate and she was left without any of her family, for the first time in her life.

From the direction of the Parc there was a tumult of shouting, bugles, drums. 'They're mustering in the Place Royale,' George the groom said, coming to stand beside her as an artillery train clattered past, gun carriages bouncing on the cobbles behind the trotting horses. He was a stolid man, good with the horses and more intelligent than his expressionless face betrayed. 'You come inside now, Miss.'

'No, I want to see—oh, look at that poor woman.' A soldier, knapsack on his back, musket slung over his shoulder, was grasping the hand of a woman with a child in her arms, while she tried to hold him back for one last embrace. 'George, I am going to the Parc.'

With the groom grumbling at her heels, Julia began to push through the crowds as the sound of bagpipes made everyone turn. 'It's the Forty-second,' someone called. 'And the Ninety-second.' The sound was deafening and yet heartening and the sight of the Highlanders swinging along lifted not only her spirits, but those of everyone around, Julia could see from the watching faces. Were the men marching here amongst those who had played and danced to entertain the guests at the ball last night?

And then, bringing the atmosphere of martial glory crashing down to earth, the market wagons started to rumble into the city, their drivers gawping about them as they found themselves in a world transformed.

Steadily the men formed up, moved off, the sounds began to fade and an uneasy silence fell over the city as the clocks started to strike seven. The flowerbeds and the paths of the Parc were crushed and rutted. Under the shade of trees, heavy wagons stood, their horses grazing under armed guard while drivers settled down to sleep on the tilt carts.

'Those'll be for fetching the wounded later,' George remarked. 'Look, Miss. There's old Nosey.' And sure enough, Wellington was riding out, his ADCs clustered at his heels.

When they had gone, it felt as if everyone had been holding their breath and now there was a collective sigh. The watchers turned and looked around, shrugged, wandered off as though they did not know what to do next.

'We must go back and get some rest,' Julia said, trying to sound positive. 'Nothing will be happening for a while now. Are you settled, George?'

'Aye, Miss. I'll be fine in the stables with the horse and the gig and my gun. The baron was worried about people stealing them, and I reckon he's right.'

Julia had not expected to sleep, but somehow she did, her dreams restless, filled with images of Hal overlain with the sounds of the morning, the tramp of marching feet, the skirl of the pipes, the rattle of side-drums. She woke from a dream of holding him, to find she was curled around the bolster, its linen cover damp with tears.

Their landlady served a distracted luncheon in the kitchen, while supervising her husband digging holes in the vegetable patch to bury their good pewter and jars of cash. Unlike some Belgians who welcomed the idea of Napoleon's return, she had only hard words for the French and was filled with pessimism.

'The Allied Army will win, Madame,' Julia tried to reassure her and received a fatalistic shrug in response. 'What is that? Thunder?' Would it be good or bad for the Allies if the rain came down?

'No, that's gunfire I reckon, Miss.' George said from his end of the table. He went outside, then came back, shaking his head. 'Long way away.'

The gunfire went on through the afternoon, getting closer and closer, more and more regular. In the city, the streets were full of carriages, horses, handcarts, and people on foot streaming towards the northern gates. Those who were not going stood around in the streets, silent except when a fresh wave of rumours reached them. The French had been slaughtered, they said. Then word came that the Belgian troops had fled, leaving the English to be cut to ribbons as almost two hundred thousand French swept over them. Julia refused to believe it. But no-one seemed to know where the battle was.

She tried to keep calm. It would do Hal no good if she made herself ill imagining the worst. It was very easy to resolve and very hard to do. Finally, with the cannon fire seeming closer yet, she left George guarding the horse and walked up to the rampart walk. There were no fashionable strollers enjoying the late afternoon air now, only crowds facing south, listening to the relentless roll of the guns.

'Wounded!' someone called. 'Walking wounded.'

It took time to make any sense of what was being shouted. Forward divisions of the Netherlands troops had met the French at a crossroads to the south, at a hamlet called Quatre Bras, and had held them until the Prince of Orange, and then Wellington, arrived with reinforcements. Gradually, more news trickled in, none of it good. The Highland regiments had suffered greatly and the Prussians were engaged some distance away and unable to join up with the Wellington's Army. The Allies were retreating towards Brussels.

'Boney's managed to split the armies then,' George said as they all sat around the kitchen table pooling what news they had each gathered. 'Cunning bugger—begging your pardon, Miss.'

'Listen.' Julia said. 'The guns have stopped. What's the time?' The clock on the wall said ten. 'Eight hours, without stopping,' she whispered. 'Eight hours.'

The night seemed endless. Just after midnight, the sound of heavy artillery moving at speed had everyone up and at their windows until the word came that it was heading for the front line. Then at six, a troop of Belgian cavalry galloped through in full retreat. Julia gave up trying to rest at that point, helped Madame make breakfast and tried to make sense of what their more sensible neighbours were saying.

'I am going down to the Hôtel de Flandres,' she told George, packing a flask of brandy and the bandages she had been tearing from old sheets into a basket. 'Monsieur Grignot says that the wounded are being taken back to their original billets because the hospitals are already full. I will look for Major Carlow there.' Finally she had admitted out loud why she had stayed. She felt slightly drunk, she realized. It must be reaction, or perhaps the lack of sleep. 'You had better stay here and guard the horses.'

'But, Miss—'

'The streets are full of decent people and the only soldiers are wounded ones: no-one will trouble me.' She jammed her plainest bonnet over tightly braided hair, picked up the basket and hurried out.

The sound of gunfire had her ducking into an alleyway, her heart in her mouth, then she realized they were shooting wounded horses. Every house seemed to have doors and windows open, and through them she could glimpse men, sitting or lying wherever there was room. The townspeople were throwing themselves into caring for the injured.

The hotel that had been Hal's lodging was as full of men as any she had passed, but she could see no blue uniforms with buff facings. One tall infantry officer leaning against the wall, with his arm in a sling and his face half covered with a bandage, seemed well enough to speak to.

'The 11th Light Dragoons?' He smiled, a lopsided grimace. 'Arrived too late to fight, came in just after darkness. They had to ride from Ninove,' he added, as though to excuse them. 'But they'll be in it now. Fighting retreat, that's what happening.'

'Retreat into Brussels?' Julia asked, feeling dizzy. Yesterday—last night—Hal had been safe. But today? Around her, the sounds of men groaning, the bustle of helpers, and the arrival of more stretchers filled her ears. The smells were all stomach-turning: blood, sweat, smoke and worse.

'No. Wellington will protect the city at all costs. Mont St Jean is where we were headed for, just south of Waterloo.' Julia pulled the brandy flask from her basket and opened it for him. 'Thank you, ma'am. Your man with the eleventh?'

'My—yes, my man is with them,' she said, lifting her chin,

feeling her pride in Hal stiffen her backbone. 'It all seems so chaotic here, I wonder how I can best help.'

'Water, ma'am, that'll be the most welcome,' the man advised her, handing back the flask.

'Then that's what I will do.' Julia found a niche with a statue in it, incongruously elegant overlooking the bloody scene. She sat her hat on its head, stuffed basket and cloak behind it, rolled up her sleeves and went to find the kitchens.

It was raining and almost dark when she stumbled out again at last. She had done all she could for the day, now she needed to wash, eat, snatch some sleep before she returned in the morning. The rain lashed down as she toiled up the hill and she tried not to think what it must be like out there in the darkness knowing that tomorrow you were going into battle.

Hal pulled his heavy felted cloak right over his head and leaned against Max's front legs. Above him, the big horse shifted, cocked up a hoof and, resigned to the rain, settled again under the scant shelter of a spindly tree. Hal reached up to make sure he had loosened the girth and that the other cloak was still over the saddle and Max's dappled rear quarters as a loud squelching announced that someone was rash enough to be moving about in the downpour.

'Who's that?'

'Trooper 'arris, sir.'

Ah yes, the man who had taken over from Godfrey at the races. Godfrey was still off sick with pains in his guts and constant vomiting. Hal wondered if the man would rather be here or on his sick bed. He knew which bed he would like to be in. A fantasy of Julia, slim and curved and pale against the dark green silk bed cover his imagination conjured up sent flickering heat into his loins and he groaned.

What on earth had prompted him to speak as he had? Hal

rubbed cold hands across his face. He must have been out of his mind. And he had hurt her too. She was growing fond of him, perhaps even, if that half-spoken word in the carriage had been what he suspected, thought herself in love with him.

She had every right to expect an honourable proposal, and she was too innocent to understand why he could not, must not, offer marriage to a virtuous, well-brought-up young woman. She deserved someone of substance, of moral worth. Someone with a future.

It was not as though she came from the sort of aristocratic background where even the daughters were well aware of the rackety lives their fathers and brothers lived.

He had no business indulging those half-understood urges towards stability and family at her expense. Look at him now! Half drowned in a sodden field and likely to come back tomorrow wounded, if he came back at all. What sort of husband would he make if he lived—leaving aside his character, reputation and general unsuitability?

So it had been right to tell her, bluntly, even if it left her hating him. But it hadn't. The memory of her innocent mouth under his, her instinctive, sensual, unawakened response filled him with a kind of humble gratitude.

Was she thinking of him? He thought she would be, safely tucked away in Antwerp. That last kiss that had turned his brain and his willpower into jelly, was not given lightly.

Of course, if he was killed tomorrow, she was safe from him, he thought ruefully. And if he wasn't, he would just have to make certain he never saw her again. She would think he was having second thoughts about her if he did, think he was going back on his word.

Hell. Hal scrubbed at his cold face again. Did it matter what she thought of him, so long as she did not make a mistake she would regret for the rest of her life?

That was a plan: be killed or be a bastard. Now all he had to do was get through tomorrow. God, he was itching to get into action. The frustration of that long, hard ride only to arrive after dark with orders to help cover the retreat, was intense.

Max shifted, his neck snaking out to bite something. 'Hey!' Hal twisted round to see what he was attacking.

'Sorry, sir. I must have got too close.' It was Harris again. 'Big bugger isn't he? Nasty teeth.'

'Yes.' Hal closed his eyes, 'He's as good as an armed body-guard.'

The rain lashed down.

'They've broken! The Old Guard has broken!'

The cry ran along the front of the Allied lines from the right flank to where the Light Dragoons fretted in reserve on the counter-slope of the left flank. Since eleven that morning when the first attack began at Hougoumont, the Dragoons had waited, their only occupation dodging fire, rallying faltering units ahead of them and making occasional forays to hold the extreme end of the line.

Now it was past seven in the evening. Hal had a hole through the top of his shako, a slight wound where a spent bullet had hit his right upper arm, and a burning sense of frustration. 'Damn it, Will,' he said to Captain Grey, who was standing beside him. 'When the hell is Vandeleur going to let us go?'

'Any minute now.' Will grinned and gestured at the rider galloping flat out from Wellington's position.

'Mount up,' Hal yelled, swinging into the saddle. 'Form line!'

There was cheering all around him as he steadied Max. Vandeleur was indicating a mass of French cavalry in front of a battery of artillery that was still holding firm. The objective was clear: take the guns.

The next few minutes were bloody, fast and deadly. The French cavalry steadied, formed up and discharged a hail of carbine fire before turning, as though on parade, and cantering to the rear through the guns. Out of the corner of his eye, Hal saw Will slump over his pommel. He reined Max back, pulled his friend straight in the saddle and turned his horse's head to the rear, sending it on its way with a slap on the rump. It was all he could do for him.

As he lowered his sabre and charged the nearest gun, he saw Trooper Harris beside him on an ugly roan, teeth bared, sabre ready. Together they charged through either side of the gun, slashing and stabbing until the gun crew fell or fled.

For a moment, they were alone on the far side of the artillery line in a swirling fog of smoke. Hal grinned at Trooper Harris and the man grinned back before he turned his horse hard into Max and drove his sabre straight at Hal's heart.

The blow took his breath with the shock and the pain, then the blade hit something, skidded, dragged down, slashing his ribs, his arm, his hip, his thigh. Reeling in the saddle, stunned by the direction of the attack, Hal tried to parry with his own weapon. Then the world exploded. He was conscious of falling, of a great roar in his ears, of pain almost everywhere and of Harris falling too. Then everything went black.

Julia, weary to her bones, sat at the foot of the stairs in the Hôtel de Flandres and wept out of sheer relief. The first word of victory had come at midnight. By dawn on the nineteenth, an exhausted city knew they were safe, that Napoleon had been defeated and the Allies were triumphant.

After a day of constant cannon fire and of rumours, each worse than the one before, it seemed impossible that it was over. Despite files of French prisoners trailing through the town and the sight of captured Eagles, the news had been constantly bad, and as late as ten that night, word was that the Prussians had not yet got through to join up with Wellington.

Some Light Dragoon officers had come in, none of them seriously wounded, none of them with any firm news of Hal except that he had been all right when they had last seen him. Knowing that a bullet could have hit him seconds after that, the news was not particularly comforting.

She must have dozed a little, despite the noise, for the next thing she knew, was someone calling her name. Blinking, Julia straightened up, stiff from huddling on the cold marble against the carved balustrade.

'Miss Tresilian!'

'Captain Grey.' She got to her feet and hurried to where he was standing, supported by an equally battered-looking comrade. 'You are wounded?' There was dried blood on his jacket and his arm was in a sling.

He grimaced. 'In and out. I'll live.' He looked as though he wished he had not said that.

For a long moment Julia stared at him before she could find the courage and the words. 'Where is Hal?'

'He didn't come back from the charge.'

The blood seemed to have drained to her toes. Julia heard a high-pitched buzz. Doggedly she fought the faintness, hung on until she could ask, 'Is he dead?'

'I don't know,' Will Grey said and she blessed him for his honesty. She could not have coped with easy lies.

'Where?' she asked, surprised to find her voice steady.

'We were far out on the left flank, east of the Charleroi road. We charged the French guns on the ridge: I last saw him as we hit the bottom of the valley.' He put out his left hand and caught hers. 'Why do you ask?'

Why? He expected her to leave Hal on the battlefield to die of his wounds or, if he was dead already, to abandon him to scavengers and an unmarked grave? Hal was her man, just like the wounded officer had said the day before. That last kiss at the duchess's ball had told her that he wanted her, even if he did not love her. Now he needed her. Whether he accepted it or not, he was her man.

'Because I am going to go and find him, of course,' she said as though explaining something very obvious to a child. 'And bring him back.'

Chapter Fourteen

The air was hot, humid and it stank of putrefaction, buzzed with flies. Three miles after they had passed through the battlements and out towards Ixcelles, Julia got down from the gig and was violently sick, then she doggedly climbed up to her seat again and, despite George's pleas to turn back, made him drive on.

The early morning sunlight filtered prettily through the leaves of the beech trees as if mocking the people beneath it. It played over the carcases of dead horses, the scattered human bodies, the pools of foul water. Progress was painfully slow: the road with its dips and summits was clogged with broken-down carts and abandoned kit, and they constantly had to stop for the wounded making their painful way back to Brussels.

'Don't look, Miss,' George kept saying as she craned to stare at every blue jacket she saw.

'I've got to,' she insisted. The light, the need to see, was why she had not set out last night. Instead, she had forced herself to eat, then to doze restlessly before getting up before dawn to pack everything she thought she might possibly need into the gig. George had stuffed a battered holdall in too, muttering that it had some 'handy stuff' in it.

They were deep into the forest of Soignes now. It seemed a dream, that idyllic picnic in the woods. Or perhaps this was the dream: a waking nightmare. The village of Waterloo, where Will Grey said some of the wounded officers had been taken, was nine miles from Brussels, the battlefield another mile or so on from that. They passed hamlets of low cottages with names of wounded officers chalked on the doors. Julia got down and checked them all, but saw none she recognized.

The gig lurched on along the deeply rutted way. It must be torment for the wounded on the unsprung wagons. If Hal was badly hurt, she had no idea if they would be able to get him back in the gig. She set her jaw against the jolting and tried to sit up straight. She was going to get him back, whatever it took. Alive or dead—or she would not be able to live with herself.

At last they made it to Waterloo village. The straggling street was lined with small houses and whitewashed cottages, all dominated by the small, domed church standing high over the deep trench of the road. Neat signs, very different from the chalk scrawls they had been passing, showed where officers had been billeted the night before the battle, and then there were the scrawled names again: Gordon, Picton, de Lancey.

'So many senior officers,' she murmured as she read them.

'Don't lead from the back, our generals,' George observed. 'He's not here, is he?'

'No.' Julia closed her eyes and took a deep breath. 'We're going to have to get to the battlefield.'

She would have nightmares about this for the rest of her life, she realized as the gig crested the incline up to the hamlet of Mont St Jean and the ground opened up before her. It was a scene from Dante's Inferno. There were bodies everywhere, heaped and singly. There were parts of bodies. There were dead horses and pitiful wounded ones, wandering amongst the men who staggered and crawled towards the Brussels road and some hope of safety and relief from their thirst and pain.

Groups of people were walking slowly among the carnage, stooping, turning over bodies. People like her, she realized, seeing a weeping woman.

'Bloody looters,' George muttered, and she saw that not all were seeking loved ones or trying to give aid.

'Where to start?' Julia forced herself to concentrate. If she let herself be swallowed up in the sheer horror of this, she would stumble around in this charnel house until she collapsed exhausted. 'Captain Grey said they were on the left flank.' George turned the horse onto a lane, and they both looked out to their right where the ground sloped down in muddy confusion to a slight valley and then up the other side to a low ridge where men could be seen dragging guns away.

'Miss Tresilian!' A figure in a filthy, tattered uniform was limping towards them. Once that jacket had been scarlet and gold. Julia struggled to recall where she had seen the officer before, then remembered: with Hal after Lady Conynham's party.

'Mr...Bredon? Rick?' She recalled the eager smile, the enthusiasm for battle. Now he looked as though he had walked through Hades. 'Are you injured?' She scrabbled in the basket at her feet and found a water flask and the brandy. 'Here.'

'Thank you, ma'am.' He took a long draft of the water then a gulp of the spirits and grinned, his teeth white in his dirty face. 'God, that's better. What are you doing here? It isn't fit for a lady.'

'Looking for Major Carlow. Have you seen him?'

'Yes.' The smile faded and he stood looking up at her, his face bleak.

'He is dead?' Somehow the question came out quite steadily, even though there was a lump in her throat and she had gone quite cold.

'No.' *Oh, thank God.* 'At least, he wasn't when we found him last night. We took him back to a hovel in Mont St Jean. Took three of us just to get him away from that damned horse of his. We took him and the trooper he was all tangled up with. The horse followed, trying to bite us, the bu—wretched creature. There was no medical help, not there then. We chalked his name up. But frankly, ma'am, I don't think he will have made it through the night. I'm damned sorry.'

'I looked, I didn't see…his name.' Her breathing was all over the place. Julia found she could hardly articulate now.

'Not the cottages on the road—they were all full. Go behind, on the right. Just a hovel, really.' He pointed. 'Ma'am.' He caught the bridle and held the horse. 'You've got to be prepared. If he's alive now, I don't think he'll last much longer; and it isn't pretty.'

'No,' Julia said, swallowing the tears. 'I don't expect it is. Thank you, Rick. I hope you get home safe, soon.'

Hal wondered, with some impatience, how much longer it was going to take to die. He had not realized that there could be this much pain. His body was not doing the decent thing and giving up, that was for sure. He couldn't even manage to faint, which would have helped.

He turned his head on the lumpy straw they had dumped him on and found that he was staring into the open eyes of Trooper Harris. Oh well, perhaps the man would finish the job he had started before that shell landed right on top of them.

'Why?' he croaked.

The other man grinned, a ghastly rictus of pain and black humour. 'Money was good.'

'That damn Gypsy, Hebden.' Hal's eyes wanted to close but now he fought to stay conscious.

'Nah.' Harris must be in a worse state than he was from that shell. Hal wondered if he had taken the full blast, ironically sheltering his intended victim. The man was grey under the blood, his lips white. 'Don't know any Gypsy. This was a gent. Hundred guineas: fifty then, fifty when he got the news you were dead. All for sticking a knife in your ribs and wrapping you up in some damn rope.' He gave a grunt of amusement that made him gasp. His eyes rolled back and he lost consciousness.

'Wake up, damn you!' Hal swore at him until one muddy-brown eye dragged open. 'What do you mean, a gent?'

'A real one, sounded like you, but older. I think. Supercilious bastard. Not that I saw him, just that one glimpse of his eyes when the light caught them. Eyes like death…' His voice trailed off into a rattling cough.

Hal lay watching the dead man, his mind sluggishly trying to make some sense of what he had said. Not Hebden-Beshaley— the half-Gypsy gem dealer was just two years Hal's senior. And even when he was speaking with care, there was still that lilt to his voice, unlike Hal's upper-class drawl. But the rope—that must be another damned silken rope, Hebden's calling card, the reference to the rope that peers were hanged with.

Got to get up. Got to warn Marcus. He tried to move something, anything—and the pain hit him like a hammer blow, leaving him gagging, the sweat soaking his body. Had he lost a leg? An arm? He tried to raise his head to look, but couldn't. He heard a horse give a sudden, sharp neigh: Max? No, he must be dead. The place he was in was growing dark now, and he sensed the darkness was within him, not the room.

Goodbye, Julia. So this is it then. This is dying…

'Hal! Hal, open your eyes! Hal, darling, please!'

And this is Heaven. That was fast, he thought hazily. *Didn't think I'd deserve Heaven. And what's Julia doing here? Or perhaps all angels sound like Julia.* But something was wrong.

'Why the hell is it still hurting?' he asked querulously.

'Because you are wounded. Lie still.'

As opposed to what? he wondered. *Saddling up for a review?* 'No option,' he managed. 'Can't move.'

'Can you open your eyes?'

It *was* Julia, he realized, dragging the lids apart and trying to focus on the intent face looking down into his. 'No!'

'Don't be silly, you've got them open.' She was crying, he realized. Smiling and crying.

'You shouldn't be here,' he managed. 'Go away.' But she was not listening to him.

'Can you get that dead man out of here, George? And then bring my things from the gig and find some water for Max?' A bulky shadow moved behind her.

Dead man? Hal's confused mind wrestled with why the body was important. 'No, strip him first. I want everything he's got on him and his pack,' he managed to get out before his voice failed him.

'But…very well. George, do that if it makes Major Carlow easier in his mind. I'll get my things.'

His eyes were closed again, but he caught a faint trace of her scent as she moved in the stuffy little room. And despite everything, he smiled as the dark took him again.

With her supplies around her feet, Julia stood and looked at Hal's sprawled body, trying to think coherently. Whoever had brought him from the battlefield had laid him down fully clothed on a thin spread of straw. The right side of his body from shoulder to knee was soaked in blood, dark now, his uniform stiff with it and covered in flies. Through ominous gashes in the fabric, she could see flesh.

She had to get him onto something higher and softer, out of his uniform and clean. That would make him more comfortable and she could see the extent of his wounds.

She began to drag straw bundles into a rough oblong, then covered the top with a deep mattress of hay. A blanket went over that, then a sheet. She rolled another blanket into a pillow and looked up to find George, his arms full of equipment.

'I've buried him under some loose earth out the back,' he said, dumping the things in a corner and going out again. He returned leading their horse and tied it up next to Max, then watered both animals. 'This big 'un's got some damage, but nothing serious,' he said. 'I'll wash him off and put some salve on to keep the flies off him.'

'Can you help me get Major Carlow onto this bed I've made first?' Julia asked, pushing her hair out off her damp forehead. 'I need to get him stripped off so I can see where he is wounded.'

'Best get his uniform off first before we move him then. You go outside, Miss, while I do it.'

'George, one unconscious naked man is probably the least shocking thing I will see today,' Julia said, taking hold of the left boot and starting to ease it off cautiously in case of broken bones.

'Right you are, then.' He took hold of the other boot and pulled too.

It took, Julia estimated, an hour to strip Hal. Below the knees, his legs were unmarked, protected by the boots. His face and left side were covered in bruises and minor cuts, but nothing serious. But a savage slash went down his right side, shallow across his chest, worse down the arm and ribs, sickeningly deep across his thigh.

'What's this?' George lifted a shattered object from over Hal's heart.

'My notebook. The sword blow must have hit it, skidded off.'

'Saved his life, I reckon,' George muttered. 'Looks like he'd just been attacked by this swordsman when a shell or something landed, took him and that dead trooper off their horses—that'll be the bruising and the smaller cuts. Just got to hope there's no damage inside where we can't see.'

Julia stared at Hal's sprawled body and told herself that fainting was optional and she did not choose to faint. It was all a matter of willpower. The buzzing faded away and she swallowed. 'We had better check his back, wash it before we lift him up.'

She had dreamed about this body, she realized as George rolled Hal onto to his left side and she knelt to wipe the sweat, dirt and blood away. Fantasised about its lean strength, imagined running her hands over the elegant muscles of his back, wondered how this man's skin would feel under her soft palms. Now, her only desire was to heal it. There were old scars, white against the lightly tanned skin and she found them reassuring. He had survived wounds before, he would again.

'Take his legs then, Miss. I'll keep him as flat as I can.' George knelt down, pushed both arms under Hal's shoulders and hips, waited until Julia took hold of his ankles and then lifted, while she swung his legs over onto the makeshift bed.

'Moving him has opened the wounds up.' Julia worried, beginning to sponge Hal's face and left side, leaving the worst until last.

'That'll need sewing,' George said, opening his mysterious bag.

'You can do it?' Julia twisted round to see him pulling a thin, curved needle and some black thread out of a pouch.

'Aye. Well, I can stitch up a horse. Can't be much different, I reckon. But we'll need to get it all clean. You leave bits of cloth in that and it'll fester. They call me a fussy old devil in the stables, but I've seen and I take note: clean wounds, clean hands and things heal better.' He squinted at the point of the needle. 'Don't know why. I use lots of brandy too, that helps.' He produced a flask and a bottle, poured dark liquid out and dropped the needle and thread into it.

Julia began to work on the wounds with the warm water he brought her, a good handful of salt dissolved in it.

'Salt water helps too,' George explained, leaving her to it and going across to see to Max. 'Don't know why that works either, but you take a horse with sores on its legs and walk it in the sea, it'll heal faster than once you don't.'

It would be worse with a gunshot she realized, making herself look dispassionately at what she was doing. A shot would force fabric deep into the flesh, a slashing wound did not. She worked her way up to his chest, laying linen cloths over each clean part of his body as she finished it to keep the flies off. As she started to work on the cut and bruised contusion where the notebook had been, Hal opened his eyes, dark, almost black with pain.

'Go away,' he croaked. 'Should be in Antwerp.'

'No,' she said firmly. 'We will make you better. Drink this.' It was clean water from Madame's big kettle mixed with brandy. She slid one arm under his head to raise him a little and held it to his lips, watching some faint colour come back into his face as he swallowed an entire horn beaker full.

'Don't want you. Go away.'

I must not be hurt by his words, she told herself. *He's in pain, he doesn't know what he is saying.*

'Julia.' His eyes were fixed on her face now, clear and forceful. Hal knew exactly what he was saying, she realized. 'Who knows you are here?'

'Captain Grey, Rick Bredon, my landlady,' she said, puzzled. 'The baron helped me stay in Brussels.'

'Rick and Will can keep their mouths shut. You can bribe the landlady. Go back to Brussels now, Julia. Go to the baron.'

'We cannot move you yet,' she said with more calm than she was feeling. 'George is going to sew up your wounds and then you must rest. All I have is the gig, you see, and I don't think we can move you in that yet, there isn't enough room for you to lie down.'

'Leave me,' he said urgently. His right hand moved as though to take her wrist and he gasped at the sudden pain. 'It is bad enough as it is, but you'll be ruined if you spend the night here.'

'It doesn't matter!'

'Yes it does! If you stay, I will have to marry you. If I live. And you cannot marry me.'

She sat back on her heels, staring at him. 'You will live,' she said as though she could make it so by force of will. 'You cannot give up. Do you hear me?'

'Yes, I hear you. You should not be here. It was…foolish. Wrong. I have no desire to marry. Not you.' The vehemence of his words exhausted him.

Julia sat dumbly looking at the gaunt bruised face, the thin white lips, the closed eyes, and she struggled not to give way to tears. *Foolish? No desire to marry… Not you.* Was he trying to drive her away with words as weapons? Perhaps he was. Hal Carlow did not know her very well, if that was so.

'Unfortunately, Major Carlow, you are going to have to

put up with me,' she said flatly. 'I cannot leave you here or you will die, and I do not want that on my conscience. When George is finished with Max, he will start on you. Do you want some more brandy?'

The bruised eyelids dragged open. 'Max?'

'He is all right, just some cuts,' Julia reassured him, trying not to feel jealous of a horse. 'Drink this,' she added, putting the flask to his lips. He was going to need it. She only wished she could drain it dry herself.

Somehow she got through the stitching without having to rush outside to be ill again, chiefly by telling herself that if Hal had to put up with it, then she certainly could. She suspected that her presence—snipping each knot for George, then bandaging behind his seemingly endless row of stitches—was preventing Hal from venting his feelings in bad language: she just wished he would let go and faint.

When it was finished and she got shakily to her feet, Hal opened his eyes and looked at George. 'Thank you.'

The groom grunted, then grinned. 'You're easier than a horse, guv'nor: never tried to kick or bite once.' He began to tidy up his things, leaving Julia alone at Hal's side.

'Who took my clothes off?'

'We did, George and I. And don't look like that: your naked buttocks are not the worst thing I have seen today, believe me.' She had actually made him blush, she realized. 'Oh for goodness sake!'

'You aren't going, are you?' he said wearily. 'You've been missing from home all day, you've been seen on the battlefield and now, unless you leave now, you'll be found here, nursing me. What were you thinking about? There is no hope for it: we are going to have to get married, Julia.'

'I refuse.' Her hands were shaking. A bandage she was trying to roll up escaped from her trembling fingers and fell into the scattered hay. 'I do not want to marry a man who doesn't want me.' She realized she had held onto the memory of that ballroom kiss believing, deep down, that he wanted to marry her. And now it seemed, she had been wrong.

The look he gave her was long, hard and unwavering. 'I never said I did not want you. I said it was wrong to marry you, but marry me you will. The lesser of two evils, perhaps. You have saved my life, Julia. Now you will take my name, whether you like it or not.'

Chapter Fifteen

Julia saw the first glimmerings of light and gave a little sob of exhausted relief. Somehow they had got through the night. Hal's pronouncement about marriage was almost the last coherent thing he said before slipping into a fever that had him tossing and muttering through the hours of darkness.

She and George had taken turns to sit by Hal's side, one bathing him with cool water while the other fetched fresh from the well behind the building. The water, by a miracle, seemed untainted although the hot night air was foul.

Now, at last, it was light; the phantoms that had hung over her shoulder all night gibbering their messages of despair had fled with the dawn. Hal was going to live, she was beginning to hope, not just to tell herself she must believe it. Now the restlessness of the night had calmed, he felt cooler when she touched his brow, laid her hand on his chest.

And she must marry him, she had decided after wrestling all night with her conscience, her desires and plain common sense. She was compromised. If she had only herself to think about, then she would refuse him, should refuse him. But there were Mama and Phillip to think about. Must they suffer because she had so hopelessly misunderstood Hal's true feelings? If she was ruined, then it would make their situation so much harder.

And Hal's strong sense of honour would be salved, she recognized that. Which had to be the real—the only—reason he was so insistent now. Whatever he said, he did not want her, she knew that. At least, he might *want* her at the most basic level that a man wanted a woman. But he did not love her. The kiss at the ball haunted her, like a book in a language she could not read. If only she was not so inexperienced, if only she could understand what that had meant to him.

George had pulled the gig into the hovel and now sat with his back against the upright supporting the wide opening, legs outstretched, one hand on the stock of the musket while he snored.

Julia dragged some hay into a heap by the side of Hal's bed, spread a blanket on top of it and curled up, trying to resign herself to this mess. She was going to marry a man whom she loved, but all that would bring him to the altar was his sense of honour. She had trapped him by compromising herself, but she found it hard to believe he would rather be dead than married. She could try and run away from him, she supposed. But she knew him too well now to believe he would let her go. This was where her heart and her desires warred with her revulsion against trapping him, however unwittingly.

And what about Mama and Phillip? If she married Hal, she would be the daughter in law of an earl. Hal might be the second son, he might not have great personal wealth, but he had connections, those essential networks of patronage and influence that would shape her brother's life and ensure her mother would always be secure and at the heart of respectable Society. Duty again: if she had cavilled at Smyth, she could hardly refuse such a match with all its advantages for the family she loved.

As a marriage prospect, Hal was far superior to any of the men she had held out hopes for. And he knew it, knew she wanted to marry. At least, she thought bitterly, he could not believe she had manufactured this battle to entrap him. What would marriage to Hal be like? The bedroom would be exciting; she knew that already. But everyday, domestic life? It was like trying to imagine a panther in a sitting room.

Her lids were closing, fight though she might to stay awake. When had she last slept? Julia tried to remember as the blissful darkness swept her away.

'Quiet, you'll waken them.'

Julia knew the whispering voice, but she could not place it, nor why there was a man in her bedchamber. Nor why, as she shifted to get more comfortable, the bed was so lumpy.

And then she heard Hal's voice. 'My God, I am glad to see you!'

She sat up with a jerk to find Will Grey, his arm in a sling, standing in the doorway with George.

'Not half as glad as I am to see you both,' he said, grinning past her.

Julia twisted round, her feet tangling in the blanket. Hal was still flat on his back, looking like death. But not, as he had yesterday, as if he might actually die. He was grinning back at Captain Grey. 'Have you got any clothes for me?'

'No, but I've got food. And I can go and get you clothes.' He walked across and sat on the end of the makeshift bed. 'Good morning, Miss Tresilian. You have him, I see.'

'He doesn't need clothes: he is not getting up,' she retorted, refusing to be drawn into an exchange of pleasantries, trying not to flinch at the captain's choice of words. 'Food would be good, but a cart we can lay him out flat in would be better. And should you be riding about? What about your arm?'

'Be careful,' Hal warned. 'She'll set George on you with a needle and thread.'

'I've already been stitched up, thank you very much,' Will said with a grimace. 'And I can ride one-handed. The question is, are you fit to be moved?'

'Damn it, yes.'

'Damn it, no!' Julia scrambled to her feet. 'He needs at least one more day and night before he is jolted over that road—if there's any road left. I heard the wounded being taken back yesterday, they were in agony.'

'True enough.' Will Grey scratched his chin. 'A horse litter would be best.'

'We have two horses, if you and George can make a litter.'

'And how do you propose to get back?' Hal demanded. 'Walk?'

Julia glared at him. 'If I have to. And stop talking, you are getting heated and your fever will get worse. Captain Grey, please come outside, you are over-exciting him.'

'Will—'

'In a minute. I think we have to accept that Miss Tresilian is in charge.' Captain Grey followed her out. 'He is going to be a terrible patient, you realize that? The last time he was badly injured, he refused to rest until our commanding officer said he was tired of Lieutenant Carlow falling flat on his face every time he stood up and ordered him to bed.' He strolled away until they were well out of earshot of the hovel and leaned against a battered apple tree. 'How serious is it?'

'I am no doctor.' Julia bit her lip. 'He was struck with a sabre over the heart, but it slid off something and sliced down through his ribs, his arm and his thigh. By some miracle, it missed any major blood vessels. We have got it clean and stitched up, and his fever is down this morning, although I don't expect it will stay down if he will not rest. But there was a shell burst very close that knocked him off his horse: I don't know if there are any internal injuries. He is in a lot of pain, I think, but he will not admit it.'

'He will tell me how he feels if I make him promise to in return for getting him back to Brussels as soon as possible,' Will said. 'I think you are right, he should not be moved today. I will go and talk to him, then we can decide what is needed and I'll ride back to Brussels and fetch it. You can ride pillion with me. Then I'll come back and that groom and I can bring him back tomorrow if he's up to it.'

'I will not leave him,' Julia said flatly. 'I do not trust him an inch. He'll be bullying poor George into letting him get up, the minute my back is turned.'

Will gave her a quizzical look, but all he said was, 'I'll go and speak to him now.'

Julia waited until he turned the corner of the shack, then ran to the other end, near where Hal's bed was, and put her ear to the wall. The planks that made the structure were full of knot holes and cracks and she could hear clearly.

'How bad is it?'

'Bloody,' Hal said his voice faint against the energy of Will Grey's.

'Internal injuries?'

'No, don't think so. I am not, so George informs me, passing blood. Hard to tell though, everything hurts. Ow! Stop that, damn it!'

'Your toes all work,' Grey said calmly. 'And your foot bends. And you can make a fist with your right hand to punch me with, even if you can't raise that arm. I don't think you've cut any tendons. It is muscle damage and you've got to keep the weight off that leg until it heals properly or you'll be lame. So now, will you stop trying to move about and do as Miss Tresilian tells you?'

'Will you please take her away?' Hal sounded desperate, Julia thought, her stomach a tight knot of misery.

'No. For a start, I am not hauling a kicking and screaming female all the way back to Brussels; and secondly, I believe her when she says you aren't to be trusted. While you've got no trousers and her in the room, you'll stay put until I come back.'

He was silent for a moment, then added, 'You know, I really thought you were going to propose to her.'

'I told you why not. At the Richmonds' affair I made a right balls-up of it, trying to explain why I wasn't going to. Must have been mad. God, I am so angry with her I could put her across my knee. I will do, if I ever get well enough. And now I must marry her, she's too compromised for me not to—Will, what the devil will I do with a wife?'

Julia got to her feet and half ran down the path that led through what must once have been a tidy vegetable plot. She scrubbed the back of her hand across her eyes and blinked hard until the nearest apple tree came back into focus. That would teach her to eavesdrop. Between them, they had compromised themselves and each other, and marriage, she supposed, was inevitable.

'Are you all right?'

Julia turned to find Captain Grey looking grim.

'No, not really,' she admitted. 'But there's nothing to be done about it. Are you leaving now?'

He nodded. 'I'll bring him clothes and I'll steal a cart if I have to and be back tomorrow. You'll make a good soldier's wife, Miss Tresilian.'

'Thank you.' Praise indeed: it was just a pity she was not marrying a soldier who wanted her. 'Take care of that arm, Captain Grey.'

Hal was lying with his eyes closed when she went back in, but he opened them at the sound of her soft footsteps.

'Breakfast?' she asked.

Hal grimaced. 'Not hungry. Coffee—now, that I could drink.'

'I'll go and make some,' George said from the back of the hovel, where he was tending the horses. 'And I'll cook something. You need to eat, Miss Julia.'

'Yes, you should.' Hal turned his head on the pillow and looked at her. 'Are you all right?'

'She needs more rest, begging your pardon, sir.' George stopped in the doorway and frowned at Hal. 'Miss Julia was down nursing the wounded at that hotel of yours for two days, getting hardly any sleep and then coming down here yester-day—that made her sick to the stomach on top of everything else.'

'What? Nursing for two days?' Hal looked from George's retreating back to Julia's set face. There were dark shadows under her eyes, her hair was escaping from its tight braids and she was pale with fatigue, not just, as he had assumed, the shock of seeing the battlefield. 'What the devil was your mother thinking of?'

'I gave her no choice. The baron has taken her and Phillip to Antwerp and I told him that if he did not help me to stay I would run away and get back to Brussels. The carriage was moving before she realized what I was doing.'

'And where have you been staying?' he demanded. This was Julia, obedient, well-behaved, sheltered Julia, defying her mother, conniving with the baron, running away…

'At our lodgings.' She began to move about the room, picking things up, moving basins. 'Madame has stayed and George moved into the stables with the horse and gig the baron left us.'

'But nursing?' Ladies did not do such things, not in public.

'They started taking the wounded back to where they had been billeted, after the hospitals filled up,' she explained. 'I knew where you and Captain Grey had lodged, and, I guessed, probably some of the other officers I had met at the Opera. So I went there and did what I could.'

Hal closed his eyes. He knew exactly what that would have been like. He knew the smells, the sights, the shock she would have been exposed to. But why? Why had she stayed when she could have got safe away?

His conscience told him: he had spoken of death, of not coming back. He had made her confront the reality of battle, and she, with the comfortable fictions of glory and flag-waving stripped away, had decided to do what she could against that tidal wave of horror. But for the wounded in general? Or for him? 'And you worked there for two days?'

'I went home at night. It was only sensible to sleep and eat and wash. I would be no use to anyone if I exhausted myself.'

'No,' he agreed, unable to think of anything else to say. Would any young woman of her background, finding themselves in the same position, do what she had done? Honoria would, he suspected, if she was helping people she knew. But Verity would just crumple in the face of that much pain and squalor. And he had been comparing Julia with his younger sister. It seemed he had missed the steel in her backbone.

Julia sat down and began to check over her basket of bandages. 'And then Captain Grey arrived and told me you were missing.'

'So you came for me. Why, Julia?' Had his fears been realized? Had he let her tumble into love with him? Must he have that on his conscience as well?

'Because I knew you,' she said, staring at him as though

he had asked a very stupid question. 'How could I not? The battle was over and you had not come back. The chances were, if you had not been killed, that you were lying on the field somewhere with no medical help and would die.'

'That applies to hundreds of men,' Hal said harshly, wondering why he needed to push her like this.

'I couldn't help hundreds,' she explained, patient in the face of his anger. 'But I might help one. One that I cared for.' He saw her closed expression and knew that was as close to a declaration of her feelings as he would get. 'Even if you were dying, it would have been a comfort to your family to know you were cared for at the end.'

It would. Of course it would, he realized, staring up into the cobwebbed gloom of the roof overhead. In all the years he had been fighting he had known the anxiety his family had suffered, their fears. But it had not occurred to him what anguish it would be to hear the details of the horrors of the battlefield and to know he had died there, perhaps lingering for days.

'Thank you,' he said at last, realizing it was not possible to say any more without shaming himself with tears. He had been angry with her for risking her safety and her reputation. She did not deserve that. She deserved that he do what he could now to protect her, and do it with good grace.

'I will marry you,' Julia said abruptly. 'You are right, I must, I see that.' The relief he felt must have shown on his face for she added, 'Then you are not angry with me any longer?' He could hear a tremulous smile in her voice.

'I am relieved. I will do my best to make you a good husband, Julia.' She bit her lip and looked away, so he hesitated over the softer words he had thought she might expect. Then the moment was gone as footsteps approached the hut.

'Here's the coffee.' She got to her feet with what he had to assume was relief at the interruption.

'I've found some planks,' George said, putting down the mug close enough to Hal for the aroma to have his mouth watering. They could have extracted any kind of confession, he realized, just by torturing him with the threat to take it away. 'Reckon I can push them under the pillow and wedge them up and you'll be able to sit up a bit.'

It hurt, but he bit his lip and kept quiet. The relief of being able to lie back and look around, not at the roof, was worth every pang. Hal took the mug in his left hand and drank, almost moaning with pleasure as the strong, hot liquid slid down. It felt as though it was replacing all the blood he had lost with liquid fire.

When he stopped drinking and paid attention to what the others were doing, he found they were inelegantly tackling fried bacon wedged between slices of bread. The smell of the hot savoury fat floated across the hut, overcoming even the coffee. 'Is there any more of that bacon?'

Julia smiled, 'Oh thank goodness, you have an appetite after all. You must be recovering.'

Hal smiled back, realizing how good it was to see her looking happy again. 'I hate to cast down your spirits, but frying bacon would make a dead soldier walk.'

After the food, he lay there, realizing just how bad he had been feeling before Julia had found him and what a miracle she and the groom had wrought between them. It would take time, but unless an infection took hold, he was going to survive this, with all his limbs intact.

Alive, intact and committed to marry the woman he wanted above all others. Why then did he feel like hell? Guilt, he supposed. In the middle of horror, Julia had behaved with courage, resource and intelligence, and it was his fault she had had to. Now she would find herself married to a man who had no idea what to do with a well-bred virgin, let alone a wife, and who was mired in a feud he only half understood.

He scrubbed his left hand over his face, shocked at the growth of beard. How long since he had shaved? Four days?

'George, can you shave me?'

'Aye, Major. I'll go and heat some water.'

'Enough for a wash,' Julia called after the groom. 'Not that you aren't clean enough already,' she commented, turning back. 'We've been sponging you all night to keep the fever down.'

'We?' Hal tried to sit up, realized he couldn't and fell back with a curse. 'You have?' Then he remembered: she had undressed him as well.

'Shocking, isn't it,' Julia said, shaking out a linen towel. 'Just imagine, I've seen a naked man. Heaps of bodies, and bits of men and disembowelled horses—not shocking at all. But a naked man, and one I'm going to marry! In truth, I am ready to sink, just thinking about it.' The corner of her mouth was twitching in an effort not to smile.

Hal tried to decide whether he was more shocked or offended. He had, he admitted, expected the sight of his body to have had rather more effect on a sheltered virgin than mere amusement. Perhaps it would make things easier when they did, finally, go to bed together. When—*if*—he ever worked out how to make love to a virgin; all he was used to was women of very considerable experience.

But now was definitely the time to change the subject.

Food, coffee, a shave and the ability to sit up and watch what was going on had wrought wonders, Julia decided, studying Hal's face from the shadows while George put away his shaving tackle. Hal was young, fit, tough—he would heal well, even though she doubted it would be fast enough for his impatient spirit.

She did love him so much: his courage and his humour

and his kindness. And his beauty. She blushed a little, thinking about that, then smiled at the recollection of his shocked reaction to the realization that she had seen him naked. Bless him, like a poacher turned gamekeeper, he was becoming positively prudish where she was concerned.

Did he secretly hate the idea of their marrying so very much? Now that the fever had gone, he was guarding his tongue and she knew she would not hear the truth, even if she asked him directly.

Chapter Sixteen

'Will you bring me the things George stripped off that trooper, please?'

Julia jumped, brought out of her reverie by the unconscious note of command in Hal's voice. He might have remembered to say *please* but he was back to being an officer.

Julia scooped them up from the back of the hovel and brought them to his bedside.

'Can you show me everything?' he asked. 'And check pockets, seams, linings.'

'What for?' Julia sat down on a milking stool she had found and picked up the jacket, trying to ignore the stains.

'I don't know.' Hal fell silent, obviously weighing something up in his mind. Julia began to feel along the seams, flexing the stiffened plackets and probing the padding. 'He tried to kill me,' Hal said suddenly, making her drop the garment.

'What, here in the hut? He was looting?'

'No, on the battlefield. He tried to get to me the night before the battle, I think, but Max went for him. I thought he'd just got too close. Then, we charged the guns. Will was hurt.'

Hal paused, obviously reliving it in his mind. 'Their cavalry ran, we got to a gun, and he turned—I thought he was going to say something, but he struck straight for my heart. I don't know why the blow didn't kill me. It was deflected off something, I felt the pain down my arm, my leg—and then there was a God-awful noise—a shell I suppose, blew us both up. I assume they picked us up together and dumped us in here.'

'This is why he didn't kill you.' Julia picked up the shattered mother-of-pearl cover of her notebook. 'You had it over your heart.'

'Then you saved my life twice,' Hal said, and his eyes were dark as they rested on the ruined book. 'Keep that somewhere safe.'

Julia tucked it into her pocket and picked up the jacket again. 'But why would a British trooper want to kill you?'

'He was paid to. He told me just before he died.' Hal took swallow of a fresh mug of coffee. 'Good money too. I was flattered.'

'Who?' Lurid visions of outraged husbands ran through Julia's mind. Or Major Fellowes. Then she remembered. 'Hebden?'

'That was my guess. But the description didn't fit.' He lay back, his head turned to watch what she was doing.

The jacket revealed no secrets, nor did the overall trousers, the shirt or the leather stock. Julia tossed each aside, then picked up a boot.

'Try the heels.' It took some prising with his pocket knife, but the heels came away at last, revealing a hiding place in each, full of gold coins. 'I think I've earned those,' Hal commented as Julia put them carefully aside. 'What about his pack? There will be a rope somewhere.'

The pack contained nothing of any interest, except a rope coiled at the bottom, just as Hal had predicted. Julia pulled it out, and it slithered unpleasantly in her hands.

'Ugh.' She dropped it on the bed, and Hal picked it up left-handed, running the multicoloured length through his fingers. 'It feels alive.'

'Silk,' he said. 'It is what they hang peers with.'

'But you aren't a peer,' Julia said, puzzled.

'No, but the man who killed Hebden's father was.' She waited, biting her lip, while Hal frowned into space.

'I had better tell you everything,' he said at length. 'You are marrying into a family in the midst of a mystery—a dangerous and probably scandalous one.'

She listened while he spoke, trying to keep the characters straight in her mind, separate the old history from the present events. 'So Stephen Hebden the jewel merchant is also a half Romany called Stephano Beshaley who blames not just the family of the man who was hanged for his father's murder—your sister in law and her sister and brother—but also the Carlows, because he thinks your father did nothing to prevent the crime. He is also bitter about his father's legitimate connections because he was thrown out of the family home and sent away to an orphanage.'

Hal nodded. So she had got that straight. 'And for some reason he decided last year to begin attacking these people he hates so much.'

'Yes. He's a couple of years older than I am. I knew him as a child, a little. I wonder if it is because he is approaching the age his own father was when he died that it is obsessing him now.'

'That is hardly a good enough reason to try and kill people.'

'Yes, but this is the first attempt at something lethal. Up to now he seems to have wanted to bring scandal and disgrace, not death.'

'You have another enemy?' Julia ventured, folding her hands tightly in her lap to prevent herself smoothing back the lock of unruly hair that kept falling across his brow. She wanted to touch him all the time: it was disconcerting and left her oddly breathless and distracted.

'A good many,' he admitted with a grin. 'But none of them with Hebden's calling card.' The rope lay like a dead snake across his thighs. 'And there's something else. Rumours are beginning to spread about the circumstances surrounding the murder. People are wondering why my father was so adamant that his best friend was guilty. Because if he were not, then the spy escaped undetected.'

'They say that your father was the spy?' she asked, too surprised to be tactful.

'No-one is saying it out loud. But it can be made to fit. If he was, then he had disposed of the two men who were about to unmask him.'

'Do you believe it?' she asked, shocked at Hal's dispassionate tone.

'No, of course not. But he isn't helping. He won't talk about it. Pages are missing from his diaries and he won't say what they contained. He's a stubborn devil.'

There is something in the way he speaks of his father, she thought, watching the long lashes come down to hide the thoughts in Hal's expressive eyes. *He doesn't hate him, or dislike him—but there is a wariness, a distance. Perhaps Hal is the black sheep of the family.*

'And why are the rumours spreading now?' Julia asked. 'Is Hebden in such a position that he could start them amongst such influential people?'

Before Hal could reply, George put his head round the door of the hovel. 'Someone's coming.'

They were so tucked away that the activity on the main road and in the village was hardly audible most of the time. Julia shivered: if they had not seen Rick Bredon, she would never have found Hal. If she had not fled from Thomas Smyth at the party, she would never have met Bredon. If Hal had not taken her back in the carriage, she would not have given him her notebook and that sabre-thrust would have pierced his chest. On such chances lives hung.

'Good morning, Miss Tresilian. Carlow, I have brought you a shirt and some loose trousers,' Captain Grey announced, striding into the hovel, a mass of white cloth flapping over his arm. 'And I've got a cart and a horse with four legs—and that, my friend was harder than taking a French gun, believe me.'

'I do.' Hal grinned back at him, then they both looked pointedly at Julia.

'Yes?' She stared back, then realized. 'Oh, yes. You get dressed, I'll just go and do something outside.' *Honestly, the pair of them will have had their clothes off in front of more women than I have had hot dinners and yet Hal won't risk me catching sight of an inch of flesh!* 'We need to pack up, George.'

Julia spread straw and then hay, then threw over blankets until the floor of the old farm cart was as soft and cushioned as she could make it, then busied herself collecting up their things while Will Grey and George brought Hal out on a makeshift stretcher. She didn't think he was going to enjoy that and he would probably swear more comfortably if she wasn't in sight. As it was, her vocabulary was considerably enriched. *He must be feeling better,* she thought, smiling. *Yesterday he hardly had the strength to curse.*

The scene, as their little procession made its way out to what had been the main road from Brussels to Charleroi, was in some ways more orderly, and in others, more shocking, than it had been on the day after the battle.

Broken-down carts, dead horses, splintered trees had all been dragged to the side so that traffic could lurch up and down the deeply rutted road. Everywhere she looked, there were freshly turned heaps of earth, some of them scarcely covering the bodies that lay beneath. In the distance, great fires burned, giving off oily smoke; Julia could only be thankful the light breeze took the smell of it away from them. The stagnant pools of foul liquid by the roadside were bad enough.

Will Grey drove the cart, George and Julia followed in the gig and Max walked beside the cart with no need to hitch his reins to it. From time to time he poked his big head over the side and blew slobbery breaths at Hal, who only laughed and rubbed the hairy nose pushing anxiously at his cheek.

Julia lost track of time as they moved slowly on, having to turn off the road into the trees from time to time to avoid a deeply mired stretch or to allow faster-moving vehicles through. They were still finding men alive, Julia saw, thankful that those hideous, greedy pyres were not taking everything.

The clocks were striking four when they finally turned into the courtyard in Place de Leuvan. Hal's eyes had been closed for miles and Will had kept turning in his seat to check on him. But as they came to a halt in the shadowed yard, he woke and took a deep breath.

'Coffee, wood smoke, food cooking and nothing, thank God, rotting,' he said. 'Julia—'

'Julia! You wicked, wicked child!' Mrs Tresilian almost tumbled out of the kitchen door, her cap awry, her face flushed. 'Madame has told me what you have been doing! You're ruined, ruined…'

'Mrs Tresilian.' Hal's voice cut through her words with their rising note of hysteria. 'We have not been introduced. I am Hal Carlow, second son of the Earl of Narborough.' Julia saw her mother go very still at the magic word, *Earl*. 'Miss

Tresilian has done me the honour to accept my proposal of marriage. I trust you have no objection.'

For a moment Hal thought Mrs Tresilian had fainted. His future mother in law's face simply vanished. Then he realized she had sat down on the step and burst into tears. Julia scrambled from the gig, sent him a rueful smile and ran to calm her mother.

'Mama, it is quite all right, I am safe. Are you and Phillip all right? We must go in; Major Carlow is wounded and we have to get him to bed right away.'

'Where?' Mrs Tresilian demanded, rising into sight again, a handkerchief clutched in her hand. 'Oh my goodness, of all the things…'

'In my bedroom, Mama,' Julia said firmly. 'And I will sleep with you. Captain Grey, I will make up the bed, if you and George can bring Major Carlow in a few moments. The first floor—Madame will show you the way. Come, Mama.'

In the silence that followed their disappearance, Will began to let down the sides of the cart. 'Masterly,' he observed. 'By the time Miss Tresilian has waved the smelling salts about and repeated your father's title a few more times, her mother is going to be killing the fatted calf for you.'

A voice from somewhere at the foot of the cart piped up, 'Is he dead?'

'No,' Hal retorted. 'I'm not, young Phillip. Just a bit battered.'

'Oh, good. Did you kill any French with your sabre? Has it got blood on it?'

'Yes and no, and will you take Max into the stable for me? I've got to go upstairs and I need George to help me.' Will raised startled eyebrows, but Hal added, 'Go, Max. Friend,' and the horse turned and plodded away. 'The boy's been up on him, Max will remember his scent,' he reassured Will who had been on the receiving end of Max's teeth before now. 'And I don't want to give him a vocabulary of military oaths or his mother will add that to the list of sins my parentage has to counterbalance.'

Getting upstairs tried both the other men's ingenuity and strength and his own endurance. Hal felt decidedly wan by the time they staggered through the door into a simple bedchamber with sprigged wallpaper and a narrow white bed next to the window. His bearers laid him down onto the clean, yielding softness, and he realized that his nostrils were full of the scent of Julia. The sensation of coming home to somewhere familiar and safe washed through him, leaving him calm and strangely light headed, as though he were floating.

Perhaps marriage would be like this, he thought vaguely.

'He must be exhausted,' he heard Julia murmur, and a cool hand stroked the hair back from his forehead. 'Try and sleep, Hal.' The hand stroked down to his cheek, and eyes closed, he turned his face into it and sighed as sound and sensation slipped away, leaving only the hazy awareness of her presence as he slept.

'Mama, please do not fuss. I really do not need a chaperone in my fiancé's bedchamber, especially when he is this weak.' That was Julia, Hal realized, surfacing slowly from sleep, wondering what the faint agitated clucking sound was. There had been no chickens in the hovel.

'Oh I suppose not. But it all seems so *sudden,* dear.' Oh yes, Mrs Tresilian, and this was Julia's bedroom and he was in her bed—alone unfortunately. 'He is such a…a *physical* looking young man,' Mrs Tresilian continued.

Hal converted a laugh into a cough and opened his eyes to find both women regarding him. His future mother in law had the expression of someone finding an exotic, and probably dangerous, animal in the room; Julia was pink in the cheeks and appeared to be suppressing a smile. Mothers in law were an aspect of marriage he had not considered.

'Good morning. How are you feeling?' Julia enquired, obviously intent on ignoring her mother's embarrassing observation. 'Shall I send George up with your breakfast?'

'Thank you, yes. I feel much better. Good morning, Mrs Tresilian. Perhaps, ma'am, it would be possible for us to discuss the situation a little later?' It seemed he had slept for more than twelve hours and he was, provided he did not try and move, feeling a sight better for it.

'Oh dear; I mean, yes, of course.'

'Captain Grey has called and he will bring the doctor later this morning,' Julia said, calmly ushering her mother out of the room. 'We can talk this afternoon, after luncheon.'

So, he had found himself a managing wife, had he? Hal gritted his teeth while George got him sitting up, then found that Julia had sent up a vast breakfast. A wife who did not believe in gruel for invalids, thank goodness. He had, he realized, committed himself to a wife who was infinitely better than he deserved. But what she had done to deserve him, other than be open-hearted, brave and generous, he could not imagine.

'It would appear from what Dr Gregson says that I am going to live, with all my limbs attached,' Hal said calmly. 'I have, beside my career as an officer, a small estate in Buckinghamshire which is in good heart and which brings me sufficient to maintain a wife and family in comfort. I can establish you, ma'am, in the country or in town, which ever is more agreeable to you. I will, of course, undertake Phillip's education.'

He paused, and Julia decided he would probably show as much emotion briefing fellow officers before an engagement. The effect it was having on her mother was, however, miraculous. She was positively beaming. No, she could not have refused Hal's offer—his order—to marry her. Whatever her scruples and the second thoughts she'd been having for the past day, her reputation, Hal's own sense of honour and her family's needs must over-ride them.

'As to the ceremony, I would propose the English church in a week's time.'

'Hal! You cannot possibly be fit by then,' Julia broke in, unable to maintain her pose of meek attentiveness any longer.

'I will be well enough to stand up for half an hour,' he countered. 'As you know, my colonel called just after the doctor. I am ordered home to recuperate and I would suggest the sooner we sail after the ceremony, the better. I regret that I will need to trouble you, Julia, to write the necessary letters to arrange that.'

'Oh my goodness.' Her mother, it seemed, was only thinking about the ceremony. 'There is so much to do! I will begin making lists at once. Your trousseau, my dear!'

'I will give you a draft on my bank,' Hal added, sending Mrs Tresilian almost running from the room to start work, without a thought to her unchaperoned daughter left behind in the bedroom.

Julia told herself that her mother's state of flustered happiness should make her happy too, but inside her stomach was a cold knot of misery. Hal, no longer the informal, friendly man he had been in the hovel, was approaching their marriage with a cool efficiency that frightened her.

'What is wrong?' He was sitting up against the piled pillows. To her critical eyes, he looked too fine-drawn and pale. Perhaps it was just the strength of the afternoon light flooding in through the window. She got up and went to sit in the chair by his bedside, trying to calm herself with the doctor's reassuring words.

'Wrong?' She made rather a business of smoothing down her skirts. He had never made any pretext of loving her, it was unfair to feel resentful that he was treating their coming union as anything but an arranged marriage. 'Nothing, really. It is just that I am concerned that you are overdoing things. It is only four days since you were wounded. We are comfortable here; your friends can visit you. I am sure that however eager they are to see you, your family would rather you waited until you were stronger.'

'And I am rushing you into marriage,' he said dryly. 'You are missing the opportunity for planning and shopping and looking forward to a wonderful day with all your friends.'

'I do not care about that.' Indignant, Julia looked up and met Hal's frowning gaze. 'But it is too soon.'

'Are you frightened?'

'Frightened?' She frowned back. What on earth had she to be frightened of now Hal was out of danger? 'Of Hebden, you mean? No. Perhaps I should be, but it doesn't seem quite real—a feud and vengeance. And I should be frightened of meeting your family, but I know I will like them.'

'Of me,' he said, holding her gaze until she realized what he meant. The blush seemed to rise from her toes.

'No!' He wouldn't release her, however much she wanted to look away. 'Of course not.'

'You are very innocent, Julia.'

'Not that innocent,' she protested. 'I know what…happens. I cannot pretend it does not sound strange, but I am sure I will soon become accustomed.' And the sooner, the better, she acknowledged, shocking herself. She wanted the wedding delayed for Hal's sake, but she wanted it quickly, for her own.

Making love did, indeed, seem a very peculiar business,

but her body was sending her quite clear messages that it understood more about it than she did. The proximity of Hal, the haunting memory of his naked form, the vivid impression of that kiss, the very fact that they were in a bedroom alone together, all produced that strange, restless sensation and an almost irresistible need to touch him.

This marriage was going to be difficult enough, but perhaps if they could achieve an understanding through intimacy, that would help with everything else.

'I hope so,' he said, turning his head away, restless, on the pillow. 'I hope that you will find marriage pleasurable.'

'At least you know what you are doing,' she said, nerves making her blurt out exactly what she was thinking.

There was a long silence, then he said, with what she could have sworn was irritation in his voice, 'I do not know what I am doing with virgins.'

'I should hope not,' Julia said, trying to make a joke of it. Hal did not reply. Tentative, she reached out and touched his forearm, the left, uninjured, one, 'Hal, I wasn't frightened before, but you are scaring me now.'

Chapter Seventeen

Her confession brought Hal's head round and he smiled, a rather rueful twist of his lips. Julia let out a breath as he moved his hand to catch hers. 'Come here then, and let me see if I can soothe your nerves.'

'I rather doubt that would be the result,' she murmured, moving to perch cautiously on the edge of the bed.

'You are going to have to do all the work,' he pointed out and the cold knot inside her began to melt at the sight of the old, familiar laughter in his eyes.

'Very well.' Cautiously, she placed her right hand on the pillow by his shoulder and leant down, eyes closed, too shy to watch his eyes change colour from troubled grey to intense blue, as they had when he had kissed her at the ball.

Julia was very aware of the smell of him, an exciting maleness beneath the overlaying scents of clean skin, soap, a herbal salve. She leaned closer and smelled the coffee on his breath and felt the heat of his body as her breasts touched the thin white cotton of his nightshirt.

And then she found his lips, warm and firm and smiling

under hers and she hesitated, unsure what to do next, confused by the difference that being above him made.

'Go on,' he mouthed silently, and her lips read the words. He had not closed his mouth on that last syllable.

Dare she? Julia let her mouth press a little more, then, when he did not move, she let the tip of her tongue slide out, between her own lips, between his. She froze, shaken by her own daring, by the intensity of initiating such a simple thing, and then Hal opened to her and his tongue found hers and touched and teased, and his hand came up to cup her shoulder, and it was all she could do not to sink down onto his bandaged chest with the need to be closer, tighter, totally entwined.

It was too much, and she needed him to guide her. She needed to hold on to him, but she did not dare in case she hurt him. She was alarming herself with what she wanted, needed. And she had no idea what to do, except that his mouth angled under hers as though seeking something. Something she had no idea how to give.

Hal was not used to virgins and the thought did not seem to make him happy, she had realized that. She must be doing this all wrong. But if she asked him, he would be too kind to tell her.

Julia sat back, stumbled to her feet, knocked into the chair and backed away, her palm pressed to her lips. Her limbs seemed all over the place, not in her control at all. 'Oh. Oh, I…' Hal's eyes were intense upon her, his body still, as it had been when he had been in such pain and stillness was the only way he could deal with it.

She felt wanton and confused, excited and ashamed of herself and humiliated by what must be a hopeless lack of natural instincts. Giving up on the struggle to find any words to express what she felt, Julia fled.

* * *

Hal put his right hand on the pew end and tried to take some of the weight off his leg. The resulting pain in his arm and side made him hiss, unable to say just what he felt under the very nose of the English chaplain.

'Here she comes,' Will said, turning from his scrutiny of the aisle and Hal forgot the pain. 'The place looks like a hospital ward, there is so much bandaging and so many crutches on display.'

'At least they are here,' Hal murmured back. 'We didn't lose all our friends.' It was not the thing to turn round and watch the bride coming up the aisle; Will, who was taking his role as groomsman seriously, had told him so. Then there was a murmur, a rustle of silk, and regardless of instructions, he turned.

Julia was on the arm of the Baron van der Helvig, a slender figure in pale primrose, her hands full of yellow and white roses and the green filigree of ferns, her face hidden by a fall of cream Brussels lace that had been Lady Geraldine's bride gift.

She looked pure and fragile and exquisite, this girl who had defied her mother and convention, who had braved the horrors of the battlefield to save him. Hal felt like a criminal who had been rewarded for his crimes when he should have been hanged. Somehow, he vowed, he was going to make this up to her, be worthy of her. She faltered as she saw his face, then took the last few steps that brought her to his side and the baron laid her hand in his.

'Dearly beloved, we are gathered here together…'

How many weddings had he sat through in the past few years? A dozen? The words and the meaning had flowed over his head, even when it had been his brother standing at his side, taking his vows. Shut in parson's pound, parson's mousetrap, yoked—all the slang expressions that had summed up how he had felt about marriage, and yet now it felt like a relief, an objective gained. It was very strange.

He repeated his vows, thinking about them properly for the first time, hearing Julia's words spoken so steadily, directly to him as though they were alone. Then Will produced the ring, and Hal slipped it on her finger and listened with total concentration as the chaplain pronounced the words that bound him to this woman.

'You may kiss the bride.'

The last time they had kissed, she had run from him, trembling and distressed. After that he had sent for Will, demanded to be taken to the Hôtel de Flandres where order was gradually being restored and he was able to have his old room back.

Mrs Tresilian had been relieved to have him at a respectable distance. Julia had been silent, except for an attempt to send George with him. But he had refused. The groom, given a comprehensive description of Hebden, the attempt on Hal's life and the possible dangers to Julia, had settled down with his shotgun to keep guard at Place de Leuvan.

Now Julia turned to him as he took the edge of lace and lifted it carefully back over the crown of her bonnet. She was pale and her eyes were huge and soft with an emotion he hoped was happiness. Or at least contentment. Perhaps that was the most he could hope for at first, to make her content.

Then she smiled at him, and Hal found he could smile back as he bent to kiss her. A sentimental sigh went round the congregation, Julia became pink and rather charmingly flustered and he turned for the endless walk down the aisle.

Bless her, he thought, as he glanced down at the brim of her bonnet. The tip of her nose was all he could see of his wife's face. *She doesn't fuss, or suggest we go out of the side door; she just lets me set the pace as though I wasn't half-crippled.*

Faces on either side smiled at them, a few sentimental ladies sniffed into dainty handkerchiefs. Many of the men there had bandaged heads and arms in slings, but they were, thank God, all there. Or almost all. Major Jameson was still in his bed, but they thought he would survive the loss of his leg. Young Lieutenant Hayden was dead, never to reduce the regimental dinner to gales of laughter with his female impersonation, never again to scrounge everyone else's second helping of pudding.

Six of his surviving sergeants and troopers were outside, sabres lifting in a flash of steel as he and Julia came out onto the steps. They walked through the arch of blades and he realized that what he was feeling—the strange, intense pressure in his chest—was happiness. Which was unexpected.

The baron's newest barouche was there at the foot of the steps, George grinning as he held the door. Hal helped Julia in, then sank down with a sigh of relief on the soft squabs beside her.

'I thought I might feel different,' she said, half laughing at herself as George climbed back onto the box. Rose petals floated in on top of them, Hal was hit by a painful shower of rice. 'Oh, my bouquet.' She stood up, turned her back and threw it so that it vanished into the press of laughing girls on the steps. 'I meant it for Felicity,' she said, sitting down again with rather a bump as the carriage moved off. 'Did she catch it?'

'I have no idea,' Hal confessed. 'I was watching you. You look beautiful, Mrs Carlow.'

'Oh.' Julia blushed. 'Thank you. I have to say, you look very handsome, Major Carlow.' She sent him a speculative look from under her lashes. 'How on earth did you get into that tight uniform with all the bandages?'

'I've lost weight and I bribed the surgeon to come and bandage me at the same time as I was getting into my uniform. So the bandages are tight and as thin as possible and my batman—who has turned up unscathed, I'm glad to say—inched me into my breeches.'

'I am glad he is coming with us,' Julia remarked, 'or I would have to cut them off you.'

'That would almost be worth sacrificing the breeches for,' Hal murmured, then could have bitten his tongue as the pretty pink blush became red-cheeked embarrassment.

'I hope the hotel in Gent is a good one,' she remarked after a pause, her voice constrained. 'The baron recommended it, but goodness knows what it is like after all the people who fled there have been crammed in.'

'I am sure it will be perfect,' Hal said. 'And it is only for one night, after all.' Lord, there he went again. Mentioning the wedding night for one thing, then speaking as though it were a matter of indifference what their accommodation would be like for such a significant occasion. 'The barge to Ostend will be very pleasant,' he promised, pushing on rather desperately. 'I have travelled by them before. There's a large public salon, and the food is excellent. And Phillip will enjoy it.'

'Yes, of course.' Julia was recovering her poise a little. 'It is kind of the baron to take Mama and Phillip to Gent. We are quite a grand cavalcade, are we not? This carriage and then the baron's and then the luggage with our maid and your batman. Oh yes, and the groom with the horses.'

'He'll go direct to Ostend and wait for us.' Hal gave some thought to that. Trooper Godfrey, who had been so sick, had recovered suspiciously fast once Harris was dead. The man was unable to account for his violent stomach pains, but Hal had his suspicions that Harris had poisoned him in order to take over the care of Chiltern Lad and get closer to his target. Godfrey had jumped at the chance to accompany Hal as groom and Hal had felt a responsibility to him, so at least he did not have to worry about the horses.

'I am glad Mama has decided to go straight to my aunt and uncle,' Julia said after a few miles of silent travel. 'Your poor family will be surprised enough to have me arrive.'

'They will be delighted to see you,' Hal said warmly, convinced of that, at least. 'Mama has been nagging me to get married for years, and she and Verity will be missing Honoria, I am sure. And Nell, Marcus's wife, is increasing again, so she will be glad of the company of another married woman of her own age. My father is not in very good health, so you will find him a trifle quiet and retiring, but you must not take that as any reflection of his feelings towards you.'

'You are close to him?' Julia asked, with a faint air of self-consciousness that had him wondering how he had betrayed the constant edge to the relationship with his father.

'No, not very,' he admitted. 'I am not, as you may imagine, the ideal son. But he will be pleased with me for finding you and will feel I have done something right for once.'

'I hope so,' she said with what he could only interpret as a brave smile. 'I have to confess that I am glad we will be going into the country almost immediately. I think I will find London rather overpowering.'

'We'll just break our journey in town. They are sure to be at Stanegate Court,' Hal said reassuringly.

'But you haven't heard from them?'

'No,' he admitted. 'Not since just before the battle. I expect the mails are clogged with all the traffic, or a bag went astray.' But either scenario left the possibility that something had gone very wrong at home, or that his family had no idea whether he had survived the battle or not. He had dictated letters, but no response had come. It was possible that he was going to surprise his family—not just by appearing on the doorstep, but with a new wife into the bargain.

'I see,' Julia said. 'We could be quite a shock then.' Hal tried to interpret her expression, but all he could read was polite interest.

Julia's stomach lurched. She tried to tell herself it was simply the effect of not having eaten since just before the ceremony so they could make an immediate start, but she knew it was not. She was here in a strange hotel, alone with her new husband. It did not matter that somewhere else in the building Mama and Philip were settling into their rooms.

'Thank you, Maria.' The maid finished fastening the row of buttons on the evening dress and patted a loose hairpin into place. Julia regarded her reflection in the long glass. Her neckline was lower than she was used to, more suitable for a married lady. She resisted the temptation to tug it upwards and then caught a glimpse of the bed in the glass. If Hal came to her tonight, then in a few hours…

The wonderful glow that had seemed to fill her throughout the wedding ceremony had all gone now. A long carriage ride with the man who was now her husband had replaced that romantic haze with so many sources for apprehension that she could hardly manage to worry about them all at once.

It seemed there was a strong possibility that Hal was going to turn up and introduce his bride to his parents when they had no idea she even existed, or before they had the opportunity to become resigned to the fact that she had neither wealth nor grand connections to bring to the match. Perhaps, she tried to console herself, they would be so happy to have Hal home, alive, even if wounded, that they would pay her no attention.

Then there was her anxiety about Hal. Was he wrong to undertake this journey so soon? She was his wife, and she felt she had failed in her responsibility to care for her husband—but the wretched man would not let her so much as ask about his wounds, let alone fuss over them. He wouldn't even wear a sling.

And then there was the prospect of the rest of the evening, of the wedding night, stretching in front of her. That bed. Before the duchess's ball, she had felt she could speak to Hal about anything; now her tongue seemed to freeze in her mouth before she could get out the simplest sentence, let alone ask him where he was going to sleep tonight.

And as for what would happen if he did come to her, she could not imagine. She could not get beyond kisses in her head. Kisses and that confusing, overwhelming feeling that he had created when he had caressed her in the woodland glade.

But first, she had to talk to him, begin the civilised routines of married life. Somehow her training was going to have to help her through, because this marriage that had begun on a battlefield was going to have to survive in a very different world.

Julia told herself that the man she loved could hardly be more difficult to converse with than Great Aunt Penelope. She ran through a mental list of topics. His country estate with the soup, the family home in Hertfordshire with the removes. Then perhaps his interest in horse breeding during dessert. Eventually it would become easier, she was sure. She would discover his interests, tell him her own and they could begin to build their own shared reality.

She would go to the other end of the private sitting room and start embroidering her new initials on some handkerchiefs, leaving him to his port and cheese at the dining table and then perhaps she should ask whether he had bought any lace for the ladies of his family and offer to do so in the few hours they had in Gent before the barge departed.

That all seemed very harmless, with plenty of scope for conversation. Julia fastened the diamond eardrops that Hal had given her, took a deep breath and opened the door to their sitting room.

'…and so that is lace for your mother and Lady Verity and Lady Stanegate.' Julia made a careful note. 'How much may I spend?'

'Whatever you think appropriate.' Hal lowered himself into the chair on the other side of the cold fireplace and stretched out his long legs slowly. Julia held her breath, waiting for a gasp of pain, but he seemed quite comfortable. 'What is it?' Bother, he had seen her watching him.

'I cannot get used to you out of uniform,' she said, truthfully. His valet had extricated Hal from his restricting dress uniform, and he was wearing loose trousers with his dark swallowtail coat. The formal severity of black and white showed off his blonde looks but turned him into a stranger, no longer either the rake or the officer, but a remote gentleman.

The evening had gone quite well, she thought. The conversation had not flagged, the topics they had discussed were personal without being intimate. It had all been very pleasant, except for that growing tension as the hour hand moved round the mantle clock towards ten.

Julia felt very aware of Hal and oddly aware of her own body. It was as though her skin was too tight, her breasts had grown heavy. There was an embarrassing and insistent pulse beating low down that made her want to shift nervously in her chair, and she was certain that Hal was purposefully averting his eyes from her neckline which felt more indecent every time she thought of it.

What on earth was the matter with her? If this was nerves, she had never felt like it before. The nearest was that long afternoon when Hal had rescued her from Major Fellowes in the forest and the aftermath of that short, passionate encounter.

The clock struck ten, making her jump. 'I think I will go to bed,' she announced, putting away the embroidery that had lain untouched for the past hour, giving Hal time to get to his feet.

She was so intent at looking at what she was doing and not hurrying him if getting up was painful, that it was a shock to find him standing so close when she finally stood up.

'It seems a very long time since I kissed my bride,' Hal said, tipping up her chin and smiling at her.

'Yes,' she agreed. In the church, with everyone watching them, the pressure of his lips had been the seal on the ceremony, part of the blessing, a sweet thing, not a carnal one.

Now the memory of how overwhelming it had been when she had kissed him as he lay in bed came flooding back. Somehow, she had to do it properly this time. Julia watched as Hal bent to her, his eyes intent on her mouth, his hand sliding round to cradle her head.

As his mouth closed over hers and he pulled her close, she suddenly realized why she had felt so strange all evening. *Desire.* Physical desire, all mixed up with love and nerves and apprehension. She wanted him, her body wanted him. It was going to be all right, but she had to be brave, to trust her instincts and learn to show him what she felt.

There was no painful bullion and braid against her bare skin above the edge of her silk gown, only the warmth of Hal's body through linen and smooth broadcloth. She moved, restless, and her nipples hardened with the friction, making her gasp as he slid his tongue between her lips and tasted her, explored her mouth, teased her until she wanted to squirm against him to get closer. But should she, with the bandages beneath his shirt?

Just as she felt emboldened to try Hal lifted his head, his eyes bright in the candlelight. 'You are very beautiful, wife. Does kissing begin to please you now?'

'Yes,' she admitted, wondering if that made her very wanton. Or whether wantonness would please him or disgust him. He was used to loose women, but men expected decorum from their wives. But decorum had not brought him into her bed so far.

'I'm glad.' He lifted his hand and brushed it gently over her mouth, tracing the shape of her lips. 'It pleases me very much.' He turned her, took her elbow and began to walk towards the bedroom door. 'You must be tired. Sleep well, Julia.'

He opened the door for her, then stepped back and turned to the other door, the door to the dressing room, and left her alone.

Chapter Eighteen

'That's Burlington House, we're almost there.' Hal pointed out of the chaise window while Julia tried to take in the sights and control her jittery nerves.

There would be only the skeleton staff of servants at the town house, she reassured herself for the hundredth time. And it was not Hal's house, even if it was his town home, so she would not be expected to give any orders to top-lofty London servants. Perhaps it was a good thing that Mama and Phillip had stopped with Uncle and Aunt Tresilian in Rochester: Phillip and a superior butler were hardly likely to make a harmonious couple.

A few days to themselves in London, the opportunity to rest and relax, to do a little shopping—to get to know each other.

Euphemisms, she chided herself sharply. *Time for him to come to my bed, that's what I mean. Oh, why doesn't he want to make love to me?* She had asked herself that over and over when the limit to Hal's physical affection seemed to be kisses, the occasional touch on her hand. Admittedly, the kisses were passionate, but they left her feeling that she would burst into flames at any moment.

They had been travelling of course—but from what she had heard, a man in the throes of amorous excitement was not to be put off by tiny cabins or the accommodations to be found at coaching inns. She could only conclude that she did not produce sufficient amorous excitement in him. But unless she had some practice, she was not at all certain how she was ever going to learn. And if they could not share the intimacy of the marriage bed, how were they ever going to become close enough to make this marriage work? Something *had* been there, so strongly between them, when he had lain with her in the grass, that day at the picnic. What was she doing wrong that he no longer wanted to caress her like that?

Or was there something she could do? Julia was not sure quite how, or whether she would dare, but she was going to find something, she vowed.

The post-chaise turned right, then stopped in front of a tall, double-fronted house. Hal jumped down and handed Julia out. 'The knocker's still on,' he said, sounding puzzled. He handed notes up to the nearest postillion who stuffed the money down his heavy leather boot while his colleague unloaded their trunks.

'Someone of the family must still be at home.' Hal took Julia's arm and climbed the steps, his limp very pronounced after the long carriage ride. 'Oh well, let's see.' He banged the knocker while Julia's heart thudded in unison.

The door swung open to reveal a tall, balding butler whose expression of dignified solemnity lasted as long as it took him to recognize the man on the doorstep. 'Major Carlow, sir! We had not hoped—Lord and Lady Narborough are in the—'

'Hal!' A tall woman hurried across the chequered floor of the hall, her hands held out. 'Oh thank God!' She threw her arms around him and burst into tears as a young woman came down the stairs.

'Is that the post? Oh! Hal!'

Julia stepped aside, as Hal was embraced from the other side, then saw she had better intervene. 'Please, do mind his arm, his ribs…Lady Verity—' She supposed this must be Hal's younger sister.

'Hal.' It was a man, rather stooped, greying, obviously an invalid. He did not come down the hall, but waited, leaning on a stick while Hal put his mother and sister gently to one side and went to him.

'Father.' Julia saw him hesitate, then he embraced the older man. 'You all seem very surprised to see me. Have you not had my letters?'

'The only letter we have had was from a Captain Grey to say you had been badly wounded, but that you had been removed from the battlefield and he had hopes of your eventual recovery,' Lord Narborough said. 'If we had heard nothing by the last post today, then Marcus was going to travel to Brussels to find out what had happened.' His voice was measured, but even from where she stood, Julia could see his hands shaking as they held his cane.

'I sent letters, I promise you,' Hal said. 'But if you have not had those, you will not know who this is.' He turned and held out his hand to Julia. 'Mama, Father, may I present my wife, Julia, the niece of Sir Alfred Tresilian of Rochester. Julia, my parents, my younger sister Verity.'

Julia dropped a respectful curtsey and her new mother in law burst into renewed tears.

'Mama!' Hal sounded shaken, but Julia realized she had expected nothing less than this rejection. Then Lady Narborough threw out her arms and gathered her into a rather damp embrace and she felt her own tears welling up with relief.

'Oh my dear! Oh, how pretty you are and what a terrible

time you must have had of it. But welcome to the family.' She kissed Julia and thrust her towards Lord Narborough before seizing Hal's hands. 'At last, you wretched boy! And the poor child arriving unannounced into a houseful of strangers.

'Now, come into the drawing room. Or should you go straight to bed? Julia, my dear. You must advise, what is to be done with him?'

'I think Hal will tell us himself,' Julia said, seeing her husband's jaw beginning to tense. 'But, for myself, I would be very glad of the opportunity to retire for a short while: we seem to have been travelling for an age.'

'But of course. Now let me see—Hal, you have your old room and Julia can have Marcus's—we have redecorated it as a guest room, not that you are a guest my dear, but it is right next to Hal with just a little sitting room between that used to be the schoolroom but you can have it as a private parlour. Wellow, do take Mrs Carlow upstairs—oh, and a maid…'

'My dear,' Lord Narborough interjected, 'You will make our new daughter dizzy. You go up, my dear, take Hal with you and we will see you later when you are rested and we are all a little calmer.'

'I will show you.' Lady Verity—the well-behaved sister, Julia remembered—stood beaming at them. Her golden hair resembled Hal's, but her eyes were a distinctive hazel green. She linked arms with Julia and guided her towards the stairs. Julia cast a glance back over her shoulder at Hal, but he nodded for her to go, so she let herself be swept along.

'We were so worried that Hal had been killed, or been horribly wounded, and it is hopeless trying to get any information at Horse Guards; they kept saying he *was* alive, but there were no letters. And here he is, perfectly all right and married!'

'He was wounded badly,' Julia interjected. 'And he is a

dreadful patient as you no doubt know, Lady Verity, so he does need to rest.'

'You must call me Verity, we are sisters.' She pushed open a door. 'Here you are. Isn't it nice? I chose the hangings. And that door there is the dressing room and that one is to the little parlour and then Hal's room is the other side of that. And you have the garden side, not like Hal who has the street, so you will be very quiet.'

'It is lovely.' Julia looked round at a room into which all the bedchambers at Place de Leuvan would have easily fitted. There was no sign of Hal, he must have gone to his own room. She eyed the interconnecting door uneasily.

'Is your maid coming later? Only you can borrow mine, her name's Miriam. I used to share her with Honoria, but she's married now and somewhere in America, would you believe?' She smiled, and Julia thought how sweet and open she seemed. 'It is so lovely to have a new sister.'

It was all going much better than he had hoped. Marcus and Nell had come and had stayed for the evening, visibly moved by the news of his safe return and unexpected marriage. Hal looked round the drawing room after dinner at his mother, sister and sister in law, all three delighted with Julia. She had relaxed, her nerves apparently subsiding in the face of the warm welcome, and his father and brother sat either side of him, watching the women.

'A very prettily behaved young lady,' Lord Narborough commented. For once, Hal decided, he had done something right as far as his father was concerned. 'I cannot imagine how you prevailed upon her to marry you.' Ah, there was the barb back again.

'She saved my life,' Hal said. 'She found me after the battle and nursed me—in a squalid hovel, just yards from the battlefield—until I could be moved. If she had not, I would be dead.'

'Then we are even more in her debt,' Lord Narborough said. Hal half regretted his words, seeing how white his father had gone around the lips, but he wanted his family to know just what they owed their new daughter.

'I think I'll take a turn in the garden.' He got to his feet with care. 'I get stiff if I sit for too long. Coming?' He raised an eyebrow at Marcus who needed no stronger hint.

'How bad is it?' his brother asked when they were clear of the half-open windows. 'You're doing a damn good job of pretending it doesn't hurt, but you don't fool me.'

'Not good,' Hal admitted. 'A lot better than it was, and the healing is going well, thanks to Julia, but the cut in my thigh was damned deep and I keep losing strength in it, suddenly. And all the internal bruising is working its way out—slowly!'

'Father's relieved to see you—you do know that, don't you?' Hal shrugged. 'He is proud of you, even if he doesn't approve of you. Do you want to talk about how it happened?' Marcus leaned against a statue of Diana.

'We'd been sitting on our backsides most of the day—it was a charge through the French artillery right at the end. The thing is, it was a French shell that took me off the horse and knocked me about—but an English trooper tried to kill me first. He was responsible for all the wounds.'

'What the hell?' His brother stood up abruptly, sending the goddess rocking on her plinth.

Hal explained. '…and I don't think it was Stephen Hebden this time. Not when Harris described someone who spoke like me, was older and who had cold eyes like death. But Harris had a silken rope. I've got it in my luggage. And Hebden was in Brussels: he bought jewellery from Julia. Snooping on me, I have no doubt.'

'You know, that ties in with my gut feeling that there is someone else orchestrating these rumours about Father. They aren't Hebden's style. Nor is murder.' Marcus began to pace up and down the flagstones. 'You realize this is the very spot where the original murder took place? No wonder it preys on Father's mind.

'But we know, to some extent, why Hebden is persecuting us all: he blames the families for his father's death. But why should anyone else? I can believe any of us individually might have made an enemy—but the Wardales, the Carlows *and* Imogen Hebden?'

'If Wardale was innocent,' Hal said slowly, 'then the murderer and spy may still be alive, still be out there.'

'In his last letter to his wife, Wardale denied it, said he suspected Father,' Marcus pointed out. 'But, if we start from the basic premise that he is innocent too—who does that leave?'

'Perhaps you should tell all this to Stephen Hebden.' Both men swung round to find Julia standing on the flags behind them. 'I came to see if you wanted tea,' she said, prosaically. 'Then I overheard.'

'You'd need a long spoon to sup with that devious devil,' Marcus said harshly. 'He almost caused my wife's death.'

'But not, I think, intentionally,' Hal said, a wary eye on his brother. 'And Hebden acts personally in his vengeance. The attack on me was planned, paid for and at one remove from the instigator.'

'I'd like to see you being so tolerant if he kidnapped Julia and threatened to ravish her. And don't forget that he tried to ruin Honoria, almost wrecked Monty's wedding. Do I need to go on?'

'No. I'll not take him into my confidence,' Hal agreed.

But despite his words, he was still brooding on the mystery as he sat in his room by the light of a single branch of candles, staring at his bare feet protruding from the hem of his silk robe and trying to work up enough energy to get into bed.

There were sounds from the little parlour that used to be the schoolroom he shared with Marcus. Julia, looking for a book, perhaps. He wondered how soon he could take things a little further without shocking her. Even thinking about it had his body tightening, his loins aching. She responded readily to his kisses now, although he often caught her staring at him, her cheeks pink with what had to be shyness. Patience had never been his strong suit, but he was certainly learning it now.

With a faint creak, the door opened. There, on the threshold, her hair loose and waving on her shoulders, stood Julia. In the flickering light he could see her toes, bare beneath the hem of her simple white nightgown.

Hal got to his feet, closing his mouth with a snap, thankful for the heavy folds of his dressing gown. He was naked beneath the robe and, suddenly, so aroused it hurt. 'Julia? Did you want something?'

Her face was flushed, and she seemed to be holding onto the door handle for support. 'I want to know if you are ever going to come to my room.'

'*What?* Why?' This was his shy, innocent bride who had fled when he had asked her to kiss him.

'Because we are married and I do not feel very married!' He took a step towards her. The pink in her cheeks, he realized incredulously, was partly indignation. 'I know I will not be very good at first, but you can teach me, can't you?'

'Julia, I told you. I am not used to virgins, I do not want to shock you. I thought, perhaps, if you got used to me and realized I am trying to reform my ways, you would come to trust me and it would be easier.'

'For whom?' she enquired tartly. Hal found his lips were twitching, despite a feeling of near panic. How could he face the French army feeling nothing but excited anticipation and yet Julia reduced him to this state of nerves?

'For both of us?' he suggested. She glared at him, and perversely he felt his spirits lifting. 'If you are sure?' He reached out a hand to his bed and tossed back the covers. For a moment, he thought she would turn and run, then she came in, closed the door behind her and walked steadily to stand in front of him.

'If it would not hurt you?' she asked. 'I wasn't sure. If it would, then it would nice just to be held, I think.'

'That might be rather more painful,' Hal muttered, earning a puzzled look. Lord, she was so innocent. A least she had seen him naked, that was one less shock, he supposed. Although what she would make of the changes that happened to an aroused man…

He blew out the candles, then moved in, finding her easily despite the darkness. He took her in his arms and kissed her, sinking immediately into the now-familiar sweetness of her response, the scent of lilac soap, the softness of her body as he held her.

Now, without corsets and layers of clothing, he could feel the yielding curves, the lovely line of waist and hip. He let one hand stray to cup her buttock and she gave a little gasp against his mouth, then pressed closer.

Emboldened, he let his fingers investigate the bows at the shoulders of the nightgown until, working blind, he freed them so that when he took his hands away and stepped back, the garment tumbled to the floor around her feet.

'Oh!'

Hal touched her, feeling with delight Julia's blushes warming her breast with imagined rose-pink. Under his palms her figure was every bit as enchanting as he had fantasised. She was small-breasted, slim-hipped, yet so sweetly curved.

Speed, that was the thing, he decided, however much he

wanted to linger. Hal shed his dressing gown, scooped her up and laid her on the bed, coming to lie on his left side beside her.

'You are the most beautiful thing I have ever seen.'

'Liar,' she mumbled. 'You cannot see me.'

'I have hands.' He began to stroke, gentling his hand along hip and waist, feeling her belly tighten as he trailed his fingers across it, then up to cup her breast. She moaned, while he caressed her until her head began to move, restless, on the pillow. His right arm ached, but he hardly felt the pain, listening to her, judging the moment to part the moist folds, slip one finger into the tender heat.

Julia gasped, tried to move away, but he persisted until she was lifting herself against his hand again and again and he could part her thighs, move over her. Hal positioned himself carefully, trying to take as much weight as he could on his uninjured left leg, nudging gently.

Yes, she was his; he could enter, so slowly, so carefully she would hardly be aware. The thought of frightening her, hurting her, made him tense. He wished he could watch her face, but she would feel safer in the dark.

And then the pain ripped through his right thigh, cramping the muscles, making him jerk involuntarily, and beneath him Julia gave a little scream, arching up, rigid beneath him. He was deep within her, her involuntary movements sending waves of sensation crashing through him, beyond his control, beyond stopping. Hal felt the orgasm take him and knew, with the last rags of his control, that he could not keep his weight from bearing down on her.

Chapter Nineteen

Julia blinked away the tears that filled her eyes. The pain had been every bit as bad as she had feared, and so sudden, but it was gone now and Hal was part of her, filling her. Although she could hardly breathe and she sensed, rather than felt, a deep soreness, that did not matter: the intimacy of their joining was breathtaking, overwhelming.

Was this what would have happened in the glade if Hal had not stopped so abruptly? Was the fear of hurting her what had been keeping him from her all along?

She was not quite sure what was happening now, or what to expect next, so she just enjoyed holding on to Hal, feeling the breadth of his shoulders under her palms, the heat of his skin, the movement of muscles, and trying to get used to the sensation of him within her. His face was buried in her shoulder, his heart was pounding and he seemed to have gone limp in every muscle, so she concentrated on lying still, her cheek pressed against his hair.

Then Hal moved with an ungainly jerk for someone who was usually so controlled, and he rolled off her body, leaving her feeling bereft. He was lighting the candle, she realized.

When he lay back on the pillows beside her and she saw his face, it was worse. Whatever had just happened, it had not made him happy.

'Hell,' Hal said bleakly, staring at the ceiling. 'Hell, I am so sorry.'

'I do not understand,' she faltered, wondering if it was her fault.

'I intended to go slowly, gently, and this bloody leg gave way and I lost control.' He turned his head to look at her. 'I hurt you, didn't I?'

'A bit,' she admitted. 'But it always does, doesn't it? The first time.'

'It doesn't have to be too bad unless a blundering cripple with no self-control makes a mess of it.'

'Oh, your leg!' She flinched at his description of himself, but there was no point in arguing about that now. 'Have you opened up the wound?' Heedless of her nakedness, Julia sat up and reached for the sheet that was tangled about his waist, trying to look at his bandaged thigh.

'Leave it!' She jerked back, wincing at his tone. 'I'm sorry. It is fine,' he said more gently, sitting up. 'You'll want to go back to your own bed.'

Julia opened her mouth to deny it, tell him she wanted to stay, to be held in his arms, but Hal reached for his robe, shrugged it on and then slid out of the bed to limp over to the washstand. He obviously did not want her to remain, so perhaps that was not something a wife should do. Or perhaps he did not want her to cling or to show affection. She was about to get up when he came back with a towel and a cloth.

'Here.' He was pale around the lips and eyes. 'There's blood.' He turned his back while she dabbed and winced.

'The sheet—' The servants would see, would know.

'They will think it is mine,' Hal said. 'I will ring for Langham, have him redress my leg. The wound has opened a little. There is no need for embarrassment.'

'No, of course not.' Julia slid the nightgown over her head and went to the door. 'Good night, Hal.'

Julia sat up in bed, fingers curled around the luxury of a cup of hot chocolate, and thought about the previous night. She was no longer a virgin, but that was about the only positive thing, that and those few moments where she had held Hal in her arms and felt the tenderness welling through her.

Instead of a husband who had not wanted to make love to her, she now had one who was blaming himself for hurting her. He had most certainly not been filled with the desire to cradle her in his arms afterwards, as she had hoped he would, but perhaps men did not like to do that. Her body and her heart ached for that comfort. This was not the marriage she had hoped for, one of sharing and confidences.

She needed advice. The image of Nell Carlow appeared, with the memory of her warm voice and the friendly smile in her hazel eyes. She was so very obviously happy with her husband, and that happiness seemed to overflow into a need for both of them to touch all the time, however fleetingly. Nell, she was sure, would talk to her.

To her relief, the breakfast room held only Verity and Lady Narborough. 'Lady Stanegate mentioned a dressmaker and some milliners last night,' Julia remarked when she was seated in front of the poached egg and toast that were all she thought she had appetite for. 'Would she mind if I called to ask her more about them, do you think?'

'She would be delighted,' Lady Narborough assured her. 'She stays at home during the mornings at the moment, which stops Stanegate fussing, but she will appreciate a visitor. It is just around the corner if you want to walk. Ask Wellow to send one of the footmen with you when you are ready to go.'

'I'll come too,' Verity said.

'No, dear.' Lady Narborough sent Julia a look that seemed to say she understood the need for one newly married young lady to talk to another. 'I want you with me this morning.'

Wondering just what Hal's mother thought she needed to talk about, if it was not hats, Julia set out with Richards the footman in attendance. It was not until she found herself seated in Nell's boudoir that it occurred to her that she had not planned quite how to phrase her questions.

'Hal must be a challenge as a husband,' Nell remarked while she was still composing herself. 'I love him dearly as a brother, but my goodness, the man is wild.'

'Not at the moment,' Julia said, crumbling the biscuit Nell had pressed upon her.

'His wounds, you mean? Yes, I suppose that would slow even Hal down. Marcus says they were severe.'

'Hal has reformed.' As Julia said it she realized how dreary that sounded. It was not a reformed rake she had fallen in love with, it was the real man with all his faults and foibles.

'Congratulations! It must be true love if you have that much control over him.'

Julia winced. 'I loved him as he was. He seems to feel he needed to change, for me. And he felt he had to marry me because I had compromised myself.'

'And saved his life,' Nell protested. 'You mean he has not told you he loves you?'

Julia shook her head. 'He said—Nell—may I call you Nell? He *wanted* me, he said, but then he told me why he could not marry me. And after the battle, when I found him, then he said he had to marry me. And now he doesn't even seem to want me either, not like…not in…'

'In bed?' Nell swung her feet down off the footstool and sat up, frowning. 'What has come over the man?'

'I think he believed that, because I was a virgin and he had lived a dissolute life, that he would shock me. He didn't seem very confident about, um, making love to a virgin.'

'But he has? You said you *were* a virgin.' Nell seemed wonderfully unembarrassed about this.

'Last night. It was a disaster,' Julia said and then, to her own surprise and shock, burst into tears.

Another pot of tea and at least three pocket handkerchiefs later, Nell sat back and laughed. 'Oh, I am sorry, I can see it is horrid for you. But to see the most outrageous flirt I know laid low by virtue really is poetic justice.'

'But what can I do?' Julia demanded. Somehow her spirits were rising, it did seem possible that there was some hope if Nell was so amused.

'Why, seduce him, of course. And learn to flirt yourself. But first we need to go shopping.'

Shopping under Nell's tuition was a luxurious adventure. It seemed London was full of small shops where one could buy the most frivolous, expensive and delightful trifles if only one knew where to look—and provided one had no care for the resulting bill.

'I haven't discussed a dress allowance with Hal yet,' Julia whispered urgently in Nell's ear. Nell was sitting at her ease, directing the assistant in a shop whose entire stock appeared to be either transparent, semi-transparent or made of lace. To Julia's dismay, the prices were in inverse proportion to the modesty of the garment.

'That is very remiss of him, but he should know he must pay for his pleasures. You do not think we are buying these things for your sake, do you? Men are very visual creatures, bless them, and we must give them something to look at. I think that sea-green gauze negligée with the matching slippers, the embroidered muslin camisoles and the Chinese silk nightgowns will do for now.'

An hour later, they emerged from another of Nell's favourite modistes, leaving an order for a delicious evening gown to be ready as soon as possible, and repaired to the nearest bookshop. 'Racy poetry and novels, that's the next thing,' Nell announced. 'And I am going to sit here and con the pages of *The Repository* for the latest bonnets.'

Julia obediently went to find the right sections, blinking a little at the choice of titles that her mama would condemn unopened as quite outrageous. They all looked wickedly tempting, and Nell had said they would put her in the mood for romance. Not that *she* needed putting in the mood...

'Are you having to buy your own love poetry, Mrs Carlow?'

Julia jumped and almost dropped her pile of books. There was the gem dealer from Brussels, the man Hal spoke of with such bitterness and his brother with such hatred. Only now, he did not look like a polite businessman; he looked dangerous. Predatory even. Or perhaps she was seeing him in the light of what the brothers had told her about him.

The shiver of sensual awareness he seemed able to produce just with a look from those bold dark eyes trembled through her. 'Mr Hebden! Are you following me?'

'What hot-blooded man would not?' he enquired, leaning his shoulder against the book stacks and smiling at her. Julia stopped herself licking her lips nervously and lifted her chin instead. 'You intrigue me, Julia. Such a very *good* wife for such a man as Hal Carlow.' He was dressed like any of the gentlemen strolling past in Piccadilly, only perhaps they did not show the glint of gold in their earlobe or wear their dark waving hair quite so long.

And their voices would not have that intriguing lilt, even

if their eyes held as much impertinent masculine appreciation. Julia felt her pulse stutter and not, she realized, entirely
through apprehension.

'What do you want, sir?' she demanded. 'If I call for help,
the proprietor will have you apprehended.'

'He could try,' Hebden acknowledged without the slightest
sign of alarm. 'He would be sorry.'

'So, not content with trying to murder my husband, you
decide to harass me?' Julia watched his face closely. If she
had not, she would have missed the brief, betraying flicker
in the dark eyes. He was surprised and Stephen Hebden did
not like finding himself at a disadvantage.

'Murder? I have not touched your husband.'

'Through your agent then.' But she believed him, believed
the surprise and the denial.

'I use no agents. The French had a good attempt at killing
Carlow, they did not need my help.'

'Someone gave it to them, Mr Hebden. You would seem
to have an ally—or perhaps a rival—in your campaign of
hatred.'

'It is not hatred,' he said, the intensity in his voice sending
cold chills that were most definitely not sensual down her
spine. 'I am the agent of a foretelling—you would call it a
curse, perhaps.' He stared deep into her eyes, and it seemed
to her, caught in their darkness, that another personality was
within him, reaching out to touch her. His voice became
lower, intense. *'I call guilt to eat you alive and poison your
hearts' blood.* That is what is promised for your father in law,
for his children.'

'No.' Julia shook her head in denial. 'I do not believe such
superstitions.' But she found—caught in the web of his voice,
those eyes—that she did.

'You do not have to believe something for it to be true,'
he said with an absolute certainty that shook her. But she

would not run, if that was what he wanted, she would not give him the satisfaction of showing him fear. She was a soldier's wife.

'Tell me,' he said, stepping forward and seizing her right wrist. Julia twisted in his grip, the cold silver cuff he wore chill against her pulse. Close-to the intensity and force of his personality took her breath away. 'Tell me what happened to Hal Carlow.'

'Let her go or I will run this hat pin through your ribs,' Nell said, stepping round the end of the shelves behind him.

He winced and opened his hand. 'Lady Stanegate, a pleasure to see you again.'

'It is all yours, believe me,' Nell said.

'The memory of your lips warms me at night,' he murmured, turning with wary grace to face Nell. 'I will leave you ladies to your browsing. Do, I beg you, remember me to your husbands.'

'Oh, Nell!' Julia leaned back against a row of lurid romances and caught her breath. 'He was demanding to know what happened to Hal and denying having anything to do with it.' She could not bring herself to repeat that curse. Not to a pregnant woman. 'Nell, what did he mean about your lips? He never—'

'He kissed me briefly when he kidnapped me,' Nell said, sticking her hatpin back with some force. 'And that is all.'

'What a relief.' Julia patted her armful of books back into order. 'He is a very attractive man, though,' she added thoughtfully. 'And he knows it.'

'If you are thinking of trying to make Hal jealous, you are playing with fire,' Nell warned, walking towards the counter. 'If he thinks Hebden has so much as breathed on you, he will try and kill him.'

'I just thought I would tease him,' Julia said, handing her books to the assistant. An idea was beginning to form, although whether she had the nerve to carry it through, she had no idea.

'Do you require both copies of this, ma'am?' The man held up Byron's *Corsair*.

'Why no. Have I picked up two in error?'

'No, ma'am. But the gentleman has already paid for this one for you.' The assistant held up a neat parcel.

'Typical,' Nell muttered. 'That is all we need, a vengeful Romany who sees himself as a romantic hero!'

Hal seemed to be dealing with the previous night's events by pretending that nothing had happened. He was polite, attentive and remote. Alert for every opportunity to carry out Nell's suggestions, she became acutely aware that he was making great efforts not to touch her.

So she touched him. When he held a door or a chair for her, she paused and laid her fingertips on his hand for a fleeting moment. When they were close, she reached up and brushed imagined flecks from his lapels; and when she handed him his tea cup after dinner, she let her fingers tangle with his. Yet all the time, she kept her eyes modestly downcast.

The results were fascinating. She found she was physically aware of him as she had never been before and, out of the corner of her eye, she could tell that he was watching her, his gaze dark and intense.

At half-past ten she went up to her room, changed into the new rose-pink silk nightgown, draped a pretty shawl around herself and went to lie on the chaise in the parlour with a book, making sure that not only was the door into Hal's room ajar, but that a candle was left burning on a shelf close to it.

Time passed and she became so immersed in her book that the sound of the door opening wide made her look up in surprise. Hal stood in the doorway, fully dressed, staring at her.

'What is the matter?'

'Nothing. I was reading. Nell and I went to the bookshop today.'

'What is it?' He came into the room and stood at the foot of the chaise, his eyes on the thin silk that flowed about her body. With what seemed to be an effort, he turned his gaze on the book. 'That is a nice binding.'

'Yes,' she agreed, closing the volume and holding it out to him. '*The Corsair,* a present from Stephen Hebden.'

'You are jesting.' Hal did not take the book, and it seemed to Julia that he had become tensely alert, although nothing showed in either his face or voice.

'No, I am not. He came up to me in the shop today. I accused him of trying to kill you, he denied it. Truthfully, I think. It surprised him.'

'And you wait until now to tell me?' Hal demanded.

'I could hardly blurt it out in front of your parents and Verity: it would have alarmed them. And you did not come in until late afternoon. I was quite safe, in the middle of a book shop in Piccadilly.'

'Quite safe! After I have told you the things that man is capable of, you think he is quite safe?' Hal was furious. Julia realized that about a split second before she discovered how exciting she found it.

She shrugged, getting slowly to her feet, allowing Hal to study the effect of her new nightgown as it moulded itself around her body. It did not seem to calm his anger. 'The man is obviously capable of all you say, and more,' she conceded. 'But he *is* extremely attractive.'

Julia almost reached her bedroom door, before Hal caught her by the shoulders and spun her round to face him. 'Do not even *think* of associating with Hebden.' He sounded as though he was using all his will not to raise his voice to her. 'Or I am going to have to kill him.'

She put up her own hands and caught his wrists. Hal freed her at the touch, but his eyes were fierce and dark and she could see the rise and fall of his chest as he controlled his breathing. He was angry and dangerous, and she had aroused those feelings because he felt—what? Protective towards her? Possessive? Hope flickered that it might be more.

Slowly she walked backwards to her own door, watching him. 'I said he was extremely attractive.' She reached behind herself to turn the handle, her eyes locked on his. 'I did not say he was more attractive than my husband.' Julia slipped through the door and closed it behind herself.

She leant back against the door panels and heard his footsteps, half a dozen strides that brought him to the door. Then silence. He was just the other side; she sensed it as strongly as though her back was against his chest, not against solid oak. Would he try and come in? Had she intrigued him enough? Or angered him—or worse, disgusted him?

Then she heard his footsteps again, going away. With a sigh, she put the book down on the bedside table and tossed the shawl onto the chair. She would try again tomorrow: she would not give up.

Hal stared at the door as though he could penetrate it by sheer will alone. All evening Julia had not looked directly at him, yet she had always seemed to be close, her fingertips touching in the most fleeting way, her scent tantalising his nostrils, his awareness of her body and his new knowledge of its sweetness threatening to overturn his control and make him forget the guilt he felt about last night.

And now…*I did not say he was more attractive than my husband*. Did Julia really mean that she *wanted* him? After the fiasco of that clumsy coupling? She had said to him that she wanted him to come to her bed, she had asked him to teach her. She wanted to feel married. But he could not risk hurting her again.

Hal turned away, back towards his own room, then stopped. He was not some inexperienced youth, even if he had behaved like one last night. There were ways to make love to his wife, ways to show her that he cared for her. He turned back, making a bet with himself. *If she still has the candle lit, I will go in, if not, I will leave her.*

He blew out the candles in the branch she had been reading by, the single one placed, he realized, to lure him into the room, then stood in the darkness looking at Julia's door. Yes, there was a thin line of light along one edge. *I* am *a lucky gambler,* he thought. But no bet had ever seemed quite so important as this.

Chapter Twenty

Hal tapped on the door and opened it without waiting for a response. His wife was sitting up in bed, her arms around her knees and her chin resting on them. She seemed deep in thought. As she heard him, she raised her gaze from the foot of the bed and stared at him, her eyes wide and dark and mysterious. Female.

'May I come in?'

Julia nodded, watching him as he came to sit on the end of the bed. It seemed she was content to let him speak.

'I thought I should treat you as though we were both inexperienced,' Hal said without preamble, thinking his way through this, explaining to himself as much as her. 'I was ashamed of my experience—of my *experiences*. I wanted to come to you like a bridegroom who had been virtuous all his life.' She frowned, a line of puzzlement between her brows that he wanted to kiss away.

'So, I tried to make love to you in the obvious, simple, way. The bread and butter way.' The frown vanished, and her lips twitched, just a very little. Heartened, he pushed on. 'The way such a virtuous man, relying on instinct not experience, would make love to his new bride. I did not stop to think that, with my leg as it is, it was a foolish thing to do and that there were many other ways to make you mine, ways that would pleasure you far more.'

'Cake love, not bread and butter?' Julia asked, her eyes alight with amusement and something he rather hoped was excitement.

'Plum cake with cream,' Hal promised, aware that he was becoming most definitely aroused. His experience in sin, he realized, was not something to discard, but a gift he could give to this woman he had married.

'Perhaps I would want cream cake every time,' she mused, making him wonder where his delusion had come from that, because she was innocent, she must also need teaching to desire.

'Occasionally, a little bread and butter is welcome,' Hal informed her, getting off the bed. He picked up the single candle and walked round to touch it to the wicks of the other dozen or so others that were placed around the room.

'All those lights?' She was biting her lip now, uncertain. Hal realized how much he wanted to see her naked.

'Of course, otherwise the cream could go anywhere.' Hal began to undress, watching her steadily to gauge her responses, trying to keep the mood light.

'That might be quite fun,' Julia said demurely, making him grin. She had courage—he knew that already—but the glimpses of a wicked sense of humour were a constant surprise.

'Perhaps another day,' he promised, down to shirt and silk evening knee breeches now. 'Come and help with my buttons?'

Julia was tempted. She felt so restless, she wanted to touch Hal so badly, but instinct was telling her to tease and to prolong. 'I want to watch,' she decided, wondering if she would embarrass him.

No, of course not: this was the rake she had fallen in love with, not the respectable gentleman he had been trying to counterfeit. Hal raised one eyebrow, then began to undo his shirt. Very slowly. It dropped to the floor and then he undid the fastenings of his breeches. Even more slowly. It seemed two could play at teasing. Julia licked her lips.

When he stood there naked, almost arrogant in his arousal, she caught her breath. She had seen his wounded body, the honed muscles slashed, the golden skin scored and bruised. Now she saw that nearly all the bandages were gone, with only a strapping round arm and thigh where the sabre cuts had been deepest. The new scars, still red, laced across older white ones, but to her they did not detract from his beauty, they were badges of honour. On his left breast, the bruised outline of her notebook was still faintly visible. Such a tiny chance, that she had thought to give it to him. And without that impulse they would not be here, in this room, tonight.

'This seems rather unequal,' he observed as she continued to stare at him.

'Mmm,' Julia agreed. Cream cakes, indeed. She wanted to…wanted to *lick* him. All over. And bite. Just there, and there…tiny, playful nips. 'Oh my,' she murmured.

'That is a delightful nightgown.'

'I bought it today. Nell took me to some of her favourite shops.'

'Now I know why Marcus looks so smug these days.' Hal took hold of the corner of the sheet and whipped it back. 'Spending your dress allowance, Julia?'

'My non-existent dress allowance,' she corrected him, reaching up her hands to flatten the palms on his chest as he leant over her, intent on the ribbons. Under her palms, his skin was smooth and hot, the muscles hard, the hair crisp.

'Such a mean husband you have,' he sympathised, leaning down, pushing against her hands so she was forced back to the pillows. 'But you have such delightful taste I can see that I must give you a large allowance, all to spend on flimsy nonsense like this. Now, how does it come off?'

Of course she had to wriggle and bat at his hands, so that he was compelled to tickle her, roll her across the wide bed, pretending to pounce until she sensed it was time to stop fighting. Julia lay still, quiescent under those clever hands while he smoothed the gown up and over and off, letting it caress her until she did not know what was his fingertips or his breath or the whisper of silk or even, as he bent his head to her breast, the brush of his hair.

Hal lay on his side and pulled her against the length of his body, then lifted her leg over his hip until she was open to him. It felt strange, but she let him do as he wished, finding she could lean in to lick along his collar bone, his neck, nip the point of his chin with her teeth, soothe with her lips. He tasted good: warm and slightly salty.

Then he began to explore her with his hands, boldly, intimately, until she writhed against him, panting, the tension mounting and knotting inside her as it had done last night. But this time she knew she was going to get to wherever that spiral of heat was taking her. And then he slid into her, easily, slowly, so that all she was conscious of was him filling her, making them one as he rocked her up, up until she was wound so tight it was impossible.

'Now,' Hal breathed in her ear. 'Come with me now.'

Where? Where… And then she knew and let go and flew with him, over the edge, up and up as he gasped her name and held her safe until, so slowly, the world came back and she was tangled in his arms on the big bed.

It was possible that she would never move again, that they would stay like this, still joined, for ever. It seemed to Julia to be a perfect fate. She closed her eyes against his sweat-damp chest and floated.

'Are you asleep?'

Julia blinked and opened her eyes to find his, blue and clear and smiling into hers, very close. She wriggled a little. 'You've gone.'

Hal chuckled. 'That happens. Now we start again. Can you ride?'

'No.' Mystified, Julia watched him roll onto his back.

'Now's the time to learn.' He lay there watching her from under hooded lids while she worked it out.

'Me? On top? Hal, that's…' Indecently bold. Indecently exciting. 'Like this?' His lean hips felt right between her thighs and she kept her weight forward, away from his wound. And beneath her, his body was stirring into life again. 'Oh yes, I see—Oh, Hal! We fit together so well.'

And he smiled and then, as she took him fully into herself and began to move, his eyes closed. 'Julia. Oh my God, *Julia!*'

The next morning at breakfast, Julia felt as though she must have *Satisfied Wife* emblazoned across her forehead. They had made love a third time before they slept and then again this morning. Then Hal had kissed her lingeringly and padded off to his own room before her maid came in.

He had put his foot through the sheet at some point, she realized, finding the maid's studious disregard of the tangled bedding and crumpled nightgown every bit as pointed as a comment would have been.

But she was too happy to be embarrassed, even though unexpected muscles ached and she was aware of her body, inside and out, just as though he was still touching her.

'Good morning, Mrs Carlow,' Hal said, sitting down again as she took her own seat at the breakfast table. He looked, and sounded, politely attentive, but his eyes, full of mischief and messages, were anything but those of a staid gentleman at his breakfast.

'Good morning, Major Carlow,' she rejoined, demurely shaking out her napkin while trying to convey that she was most willing to try whatever that mischief was suggesting.

No-one seemed to notice the by-play. Lord Narborough, looking rather better that morning than he had for several days, settled back to his perusal of the newspaper while his wife discussed the desirability of harp lessons with Verity.

'Would you like to go for a drive, Julia?' Hal asked. 'It would be a pleasant day for a ride, but, of course, you do not ride, do you?'

'Not yet,' she said, compressing her lips. 'You must teach me.' Oh but he was wicked, and she did love him.

Everything was perfect now, except for that one small detail, she thought, the desire to smile fading. He had never said he loved her, not even in the extremes of passion or those precious intervals while he had held her in his arms before they slept. But that was too much to hope for, she supposed. After all, this was a marriage of necessity, not a love match. Hal enjoyed her in bed, he desired her, he appeared to like her company—that was all far more than she had ever looked for in marriage. *I must not be greedy,* she thought.

'I will see you in the hall in an hour then?' Hal folded his own newspaper and got up. Julia agreed, managed a smile, and was promptly appealed to for support by Verity whose godfather had promised her a harp if she wanted to learn.

'Only I don't know if I do,' she said. 'It isn't like the piano—everyone has a piano and it can be fun as well as something one has to do at parties. The harp always seems such a performance.'

'It does make the player appear very graceful and feminine. Perhaps Lord Keddinton thinks it would be a useful accomplishment for the Season,' Julia suggested.

Verity wrinkled her nose. 'I suppose you mean it will help attract gentlemen. I don't want the sort of gentleman who would like me because I can play the harp. I want someone dashing, like Hal or Marcus. Or Gabriel,' she added, with a wary eye on her mother who pursed her lips slightly at the mention of her son-in-law's name.

'Some excitement is good,' Julia conceded, wondering what well-behaved, sheltered Verity would make of a dashing and dangerous suitor if she found one. He would probably scare her to death. 'But I do not think you can predict in advance the kind of man you will want to marry. I thought I wanted to find someone very ordinary and stolid.'

'And instead you fell in love with Hal.' Verity beamed at her, ignoring Julia's blushes and her mother's *tut* of disapproval.

And thank goodness Hal was not in the room to hear that, Julia told herself. She hoped he believed she had gone to the battlefield out of friendship, not because her deeper feelings were engaged. If he thought that, he might easily think she had compromised herself deliberately. She was not certain which was worse: that he might think she had set out to entrap him as a husband, or that he guess she loved him and he, not returning that sentiment, pitied her.

'I am sure Verity will find someone entirely suitable,' Lady Narborough pronounced, rising gracefully from her place. 'Unlike dear Honoria, one can always rely upon Verity to do the right thing.'

'That is a most provocative bonnet,' Hal observed when Julia came down to the hall for their drive. 'There is the smallest area of tender skin just between the ribbon and your ear that makes me want to nibble.'

'Ssh!' Julia cast a hunted look round for footmen. 'Oh thank goodness you are leaving your tiger behind,' she added as the lad let go the horses' heads and Hal sent them off towards Piccadilly at a smart trot. 'If you are going to say such shocking things I most certainly do not want an audience.'

'Neither do I,' he admitted. 'But that was not the main reason I wanted to be alone. Green Park or Hyde Park?'

'Green,' Julia decided. 'So much quieter.' She felt slightly apprehensive, his tone was so serious all of a sudden. 'What is it you want to talk about?'

'Hebden. Or Beshaley, to give him his Romany name.' Hal negotiated the gates and guided the horses away from the reservoir with the strolling pedestrians enjoying the summer morning sun on its banks. 'I realize you were only trying to provoke me last night, but I need you to be careful with that man, Julia.'

'If he has done all these things, why not have him arrested?' she asked. 'Or call him out.'

'If Marcus or I called him out he would avoid the challenge.' Hal reined the pair into a walk. 'He has no concept of honour. He is not a gentleman, even though he was brought up as one as a child—until his father was murdered and the family threw him out. Now he has the talents and the instincts of a gutter rat.'

He drove in silence for a few moments. 'And the things he has done are not for public consumption; they affect the honour of wives and sisters, young women like Mildenhall's new wife who is Hebden's own half-sister. Or they cannot be proved against him—the attempt to give my father heart attacks, for example. He's as slippery as a snake and as elusive as smoke, damn him.'

'It all goes back to that murder,' Julia mused. 'It seems strange to me: the man was hanged, so why does this still continue?'

'Unless he was innocent,' Hal said, reluctantly.

'Who is the obvious suspect if—Wardale was it not?—was innocent?'

'My father.' Hal sounded grim.

'They suspected no-one else was involved?' He shook his head. 'But the man who paid the trooper to try and kill you was not Hebden, yet there was that silken rope, so we know there is someone else connected with this,' Julia said, trying to work through it logically.

'But why the devil would they get involved in Hebden's vendetta now if they are the real murderer?' The horses, finding the reins slack on their necks, stopped. Hal did not appear to notice.

'Guilt?' Julia suggested. 'After all these years, preying on their minds until they become unhinged? Hebden's activities are making you all focus on that one event. Perhaps the guilty man thinks you and Marcus have discovered something and are getting close to unmasking him; that might explain an attempt at murder.'

Hal gathered his team and set them off walking again. 'Well, we haven't. In truth, we never questioned Wardale's guilt, because to do so would have been to believe our father sent an innocent man to the gallows. He had no doubts then that his friend was guilty. After all, he came upon him, the knife in his hands, kneeling over Hebden as he lay dying on our terrace. And we have no proof now, just supposition.'

'Was it in Hertfordshire?'

'No, here at our London house. And Wardale was having an affair with Hebden's wife, to make things worse. My father strongly disapproved.'

'Wardale made no counter-accusation?'

The horses broke into a trot, as though Hal had given them a signal. He reined them back. 'He wrote a last letter to his wife protesting his innocence and voicing his suspicions of my father. Nell showed it to Marcus and he told me of it.'

'Oh dear.' Julia tucked her hand under Hal's elbow, feeling the need to offer some comfort. 'But Nell cannot believe Lord Narborough guilty. However much she loves Marcus, she could not be on terms of such affection with Lord Narborough if she believed he had killed her own father.'

She thought some more as the horses took them into the shade of the elms. 'Let us assume Wardale was innocent, and accept, of course, that your father is too—for, if nothing else, your own father would not plot to kill you.' Beside her, Hal stiffened. That friction again. 'That means we are looking for a very clever man who was in the right place at the right time to kill a man he knew was a threat to him.'

'We?' Hal queried.

'I am your wife now.' She leaned against his shoulder, thinking happily of last night. 'And I am not going to sit around in ignorance expecting to be protected.'

Hal squeezed his arm against his side, trapping her hand more firmly. 'Then do not treat Hebden lightly.'

'We know he cannot have been the original murderer. Does Lord Narborough not suspect who it might have been?'

'They operated in isolated groups for security. The three of them were trying to trace one French spy, to read his coded messages. They reported to a minister now dead. Even Veryan has not been able to trace any likely contacts or points of weakness, and he has better access than anyone to the files.'

'Veryan?' she queried. 'Lord Keddinton, Verity's godfather?'

'Yes. He was a junior secretary at the time, so he knew nothing of it then. But last year, when Hebden began his campaign, he looked for clues, even set his new assistant on it. Nothing.' He frowned. 'And the young man met with a fatal accident shortly after he began the task. At the time it just seemed to be a random tragedy. Now, I wonder.'

'Hebden is an intelligent man,' Julia observed. 'Amoral, dangerous and vengeful—but also clever. If he believed your father and Wardale innocent, then he would be a powerful ally.'

'No!' Hal said, reining in and turning on the seat to face her. He jammed the whip in its holder and took her chin in his free hand. 'No, no and no, Julia. Marcus is right: we avoid that man like the plague. He can never be anything but a threat. I don't know what he does to women—you all seem mesmerised by him.'

'No, you wouldn't understand,' she agreed. 'You are too close to see it. And you are a man. But he is very like you.'

Chapter Twenty-One

'*What?*' Hal's furious bellow had his leader rearing, sending the curricle slewing sideways across the drive. It took a moment to settle the animal. Julia kept quiet, clutched the side rail and concluded that frank speaking was not always ideal in marriage.

'You are comparing me to that bastard?' Hal finally demanded. 'Are you all about in your head?'

'Not in your morals or your honour, of course not,' she said, half fascinated, half wary of the storm clouds in his eyes. 'But you wonder why he is attractive to women. You are both very beautiful, very male, very fit young men with indecent amounts of charm.' Hal snorted. Julia noted the flush on his cheekbones and concluded that he was rather flattered by the description.

'He uses all that, quite deliberately,' she said, thinking about Hebden, how he had looked at her, how he had used his voice and his body. 'Looking back, he was as calculating as an actor. He knows perfectly well how attractive he is and he wields his personal attributes like another weapon, with calculation. Heaven help the woman he unleashes that on without any artifice and in all sincerity.' Hal glowered.

'You, on the other hand, are a gentleman. All that arrogance and self-confidence is quite natural, quite unconscious.' The glower became a scowl. 'The charm is used with good manners and restraint—which makes it just as lethal for poor, unsuspecting females. We are apt to believe in it, you see.'

'Apt to believe I am a flirt and a rake, you mean,' he said harshly.

'Well, of course. Hal, I might not be very experienced, but I am female! And I cannot imagine anyone *without* your charm and address—and looks—being much of a success as a rake.

'And I cannot pretend I do not enjoy having a husband who is—' she felt the blush but carried on anyway '—experienced and attractive.' He smiled at her, but she could see he was troubled. 'Hal—what is it? Why are you and your father so constrained with each other? I see him and Marcus talking together, easy with each other. You and your father are always so polite, so distant. And why do you say things that make me think that you are not always happy to be the rake you say you are?'

For a long moment she thought he would not answer her or would pretend he did not understand. 'I'm the second son, of course. And I was always the wild one. Marcus is serious. He will make an excellent earl one day, take his seat in the House, do all the right things. He even managed to lose his virginity in the correct manner   discreetly at the age of seventeen in a fashionable bordello that he had carefully researched beforehand.

'I, on the other hand just found girls—and sex—almost too good to be true. I was not the most attentive scholar at the best of times, if the subject was not military history or mathematics, so I'd give our tutor the slip and be off, exploring this much more interesting subject. I'd get beaten when I got back, but that seemed a fair exchange for kisses and exploratory fumbles in haystacks.'

The horses were ambling now, the disciplined hand they were used to slack on the reins. Julia kept quiet and let him talk. 'And then, of course, the inevitable happened and I thought I had fallen in love. The trouble was, she was not some willing milkmaid who had spent a few years being tumbled by rustic swains and knew what she was about. This was the squire's daughter.'

'How old were you?'

'She was seventeen. I was fifteen. Looking back I'm not sure who seduced who, but there we were one summer's afternoon in the long grass of a woodland glade—' Julia gasped. 'Quite. Just like the glade where you and I…met. I was clumsy, but enthusiastic. I have no doubt we were making a great deal of noise. And then a riding crop landed hard across my adolescent buttocks and there we were surrounded by my father, her father and his head gamekeeper.'

Hal collected his team and drove in silence for a few minutes. 'They arrived in the nick of time or I'd have found myself a very young bridegroom, but you can imagine, perhaps, the impact of it all, being hauled off a sobbing girl while three large men yell at you that you are a *whoreson, rakehell, good for nothing young goat.* My father was deeply disappointed in me: I was turning out even worse than he expected. He has a strong moralistic streak and my behaviour deeply offended and distressed him, I can see that now.

'I could have reformed, been penitent, returned to my books and forswore women. Instead, I set out to prove him right, and I also set out to make sure that no woman ever had cause to complain of my performance in bed.'

Julia digested this, swallowed several forthright comments

on the behaviour of her father in law, and said, 'But you like women, don't you? Not just the sex. That's why you flirt.'

'True.' There was a hint of a smile at the corners of his mouth now.

'Are you really worried about reforming for me? I wish you would not: I like you as you are.'

'Loose women as well?' he asked, eyebrows lifting.

'I hope not, if I am honest,' she said. 'But I would be hypocritical if I objected: you married me to save me from being compromised. It is not as though you promised me a love match.'

'No, I didn't, did I?' he said slowly. 'But I promised you fidelity at the altar. I never meant to marry, I never expected to find a woman who would accept me as I am. There will be no other women, Julia. Only you.'

'Good,' she murmured, resting her head against his shoulder for a moment. 'I am glad.'

They did not speak after that, driving in what seemed to Julia to be a companionable silence around the park and back to the house. Not a love match, but no other women either. If Hal said that, then she trusted him. And, of course, it was best to harbour no foolish fantasies about his feelings for her. She had always known that love was too much to hope for in marriage.

'I'm thinking of going to Risinghall,' Hal remarked at breakfast two days later. Julia looked up from her egg, wondering why he had not mentioned his Buckinghamshire estate earlier. 'It occurred to me while I was shaving,' he explained, smiling at her. 'The weather is holding, everything here is quiet. It is about time you saw your new home.'

And perhaps as we drive down, we can discuss what he expects me to do, she thought. *Live in the country while he is posted to goodness knows where? America probably.* She dug the point of her spoon into her boiled egg, the certainty stealing over her that she would not be happy to live like that. Other officers' wives followed their husbands, she knew. It could not be harder than that hovel in Mont St Jean had been. But would Hal allow it?

'Not until Monday, I trust,' his mother said, cutting across her thoughts. 'I am sure Julia will not wish to travel on a Sunday.'

'True, Mama. We will do that then, the day after tomorrow, if it will suit you, Julia?' He drained his coffee and stood up.

'Yes, of course, if that is convenient for Lady Narborough. Hal, might I have a word before you go out?' She was not going to wait, she decided. They would have this out now.

'Of course. I will be in the library when you are ready.'

She went to find him twenty minutes later, feeling rather less like a new bride who had woken that morning to her husband's caresses and more like a candidate for a housekeeper's position.

'Hal, what are your intentions when your wounds are completely healed?' she asked without preliminaries, as she sat down on the opposite side of the library desk.

'To go to Horse Guards and ask about my next posting.' He put down the pen he was holding. 'I thought a week or so in Buckinghamshire should see me fit. You will like it down there: it is peaceful and very beautiful. One of these days, when I sell out, I think I will start breeding horses there. You can come up to London with me when I return, if you like, or stay.'

'And live here, if I come back?'

'We can find our own town house if you wish,' he offered. 'I expect you would like to be close to mother and father and to the Stanegates' house.'

'I meant, you would not want me to come with you, wherever you are posted?'

'No!' The idea had never occurred to him, she realized with a sinking heart. 'For Heaven's sake, Julia, wasn't your last experience of military life enough?'

'I would rather know what was happening, share things, see things, than stay here out of touch.' *Out of your life.* 'I would not get in the way or interfere, I promise.'

'I am not worried about you interfering, I am worried about your safety. And your comfort,' he added.

'Many officers' wives followed their husband in the Peninsula, I know,' she retorted. 'If you teach me to ride, I will be able to get out of danger, won't I? And as for comfort, I do not expect pampering. I expect to do my duty as your wife and that, I believe, means being with you.'

'Your duty,' he said flatly. 'I see.'

What could she say? That she loved him and could not bear to be parted from him? And then what would he say to cover his dismay at discovering that he had to bear the burden of her emotional attachment as well as his responsibility for her welfare?

'No,' he repeated. 'I am sorry, Julia, but that is final.'

I will not argue, not now, she told herself, closing her lips on all the arguments. *He can change his mind—he married me when he was determined not to. I just have to find the right approach and the right moment.*

'I understand,' she said, attempting wifely meekness. Hal narrowed his eyes at her but did not pursue it. 'I will go and organise an early departure for Monday, shall I?'

'Yes,' he agreed. 'That would be best. I will see you at dinner.' And he went out without dropping the passing kiss on her cheek that had become his custom.

'That was an excellent sermon,' Lady Narborough remarked, leading her party out of the precincts of St James's

Palace and onto the gravelled walk bordering Green Park. 'One can never be certain, with the Chapel Royal, if one will be honoured with the Royal dukes and their habit of talking throughout the service.'

Julia, on Hal's arm, rather thought she would have liked to see one of the corpulent and blunt-spoken brothers of the Regent, but deemed it tactful not to say so.

Marcus was escorting his mother, while Verity walked with her father in front. 'Are you sure Father will be all right walking?' he murmured to his mother. 'He could have gone with Nell in the barouche. I can still go back to St James's for a cab.'

'I think the fresh air will do him good.' Lady Narborough studied her husband's erect back. 'His colour is better and he has his stick.'

As she spoke, Lord Narborough flourished it in greeting and a group that had been walking across the grass towards them waved back.

'The Veryans,' Hal explained. 'Viscount Keddinton is an old friend—a junior colleague of my father's when…when there was the trouble, and he is Verity's godfather. I mentioned him the other day.'

'I remember. He wants to give Verity a harp.' Julia nodded. 'Those are his daughters, I have seen them with Verity.'

'And Alexander, his son. He's up at Oxford, a don of sorts, I believe. Mama thinks he would do for Verity.'

'Really?' Julia studied the young man as he approached. His father was tall, slim and dryly elegant and looked intimidating intelligent. The son was a blurred copy: shorter, plumper, less perfectly tailored, but his pale eyes were as sharp and assessing as his father's. He certainly did not look like the dashing hero of Verity's innocent daydreams.

There was a flurry of introductions. The Misses Veryan

talked to Verity about new gowns and ignored Julia. Mr Alexander Veryan positioned himself where he could look at Verity and made rather laboured conversation with Lord and Lady Narborough, and Lord Keddinton came to shake hands with Julia.

He had a certain astringent charm, Julia decided, and he would probably be excellent company provided one said nothing foolish and did not allow oneself to be intimidated by him. 'What a very pretty rose,' she remarked, seeing his buttonhole. The slim white bud had petals edged with green.

'Unusual, certainly. Allow me, Mrs Carlow.' He plucked it from his coat and handed it to Julia.

'Why, thank you, my lord.' Julia twirled it under her nose, inhaling the sweet apple scent of the rose and the tang of the herb backing it. 'Rosemary, I would never have thought of that. It goes so well.' She tucked it into the top button hole of her pelisse as the three of them walked to join the others.

'Very good to see you out and about, sir,' she heard Alexander Veryan saying in his carrying, lecturer's voice. 'Nothing like making an appearance to put a stop to all those rumours.'

'What rumours?' Lord Narborough said. Hal swore viciously under his breath and took an urgent stride forward.

'Why, about that murder and the hanging all those years ago,' Alexander went on, apparently unaware of both Carlow sons bearing down on him and of Lady Narborough's white face. 'No-one who knows you takes any notice, naturally. Still, nasty to have talk about French spies, just now. Although *I* do not consider it the slightest bit suspicious that you did nothing at the time—why should you have if the man was guilty?'

'Alexander!' Lord Keddinton's voice cut through his son's chatter. 'Damn it, do not repeat that vicious garbage.'

'I just thought I'd congratulate Lord Narborough on facing it down—oh, I say, sir! Are you all right?'

Marcus and Hal reached their father as he toppled, his left fist clenched over his heart, his lips blue. Lady Narborough swayed and Lord Keddinton caught her in his arms as Verity screamed.

Julia saw a barouche proceeding sedately along the nearest ride and ran, casting aside her prayer book and parasol. 'Stop! Please stop!'

When she returned with it, the owner, an elderly widow, urged her two stout footmen to help. Between them they got Lord and Lady Narborough into the carriage, Hal climbed up with the driver and Marcus swung up behind.

'As fast as you can, Roberts!' the widow called as Hal gave him the direction.

'Go on,' Julia urged, 'I'll bring Verity home.'

Verity, in tears, was being held firmly to Alexander Veryan's shoulder. His father looked grim.

'Will you please go and get a cab, Mr Veryan,' Julia said, disentangling her sobbing sister in law from his arms. 'We will follow.'

'Miss Carlow needs my support—'

'I feel, sir, that you have done more than enough for one day,' Julia snapped. 'Verity, take my handkerchief and blow your nose. Weeping is not going to help. Thank you, my lord.' Keddinton handed her her parasol and prayer book as his son hurried off towards the Palace.

Julia led Verity, hiccupping into the handkerchief, after him.

'My son was appallingly tactless,' Lord Keddinton remarked. 'I fear that the rather sheltered academic life he leads has not given him the Town bronze necessary to deal with such delicate matters.'

Julia merely nodded, intent on getting Verity into

the hackney carriage before anyone observed her tear-streaked face.

'Please tell Lady Narborough that I stand ready to do whatever is in my power to assist,' Keddinton continued as he stood by the open door. 'Alexander will, of course, write to apologise.'

'Oh, he meant no harm,' Verity said anxiously. 'But Julia, please can we go?'

'Yes, of course. Thank you, my lord.' Julia sat bolt upright away from the dingy squabs and held Verity's hand as the cab rattled up St James's Street. Despite the calm face she showed Verity, butterflies were fluttering in her stomach. Hal had told her about these rumours, but he had thought they circulated only amongst a small, discreet group. If the likes of Alexander Veryan was prattling about them, who else was?

And, anxious though she was for her father in law, Julia realized her greatest fear was for Hal. He would be furiously angry now, set on finding the truth at whatever personal cost. Someone had tried to kill him once—what would happen if Hal threatened them directly?

By the time they got to the house, Lord Narborough was in bed, the doctor had been summoned, and Hal and Marcus were in heated discussion in the library. Julia took Verity off to the drawing room and tried to keep her distracted until the doctor arrived.

Finally, Lady Narborough came in and sank onto the chaise. 'Well, my dears, that was a bad attack, I am afraid. The boys are with him, watching while he sleeps.'

Verity jumped up to pull the bell for tea, then sat by her mother, worrying her lower lip with her teeth. 'Poor Papa. I do not understand why Alexander upset him so. I am sure Alexander did not mean to say anything alarming.'

'It was about some business long ago that has always distressed your father, my dear.' Lady Narborough patted her daughter's hand. 'Would you call your maid and walk round to Bruton Street to let dear Nell know what has happened. She will be worried that Stanegate has not returned home and sending a note may alarm her. Whatever you do, Verity, make sure she stays at home. She must rest, in her condition.'

'Yes, of course, Mama.' Obviously happy to be able to do something, Verity hurried out.

'That wretched, wretched man,' Lady Narborough said vehemently, the minute the door closed behind her daughter.

'Mr Veryan? He was certainly most tactless,' Julia agreed.

'No, dear Alexander is simply gauche. An admirable young man, very steady and reliable, but not the sophisticate his father is. He will do excellently for Verity.' Fortunately Julia managed to control her expression: it seemed she was the only one who felt Alexander Veryan was completely unsuitable for her sister in law. But that was hardly the problem just now.

'Who then, ma'am, is rousing your ire?' She poured tea and placed a cup beside her mother in law.

'Wardale,' Lady Narborough almost spat the name.

'Nell's father, Lord Leybourne? The man who was hanged for the murder?'

'Oh, I do my best to keep my lips closed for dear Nell's sake, and I know she cannot believe other than that he was innocent—he was her father after all and she is loyal. But he was fornicating with Hebden's wife, he wrote letters as good as accusing George of the most dreadful things—and he would not admit his own guilt! So poor George had the added burden of having to support the truth in the face of those denials. It broke his health, almost broke his spirit.' Lady Narborough stirred cream into her tea as though stabbing the long-dead man.

'I know I did right to keep that letter from him,' she murmured. 'Goodness knows what poison Will Wardale would have spread with those final words.'

'A last letter?' Julia put her own cup down with a rattle. 'From Nell's father? And you did not read it, ma'am?'

'Read it? I did not so much as open it.'

'So it was destroyed,' Julia sat back with a sigh. It could have held a clue, something that Hal might interpret. But it was too late now.

'Destroyed it? Oh no. I did not feel I should do that.'

Julia sat up again, trying to speak calmly. 'So what happened to it?'

'Why, it is in my file of old letters.' Lady Narborough appeared to focus on her properly at last. 'You think it might be helpful?'

'Perhaps, ma'am. If you could give it to Hal and Marcus to read—'

'No.' The older woman got up. 'There might be something it to distress them and *I* certainly do not want to read it. You must.' She swept out leaving Julia staring after her.

'Me?' she said faintly into the empty room.

Chapter Twenty-Two

'There.' Lady Narborough thrust a sealed letter into Julia's hands. 'Read it and see.'

The paper was of poor quality, yellowing and dirty. The seal was just a brittle lump of candle wax that splintered under Julia's fingers. She pressed it open and read.

~~Carl~~ *George,*

They'll be coming for me soon, so this is the end. I haven't slept all night, racking my brains—as though the months in here have not given me time enough for that.

And it seems to me that perhaps I was wrong about you. If I was not, you'll read this and laugh at the poor gullible fool that I am. All I know for certain is that I did not kill Kit, that I am not a spy. And I think I know you—we've been friends long enough, damn it—to finally accept you think you are doing what is right, the honourable thing, you stubborn principled prig. God, I've been angry with you George, but I am

*going to die in an hour, I can't go to my death angry
at my oldest friend.*

*Because you genuinely believe I'm guilty, don't you,
George? And, if I am guilty, your sense of honour tells
you that justice must take its course. I'm an adulterer,
I admit that, but nothing else, I swear to you on my
children's souls.*

*So listen, George, and do this for me and for
Catherine and the children. Look after them—I've
written the address where they will go at the foot of
this—show it to Catherine, she'll take your help then.
And find who killed Kit, who the spy is—because Kit
must have been close, the clever devil. Too close to
live.*

*That drunk of a parson will be here soon to pray over
me, so goodbye, George. I hope I am right about you,
finally.*
Will.

Julia stared at the desperate scrawl in the faded brown
ink. They could not show this to Lord Narborough, it would
kill him, and she must prevent the other woman reading it
and realizing she had snatched away help from the surviving
Wardales.

'What does it say?' her mother in law asked, her voice
fearful. She did not hold out her hand for it.

'That he is innocent,' Julia said, swallowing hard against
the tears that were blocking her throat. This was Nell's father's
last testament. The stench of the prison, the fear soaked into
the stones of the cell, seemed to ooze out of the paper, but so
did the spirit of the man who had written those words. She
believed him.

'May I give this to Hal?' she asked when she had her voice
under control again.

'Yes, if you think it will help.' Lady Narborough drank the last of her cold tea and got to her feet. 'I will go up to George again, you talk to Hal and Marcus, my dear; I will send them down. I do not care what you do, just do not let George see that letter.'

Julia waited at the bottom of the stairs for the men. 'How is he?'

'Worse than I have ever seen him,' Marcus said, running both hands over his face then raking them through his hair in weary resignation. 'The doctor thinks he will pull through, but he will be an invalid for a long time. Perhaps for ever.'

'What is that?' Hal nodded at the grubby paper in Julia's hand.

'Come into the drawing room and have some tea, and I will tell you.'

When they had both read the document, she thought they were as shaken as she was. More, no doubt, for they had lived with this story almost all their lives.

'Hell's teeth,' Hal said at last, without apology.

'Quite.' Marcus stared at the letter. 'Do you believe him?'

'Yes,' Julia and Hal said together.

'Why should he lie, then of all times?' Hal asked. 'The man would have had to have been twisted beyond belief to have written that minutes before he died if it were not true. My God, if father sees it—'

'He must not,' Marcus said. 'You realize what this means, don't you? There is a murderer and a spy to find.'

'You have a potential ally,' Julia ventured. 'Stephen Hebden.'

'What! That bastard? He is no-one's ally, he's a dangerous vengeful maniac.'

'He wants vengeance on the man who killed his father,' Julia said patiently. 'He thought it was Nell's father, so he attacked his family. He felt betrayed by his own father's legitimate family, so he attacked them. He thought your father betrayed his by his inaction, so he hates all of you. If he hears the rumours, he might suspect your father of the murder or of being a spy.

'Yes, the man is dangerous,' she agreed, leaning forward to urge her words on them. 'But he also acts outside the law with amazing ease, and he is unscrupulous and obsessive. He can do things you never could—never would. If you can convince him with this letter that both Wardale and your father are innocent, then you will have him on your side. And never forget you have a present-day attempted murder to solve.'

She saw Hal look at his brother. 'I did suggest '

'No.' Marcus slammed his fist down on the table by his side, making the fragile piece rock. 'You know what he did to Nell, what he threatened. I will not go near him unless it is to put a bullet in him—she is your sister now, you swear to me you will never go to him for help.'

'I swear,' Hal said, reaching to clasp his brother's hand.

Julia's heart sank. She could understand, she could sympathise, but she was certain in her heart that they were wrong. Their half-Romany nemesis could be a powerful weapon on their side.

The letter had fluttered to the floor when Marcus thumped the table. Julia picked it up and slipped it into her pocket. *She* had promised nothing.

It was a long Sunday. They all sat around, not knowing what to do to help, yet feeling it was wrong not to be there. Julia woke the next morning to find Hal's side of the bed unrumpled and the bed in his dressing room untouched. As she was looking at it he came in, yawning.

'I sent Mother to bed at two,' he explained. 'And packed

Marcus off back to Nell at the same time.' Julia put an arm around his waist, tugging him towards the bedroom.

'Come and undress, get into bed,' she urged. 'How is your father now?'

'Better, a little. Mama is with him again.' Hal tossed his coat aside, he seemed to have discarded his neck cloth long since. Julia began to unbutton his shirt when he made no effort to do it himself. 'His lips aren't so blue and he seems to be sleeping.'

'And so should you,' Julia said, attacking his breeches fastenings. 'Come on, help me. And then I will get dressed and see if your mama needs me.'

By luncheon, Hal was up again and Marcus had returned with Nell. Between them, they devised a rota for sitting with the patient; Julia insisted on taking the hours between dinner and midnight. Which left her, she calculated, enough time to locate Stephan Hebden.

As everyone dispersed after the meal, she found the butler alone. 'Wellow, whereabouts does Viscount Mildenhall live?'

'Hanover Square, ma'am.'

'Thank you. I wish to visit Lady Mildenhall. Is one of the footmen free?' Julia had read enough Gothic novels where the intrepid heroine plunges off into danger without so much as a note left behind her not to take precautions—like one of the Carlows' strapping footmen.

'Certainly, ma'am. Richards is available. Do you require a carriage?'

'The small town coach, if you please. I will be down in fifteen minutes.'

Julia had not become accustomed to the luxury of being able to take a carriage for distances she could easily walk, but she had no idea where she might locate Hebden, and she did not want to have to rely upon hackney carriages. Always assuming his half-sister was at home and would receive her: without her help, Julia would be at a standstill.

But she was in luck. Not only was Lady Mildenhall at home, but positively eager to receive a visit. Julia liked her on sight, with her flyaway brown hair and her candid grey eyes. She looked, Julia thought, nothing like her half-Romany brother.

She waved Julia to a chair and sank back into her own with a grimace. 'Oh my, another four months still to go,' she lamented, resting a hand on the swell of her very pregnant belly. Julia did some quick mental arithmetic and hid her smile behind an expression of sympathy. The Mildenhalls had been married just five months: she wondered if she would begin increasing so soon and what Hal's feelings would be if she did.

'So, you are Hal's new wife, Julia! He was at my wedding and my step-brother was teasing him about settling down— and here you are, married.'

'Indeed, Lady Mildenhall. That would be Captain Bredon? I met him in Brussels and then, after the battle, he helped me find Hal. I think that saved Hal's life.'

'You must call me Midge,' Lady Mildenhall said with a friendly impetuousness that Julia guessed was habitual. 'I have been dying to meet you. I am so glad you saw Rick. Tell me, truthfully, was he badly hurt? He writes that he had just a scratch, and he is still over there and *seems* to be all right—but one can never tell with him.'

'Rather more than a scratch,' Julia admitted. 'But nothing worse than weariness, cuts and bruises. He was walking and had the use of all his limbs when I saw him, I promise you.'

'That is a relief.' She blinked hard for a moment, then

smiled. Julia suspected that Midge was rarely cast down for long. 'It is good of you to come and visit.'

'I am afraid I should have waited and called with my mother in law, or Lady Stanegate,' Julia admitted. 'But I need your help, you see.'

'Oh.' The ready smile faded. 'What has Stephen done now?'

'Nothing,' Julia hastened to assure her. She was not going to tell tales of teasing encounters in book shops or the mystery of the attack on Hal. 'I think I have found something that will convince him to halt his campaign of vengeance.'

'Oh, thank goodness.' Midge closed her eyes for a moment. 'He is not the evil man they make him out to be, you know. He has had such cruelty in his life.' She bit her lip as though to stop herself pouring out the entire story, then smiled, a lopsided smile that suddenly made Julia see a fleeting similarity to Stephen. 'What can I do?'

'Help me find him. There is a letter I must show him. Is he in London?'

'Yes. He has a house in Bloomsbury Square. Here.' She took some paper from the table beside her, scribbled a few words. 'There's the number—and a note to his man to admit you—the servants defend the house like a fortress.'

I'm not surprised, Julia thought grimly. Stephen Hebden made enemies, it seemed, as easily as breathing. 'Thank you, I do so hope this will put an end to this awful feud.' She got to her feet.

'But won't you wait, take tea? Monty will be home at any moment, I do so want him to meet Hal's wife.'

'I will come back,' Julia promised, taking the note and gathering up her things. 'But I must hurry now.'

The streets were crowded, and Julia was soon lost. Bloomsbury Square must be somewhere close to the British Museum, she supposed, although she had not visited this temple to learning. Hal had expressed himself forcibly on the subject of fusty holes when asked to accompany her.

But she could not think about Hal now; she must focus on convincing Stephen Hebden that his campaign of vengeance had missed its target. As the carriage drew up, Julia looked out at a terrace of pretty town houses with ornate iron balconies running right along at first-floor level. It seemed an improbable home for a half-Romany adventurer.

She paused on the edge of the pavement, her hand still resting on the footman's arm. The clock of some nearby church struck three. 'Richards, if I am not out by the time that clock strikes four you must go immediately to find Major Carlow, or, failing him, Lord Stanegate. Tell them where I am. And take no notice if anyone from the house comes out and says I will be longer. Do you understand?'

'Ma'am.' The footman looked distinctly unhappy. 'Should you be going in there? The Major won't like it, not if it's somewhere that isn't safe, he won't.'

'One of Lady Mildenhall's relatives lives here,' Julia said lightly. 'I am probably being over-cautious, but as I have never called on them before…'

'Very well, ma'am.' Still looking less than happy, he mounted the step and banged the knocker.

The door opened to reveal an impassive Indian in a green coat. Trust Hebden not to have a conventional butler like everyone else. 'Good afternoon, I am here to see Mr Hebden,' Julia said brightly, holding out her card.

'You have the wrong address, *Mem Sahib*.' The man did not glance at the card.

'Mr Beshaley then.'

'I am sorry, *Mem Sahib*.' The door began to close.

Julia stuck her foot out, jarring her toe. 'I have a note from Lady Mildenhall.' She flourished it under his nose—which someone appeared to have recently broken—while rubbing the wounded toe on the back of the other calf.

Without a word of apology, the man stepped back, holding the door. It shut behind her the moment she was through.

'Stephen *Sahib* is in his workshop.' The Indian took her card, turned his back and moved silently across the hall. Julia followed, through the green baize door, down three stone steps and into the kitchen. The man kept going, pushed open a door at the far end of the kitchen and announced, 'Carlow *Mem Sahib*, from Imo *Mem Sahib*.'

Julia stepped past him into what must once have been a long washhouse. Now it looked like the workshop of an eccentric alchemist. Shelves and cupboards lined the walls; strange tools hung from hooks; jars and boxes were stacked everywhere; a sword was propped against a vast safe in one corner. A bench, covered in stretched leather that had been caught up to make a trough at the front, ran under the barred windows and in the middle stood a small brazier, glowing red despite the warmth of the day.

As Julia stared, the man bending over it dropped something into a crucible and a cloud of evil-smelling vapour puffed up. She choked, fanning herself with her hand.

'My dear Julia!' Hebden strode out of the cloud of smoke, put an arm around her shoulders and guided her to a high stool by the part-open window.

'Let go.' She coughed and batted at him with her hands, but he laughed, stooped and kissed her right on her parted lips.

The shock took what little breath she had left. Pressed against the high back of the stool, Julia fought her instinctive response. She was on the verge of kissing him back, she realized, outraged. His mouth was firm and he tasted spicy. Something in the smoke, she thought hazily, then found the strength to raise her right knee sharply, even as she jerked her head back.

He dodged with a fencer's agility, laughing at her as he stepped out of range. 'I thought you had come to say *thank you* for my gift of Byron's verse,' he said, dark eyes soulful. 'I am wounded.'

'But not wounded enough,' she snapped. 'Listen, Mr Hebden or Beshaley or whatever your name is '

'I have so many.' He was still smiling. 'Call me Stephano. If you have not come for my lovemaking, then how may I be of service?'

'You can listen to the truth for once and stop these attacks on my family and their friends,' she said, ignoring his question. If she took exception to all his outrageous remarks, she would never get through this.

He spread his hands in a gesture inviting her to proceed, hooked a foot through another stool, and pulled it close so that when he sat his knees were within six inches of her own. 'I listen, beautiful Julia. And then we will go somewhere more…comfortable.'

Chapter Twenty-Three

Hal rode slowly up Whitehall, his uniform uncomfortable after weeks in civilian clothes, the rigid stock chafing under his chin. So, report back in a month and they would tell him their decision. The West Indies, India or an English garrison.

He realized he had no appetite for an English posting. What would it be? Endless drills—or subduing rioting factory workers? That was not why he had joined up. And India or the West Indies were a hell of a long way away. A long way from Julia.

He did not notice the tall grey stone buildings as he passed, or the busy traffic. Max knew where he was going and walked steadily on.

Hal's imagination was full of lush green Buckinghamshire meadows with soft-eyed brood mares nudging their spindly-legged foals into their first steps. And a small child laughing in a woman's arms. Julia's arms.

He could not take her with him as she asked: not to the heat and the disease. She was too precious to risk like that. And too precious to leave behind. But he had to choose. Somehow.

He was still deep in thought as he reached the house in Albemarle Street and dismounted. A shout and the clatter of hooves roused him.

'Carlow!'

'Monty?' His old comrade reined in the team of chestnuts pulling his high-perch phaeton. 'What's up?'

'Your wife,' Mildenhall said urgently. 'Is she home?'

'Of course she's home.' The front door opened. 'Wellow, where is Mrs Carlow?'

'She went to visit Lady Mildenhall at about two, Major. She took the small town coach and Richards. She has not yet returned.'

Hal pulled out his watch. 'And it is just past three. Not so long for a call, Monty.'

'But she left our house almost at once; she came to ask Midge for Hebden's address.'

'What?' Hal felt the blood drain from his face. 'And Midge gave it to her?'

'Yes. Apparently your wife told Midge that she had something to tell Hebden that would stop his campaign of vengeance.'

'Hell and damnation—the man is here, in town?'

'Yes, Bloomsbury Square.' Monty began to turn his team. 'North side.' He gave the number as Hal swung back into the saddle. 'Don't try the main street, there's a brewer's dray overturned at the bottom of Tottenham Court Road—chaos. I'll follow, fast as I can.'

Hal set his spurs to Max's sides and the big grey took off at the gallop towards Oxford Street. His sabre bumped his leg as he made the turn into Bond Street, and he checked the saddle holster. Yes, his pistols were there. He was going to need those.

Nell took the old, much-folded paper from her pocket and held it up. 'This is the last letter that William Wardale, Earl of Leybourne, wrote, minutes before he was hanged. If ever a man is going to tell the truth, surely it is on the verge of death.' The beautiful brown eyes watching her sharpened, lost their mocking, sensual smile. 'Listen, he swears on his children's souls that he is innocent.' She read that impassioned statement, then watched as the colour leached from under Stephen Hebden's golden skin. His eyes widened.

'I believe him—so do Hal and Marcus. Wardale was not your father's killer, Stephano, and neither was—' Julia broke off as he swayed, his hands coming up to clutch at his temples. Staring into his wide eyes, she saw the pupils contract to pinpricks. 'What is it? You are ill, let me call for help.' She began to scramble down from the stool, bumping into his legs as she did so.

'He swore on his children's souls. He swore as he was about to die?' Stephano seized her by the forearms so she was trapped between his thighs. 'And now they prosper, they thrive. They are happy, all of them.' He was talking to himself, she realized, not to her.

'Let me go, Stephano, I do not understand.'

'The curse,' he muttered. '*The children will pay for the sins of their fathers.* He did not sin. *He* did not.'

'You are frightening me, and you are not well.' Julia tried to free a hand. 'Let me get help.'

'No.' He was on his feet now, pulling her tight against him, her face pressed to his shirt, his own cheek against her hair. He needed someone—something—to hold onto, she realized. She doubted he even realized who he was holding.

Distantly there was a crash, then shouting. 'Stephano,' she said softly. 'Stephano!' He winced as though she had struck him. The workshop door banged open.

'Julia!'

The man holding her jerked round, one hand still circling her arm.

'Hal!' He was in uniform, she realised. His sabre was in his hand and murder in his eyes. 'Hal, he has not hurt me. He isn't well.'

'He'll be dead in a minute, that will cure him,' her husband said, slamming the door. He spun a chair towards him and jammed it under the handle. 'What has he done to you?'

'*Nothing*. Hal, I came to tell him about the letter because you could not, that is all. And then he became ill. I was supporting him.'

Hebden pushed her back a little. His eyes were focused again, although the planes of his face were sharp and drawn as though he was in pain. 'So sweet, your wife's mouth, Carlow, so generous her kisses.'

'You fool,' she snapped at him. 'Do you want him to kill you?'

'He can try.' And suddenly there was a knife in his hand, a slim, wicked, curving blade.

Hal edged forward, his own weapon up, *en garde*. He had pushed his pistol into his uniform sash and his eyes were locked with Stephano's as the men faced each other, the glitter of lethal metal stained red by the light from the glowing brazier. Julia backed away, her skirts swinging, and something fluttered, the brazier flared up, and Stephano lunged.

As the sabre deflected the knife with a scream of steel on steel, she saw what had burned—the letter, her evidence. Gone. The writing stood out clearly on the blackened paper for a moment *On my children's souls…* Then Hal lunged again and the wisp of ash whirled and fell apart.

There was shouting from the kitchen, banging on the door. Distracted, Julia glanced away. When she looked again, Stephano had a sword in one hand, the knife in the other. Whatever had made him so ill before had vanished and he was fighting with a vicious grace.

They seemed evenly matched. Julia thought of Hal's

wounds, barely healed, and prayed as the two men fought up and down the crowded workshop, sending jars crashing, stumbling against packing cases as they went. At the door the thudding got louder. And then another voice, one she did not recognize, was out there, barking orders. Suddenly, it all went quiet and she could hear the duellists' breaths rasping as they sweated, lunged and parried in the centre of the room.

Stephano reached out with his left hand, seized one of the tall stools and swung it. Hal jumped back; it hit the brazier, and the whole thing toppled, spilling burning coals out across the floor at Julia's feet. The kitchen door burst open bringing with it a rush of air. A sheet of flame shot up in front of her and she staggered back, unable to see a way through it.

'Julia!' Hal came through the flames, sabre in hand, his face smoke-blackened, his teeth bared. Like Lucifer from hell, she thought wildly. *My fallen angel.* He took hold of the bench, heaved it across the fire, picked her up and took her across the makeshift bridge to safety.

'Are you hurt?' he demanded, looking down into her face with fierce intensity.

'No, no Hal, I…' Her voice broke as she began to cough. The smoke swirled around them.

'Get your wife away,' the voice she had heard giving orders shouted. 'I'll help them put out the fire.'

'Let him burn,' Hal snarled back.

'He's my brother in law,' the other man retorted. *Mildenhall? So that is how Hal found me,* Julia thought, struggling to try and stand. Hal simply tossed her over his shoulder and went through the door, pistol in hand. Julia twisted her head to try and see. The kitchen was full of servants, the Indian grasping a curving knife. As Hal passed, they ran for the workshop where Midge's husband was yelling for water.

'Are you hurt?' Hal asked again as they emerged onto the street.

'No. Hal, put me down.' In reply he simply tossed her up in the air and she found herself perched on a saddle, her hands clutching wildly at a long grey mane. 'Max! Hal,' she protested as he swung up behind her, shifting her in his arms until she was sitting across his thighs. 'You cannot ride back through the street with me like this.'

'Watch me,' he said. 'Unless you want me to stop here and shake you until your teeth rattle?'

'You are angry with me?' she ventured, as Max made his way along Great Russell Street. With her face pressed against Hal's uniform jacket and its painful rows of braid and buttons, she could not see his expression. But she could smell the smoke and sweat on him and feel his heart thudding against her cheek as the rate slowed back to normal. They were both safe. And behind them, with so many helpers, the fire would be out soon. She was not, thank God, responsible for Midge losing her half-brother.

'Livid,' Hal said tersely, then did not speak again. Julia closed her eyes, clung on and found she really did not care what sight they presented as the big grey charger trotted through the crowded streets, its smoke-stained rider clasping her safe in his arms.

'Max is outside,' Hal said to Wellow as he strode into the hall at Albemarle Street, Julia in his arms. 'Have a groom take him round to the mews and send hot water up. And Wellow—'

'Yes, Major?' the butler said calmly.

'There is no need to tell anyone that we have arrived home somewhat…dishevelled. I do not wish to be disturbed: have dinner sent up.'

'Certainly, sir.'

'Oh, and Wellow. Please send to my brother and ask him to come round and take over the night watch with my father.'

'There is no need, Major. The staff have expressed a desire to assist. Felling and Langham will take the first part of the night, Mrs Hoby and I, the second. His lordship is resting quietly, I foresee no cause to expect alarms in the night.'

'That is damned decent of you, Wellow.'

'A privilege, Major. I will organise the hot water now.'

Hal swept upstairs, kicked open the door and dumped Julia unceremoniously in the middle of her bed. 'Get undressed.'

'Why?' she demanded. He was still blazing with anger, his eyes vividly blue as he faced her, his hands clenched.

'Because when I have washed this soot off I am going to remind you who you are married to.'

'Like some Turkish sultan dragging an unwilling slave back to the harem?' She scrambled up until she was sitting, the better to glare at him as he started wrenching off his uniform.

'You are unwilling?' He paused, his fingers stilled on his sword belt.

'I—'

There were sounds from the dressing room. Hal swore under his breath and went into the room, banging the door behind him. Julia sat where she was, staring rather blankly at the sabre in its scabbard leaning against the dressing table.

Hal remerged, shirtless, his hair wet, scrubbing at his face with a towel. 'Now. Talk to me.'

'I went because you cannot,' she said, her hands knotted in the sheet as he stood there watching her. 'I went to convince him that Wardale was innocent, and he believes it. I want help to find out who tried to kill you. But you arrived before

I could talk to him about that, or your father, and the letter fell into the fire and is gone.

'He kissed me,' she said, talking doggedly on in the face of Hal's lack of response. 'He kissed me because he can no more help himself than a cat can stop teasing a mouse it has caught. He did not hurt me and he did not frighten me. I told Richards that if I had not come out in an hour, he was to go and fetch you.'

Hal turned his back and walked to the window. 'I thought he had taken you. That he would…harm you. And then, I thought the fire…that you…Julia, have you any idea the hell it is, loving someone and knowing they are in danger? Perhaps dead? And feeling so powerless. I love you so much, and I saw his hands on you, saw the fire—' He laughed, a short, harsh sound with no amusement in it.

For a moment, she hardly understood the words or their meaning. Then, when he stayed with his hands braced against the window frame, head bowed, she climbed off the bed and walked to him, laying her hands, and then her cheek, against his naked back.

'Yes, I know what it feels like,' she said, schooling her voice so it would not shake. 'I fell in love with a soldier and I saw him go to war. And then he did not come back and I thought he was dead. So I went to find him, and I watched over him, thinking he would die and that my love would not be enough to save him. Yes, it is hell, and I am sorry I put you through it.'

Under her palms, she felt the muscles tense, and then Hal turned, catching her by the shoulders so he could look down into her face. 'You love me? I thought…I knew you wanted to marry *someone* and you liked me, perhaps wanted me—a little. But I knew you should not marry a man like me, a man with my past, my reputation. I wanted you to stay innocent, to find someone worthy of you. I knew I should go and never see you again. And then you were compromised—'

Hal closed his eyes, a man confessing. He was unable, she realized, to believe this would be all right. 'I felt guilty. I had what I wanted, what I desired, although I did not realize then that I loved you. I have never been in love before,' he added ruefully, opening his eyes to smile at her. 'The one thing I wanted and should not have and yet I was forced by honour to take it.'

'I've loved you for so long. I realized at the Review,' Julia said, putting up her hands to frame his face, rubbing with her thumb at a last smudge of soot on one sharp cheekbone. 'And I love you now, with all my heart. And I like you very much, when you aren't cross with me. And I want you all the time, cross or not. And I cannot imagine what I have ever done to be worthy of a husband like you.'

Hal's mouth on hers was simply bliss, simply comfort and excitement and loving and friendship and relief, all together, all at once. She cried a little, wriggling close into his embrace and he must have felt the tears, for he lifted his head and touched them away with gentle fingers.

'Love me, Julia? Now?'

'Yes. Yes please. Bread and butter loving so I can feel the weight of you and look up into your eyes.'

He laughed and lifted her and laid her on the bed, smoothing away her clothes with the expertise that had once so shamed him. He shed the remains of his uniform and came to lie over her, and she curled her legs around his narrow hips and felt him press intimately close, wanting her. 'Yes,' Julia murmured, her fingers tight on his shoulders. 'Yes, now Hal.'

And he stroked smoothly into her as she sighed and arched up to take him, matching his rhythm, reading his eyes and listening to his voice as the words of love became gasps and he groaned and stroked higher and deeper into the yearning heat of her. The bliss began to ravel and build, and she read his in his face and in the tension of his body, and she matched him, urgent now until he went still, gasped for breath, surged one more time and she went with him, tumbling into the light.

Julia came to herself held tight in Hal's arms. She wriggled until she could sit and look at him sprawled in elegant, indecent abandon amidst the wreckage of the bedclothes.

He put up a hand and stroked it down the side of her breast, making her shiver. Then the thing she had not been wanting to think about came and dug its claws into her heart, and she felt the chill touch the warmth of her happiness. 'You were wearing your uniform when you came for me,' she said.

'Yes, I had been to Horse Guards.'

'You have a posting then.' *I will be brave about this.*

'They said if go back in a month they will tell me.'

'I see. We have a month together: that is more than I feared.'

'You will not insist on following the drum?'

Julia reached out and brushed the still-damp hair back from his forehead. 'No. It would worry you and distract you. You were right. I married a soldier, I must accept all that it means.'

'You will not have to, my love.' Hal caught the hand that was stroking his hair, pulled it to his mouth and kissed it. 'I am selling out. I will breed horses in Buckinghamshire and we will buy a Town house so we can be frivolous and sociable when it suits us—and you must tell me how many bedrooms we must look for.'

'For the children?' she asked. *Oh, my brave, wicked rake. You are going to make such a perfect father.* And he was not leaving her. He wanted to stay of his own free will.

'I had this daydream as I was riding down Whitehall,' Hal

said. 'Max was looking over his stable door at a brood mare with a long-legged foal at her side, and I was watching my wife and my child playing in the long, soft spring grass. And I thought, that was what it would be to be happy.'

'Oh.' Enchanted by the vision, Julia smiled down at him. 'A baby for next spring? Hal, there is no time to lose.'

'That is what I thought, my love,' he agreed, serious except for the wicked sparkle in his eyes as he pulled her down and kissed her. 'There is no time to lose—and all the time in the world for loving.'

* * * * *

Author's Note

Much was written about Brussels in the months leading up to Waterloo by those who were there. I have relied heavily on these original accounts to understand Julia's life in the city and what it was like both there, and on the battlefield after June eighteenth.

I have taken liberties with a few dates and facts: the picnic in the Fôret de Soignes did take place, but rather earlier. There were numerous horse races, but not one on the day Hal won. As far as I know, no Brussels church had a stained-glass window with the fall of Lucifer.

But the words of Wellington and Lord Uxbridge are as I report them, the Duke of Brunswick did drop the young Prince of Ligne, Madame Catalani did sing at the Opera during June 1815. I used Captain Mercer's memoirs extensively for the great cavalry review at Ninove.

Brussels has changed greatly since 1815, but the Parc is still there and families still picnic in the Fôret de Soignes. There are few traces now along the road to Mont St Jean of the brave men who marched along it, or relics of the terrible journey back to the city for those wounded. But the church in

Waterloo still faces the inn where Wellington had his head-quarters and the museum there preserves the table where he wrote his orders and many other relics of all the armies.

Julia nursed Hal in a hovel, just as Lady de Lancey did her husband of only a few weeks, but with a much happier result. Magdalene de Lancey's moving and tragic story is told by David Miller in *Lady de Lancey at Waterloo*. I also found his book *The Duchess of Richmond's Ball* very useful. Amongst the memoirs of those present I used Cavalié Mercer's *Journal of the Waterloo Campaign*; *The Days of Battle or Quatre Bras and Waterloo* by An Englishwoman; *The Capel Letters*; John Scott's *Paris Re-Visited in 1815 by way of Brussels and Waterloo* and *The Letters of Spencer Maden*.

Nick Foulkes's *Dancing Into Battle: a Social History of Waterloo* is a highly readable account that brings together a wealth of these original documents.

Harlequin Presents® is thrilled
to introduce the first installment of
an epic tale of passion and drama by
**USA TODAY Bestselling Author
Penny Jordan**!

*When buttoned-up Giselle first meets
the devastatingly handsome Saul Parenti,
the heat between them is explosive....*

"LET ME GET THIS STRAIGHT. Are you actually suggesting that I would stoop to that kind of game playing?"

Saul came out from behind his desk and walked toward her. Giselle could smell his hot male scent and it was making her dizzy, igniting a low, dull, pulsing ache that was taking over her whole body.

Giselle defended her suspicions. "You don't want me here."

"No," Saul agreed, "I don't."

And then he did what he had sworn he would not do, cursing himself beneath his breath as he reached for her, pulling her fiercely into his arms and kissing her with all the pent-up fury she had aroused in him from the moment he had first seen her.

Giselle certainly *wanted* to resist him. But the hand she raised to push him away developed a will of its own and was sliding along his bare arm beneath the sleeve of his shirt, and the body that should have been arching away from him was instead melting into him.

Beneath the pressure of his kiss he could feel and taste her gasp of undeniable response to him. He wanted to devour her, take her and drive them both until they were equally satiated—even whilst the anger within him that she should make him feel that way roared and burned its resentment of his need.

She was helpless, Giselle recognized, totally unable to withstand the storm lashing at her, able only to cling to the man who was the cause of it and pray that she would survive.

Somewhere else in the building a door banged. The sound exploded into the sensual tension that had enclosed them, driving them apart. Saul's chest was rising and falling as he fought for control; Giselle's whole body was trembling.

Without a word she turned and ran.

Find out what happens when Saul and Giselle succumb to their irresistible desire in

THE RELUCTANT SURRENDER

Available January 2011 from Harlequin Presents®

HPEXP0111

A Romance

FOR EVERY MOOD™

Spotlight on

— Classic —

Quintessential, modern love stories
that are romance at its finest.

See the next page
to enjoy a sneak peek from
the Harlequin Presents® series.

MARGARET WAY

Wealthy Australian, Secret Son

Rohan was Charlotte's shining white knight
until he disappeared—before she had
the chance to tell him she was pregnant.

But when Rohan returns years later as
a self-made millionaire, could the blond,
blue-eyed little boy and Charlotte's heart
keep him from leaving again?

Available January 2011

HRI 7704

Silhouette *Desire*

HAVE BABY,
NEED BILLIONAIRE

MAUREEN CHILD

Simon Bradley is accomplished, successful
and very proud. The fact that he has to
prove he's fit to be a father to his own child
is preposterous. Especially when he has to
prove it to Tula Barrons, one of the most
scatterbrained women he's ever met. But Simon
has a ruthless plan to win Tula over and when
passion overrules prudence one night, it opens
up the door to an affair that leaves them both
staggering. Will this billionaire bachelor learn
to love more than his fortune?

*Billionaires
and Babies*

*Available January
wherever books are sold.*

Always Powerful, Passionate and Provocative.

Love Inspired®

Bestselling author

JILLIAN HART

brings readers another heartwarming story
from

the
GRANGER
FAMILY
RANCH

To fulfill a sick boy's wish, rodeo star Tucker Granger surprises
little Owen in the hospital. And no one is more surprised than
single mother Sierra Baker. But somehow Tucker ropes her heart
and fills it with hope. Hope that this country girl and her son
can lasso the roaming bronc rider into their family forever.

Look for
His Country Girl

*Available January
wherever books are sold.*

Steeple
Hill®

www.SteepleHill.com

LI87643

REQUEST YOUR FREE BOOKS!

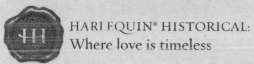

HARLEQUIN® HISTORICAL:
Where love is timeless

2 FREE NOVELS PLUS 2 **FREE GIFTS!**

YES! Please send me 2 FREE Harlequin® Historical novels and my 2 FREE gifts (gifts are worth about $10). After receiving them, if I don't wish to receive any more books, I can return the shipping statement marked "cancel." If I don't cancel, I will receive 6 brand-new novels every month and be billed just $4.94 per book in the U.S. or $5.49 per book in Canada. That's a saving of 20% off the cover price! It's quite a bargain! Shipping and handling is just 50¢ per book.* I understand that accepting the 2 free books and gifts places me under no obligation to buy anything. I can always return a shipment and cancel at any time. Even if I never buy another book from Harlequin, the two free books and gifts are mine to keep forever.

246/349 HDN E5L4

Name _____
(PLEASE PRINT)

Address _____ Apt. #

City _____ State/Prov. _____ Zip/Postal Code

Signature (if under 18, a parent or guardian must sign)

Mail to the Harlequin Reader Service:
IN U.S.A.: P.O. Box 1867, Buffalo, NY 14240-1867
IN CANADA: P.O. Box 609, Fort Erie, Ontario L2A 5X3
Not valid for current subscribers to Harlequin Historical books.

Want to try two free books from another line?
Call 1-800-873-8635 or visit www.morefreebooks.com.

* Terms and prices subject to change without notice. Prices do not include applicable taxes. N.Y. residents add applicable sales tax. Canadian residents will be charged applicable provincial taxes and GST. Offer not valid in Quebec. This offer is limited to one order per household. All orders subject to approval. Credit or debit balances in a customer's account(s) may be offset by any other outstanding balance owed by or to the customer. Please allow 4 to 6 weeks for delivery. Offer available while quantities last.

Your Privacy: Harlequin Books is committed to protecting your privacy. Our Privacy Policy is available online at www.eHarlequin.com or upon request from the Reader Service. From time to time we make our lists of customers available to reputable third parties who may have a product or service of interest to you. If you would prefer we not share your name and address, please check here. ☐

Help us get it right—We strive for accurate, respectful and relevant communications. To clarify or modify your communication preferences, visit us at www.ReaderService.com/consumerschoice.

HHIOR